Supacar

By

GA Howie

© 2022

Published in Australia in 2022 by;
Trenwick House Publishing.
www.trenwickhouse.com.au

ISBN 978-0-6451626-2-2

Printed by;
IngramSpark

NATIONAL LIBRARY OF AUSTRALIA

A catalogue record for this work is available from the National Library of Australia

Supacar

Trenwick House
Publishing

I want to dedicate this book to my mum, Marie Howie (1937-2021). She may be no longer with us in person, but she will always be with us in spirit.

Previous Jake North Releases

Spiral

Previous Releases by GA Howie

Prissy DuPonce

Prologue

Phone on the desk

Rattling and vibrating

Greetings

Confirmations

Travel plans

Appointments on return

Paperwork in the mail

Thanks for the doctor.

Phone back on the desk

Graffitied pictures

Disfigured pictures of two men

Disfigured pictures of racing cars

Darts aimed

Darts thrown

'Never again will I be denied.'

'If I can't have it, then neither can they.'

The voice was bitter and angry.

Laboratory

1

1.1

Monday, December 28,

Teri Hardy-Shannon had enjoyed Christmas with her family, but it was time to get back to work. Her father insisted the work could wait until after New Year, but Teri persisted.

She parked her car in the garage below the research facility, entered the building and began her ascent to the lab. She arrived about ten a.m.

As was their rule, from the moment Teri logged into the isolated lab, every action was entered on the computer and recorded by camera. They had installed a camera in each of the four corners, so as not to miss anything. There were also two more cameras focused on the rat, who had been named Charlie, in its controlled environment cage (CEC) in the centre of the room. The CEC was less of a traditional cage as it had acrylic sheet walls, one of which had thick rubber gloves fitted. The top was half acrylic sheet, half wire.

'It's ten-fifteen a.m., December 28, and I am reviewing a sample I left last week,' Teri said into a mic pinned to her lab coat. 'There appears to be some very minor mutations to one of the protein strands. This original sample is designated LS782-176 and with this mutation, I am labelling it LS782-176a. I will administer five milli-units of the newest serum to Charlie and see how he goes. The previous three samples of the serum do not appear to have made any difference to him and he seems to be the same since I left him last Friday, apart from needing a top-up of his food and water. It's possible his appetite has been increased as I'm sure there was more than enough to last him the few days I have been away. I will take samples and run tests.'

Teri administered the dose she wanted to test on Charlie.

It was turning into a long day for Teri as there were no obvious reactions in Charlie.

Teri stood by the cage.

'It's now four-thirty p.m. and has been just over six hours since I administered LS20-176a with no obvious reaction.'

Teri turned and retrieved a small dish containing a syringe.

'I will extract a blood sample and examine it for any molecular changes.'

Teri placed the dish into a small drawer and pushed it into the cage. Next, she walked around to the side and placed her hands inside the gloves and leant forward. She reached out and began to pat Charlie, soothing him. It responded and when she felt right, Teri grabbed the syringe and drew a sample of blood. The rat flinched but did not react.

Teri placed the plastic tubes with the blood sample back into the kidney tray. She then placed it in the secure compartment and slid it out of the cage. After taking her hands from the heavy rubber gloves, she transferred the sample to a number of vials, labelled them and placed them in the same dish.

She turned suddenly when she heard the cage rattle. The rat had begun to convulse. Teri returned to the cage, placed her hands into the gloves and reached for the rat. Initially it allowed Teri to soothe it but when the rat began to convulse again, it became violent and tried to bite her. The rat squirmed in her grip until it was free. Before Teri had a chance to remove her hands, the rat leapt onto one of her arms and sunk its teeth into her. Teri batted to rat off her arm and removed her hands.

Thinking the thickness of the rubber gloves would protect her, she was visibly surprised to see teeth marks on her forearm. She recorded what had happened, bathed her arm, took her own blood and tissue samples, and continued her observations. She marked her notes with the agreed condition level, which automatically sent notifications to the other scientists and research assistants.

Teri's back was turned to her computer screens when she heard the rat scream. As she turned to observe, the rat convulsed violently and began to swell. It got to the point where its skin began to tear. Within five minutes, the rat was a bloody mess of torn skin and rapidly expanding internal organs. Teri dared to move closer but before she could get two paces, the rat exploded onto the sides of the acrylic sheet walls. Teri doubled over, clambered for a bin, and vomited.

Sipping some water, she sat down, upgraded the condition level, which sent out an urgent message to the others who responded with their intention to attend the lab as soon as they could get there.

1.2

Monday, December 28,

Teri thrashed around on the floor violently, crying out for help. Uncontrolled, her arms and legs hit cabinets and drew blood. One leg had obviously broken. In a moment of calm, she rolled over and saw her colleagues at the window. She crawled towards the nearest console and painfully drew herself up.

She pressed a button on the desk. 'Don't come in,' she said. 'Aaarrrggghh.' Teri fell to the floor, writhing and thrashing once more. With the comms still open, her colleagues heard her screaming in agony. Her final words before the room went quiet was, "Watch the recording".'

Teri lay in a crumpled and bleeding heap against the desk. A small pool of blood began to spread around her open wounds.

With her colleagues in shock, they stood for several minutes before they could move.

'We have to get in there and get her out,' said one man.

'We can't go in there, Fairfax,' said the older of the women watching, stopping him from unsealing the room. 'We don't know what's happened. We don't know if it's airborne or not. If she's quarantine -sealed the room, we can't even open it if we wanted to until we know for sure.'

Fairfax placed his hands on the glass. Tears streaming down his face, sobbing. 'She's my daughter.'

Prof. Fairfax Hardy-Shannon was the co-owner and senior researcher at Balcher Research At 64, and only 178 cm tall, with a solid build, he still made an impression.

Added to this, his thinning grey hair, reddish-grey trimmed goatee and moustache, fair complexion, deep blue eyes, rectangle-shaped metal rimmed glasses, seemed to conflict with everything else.

'We can't leave her like that, Eleanor,' said Fairfax, turning to look at her.

Eleanor walked over and hugged him. Prof. Eleanor Balcher, 67, 183cm tall, medium build, dark hair with wisps of grey, light grey eyes that give her a ghostly appearance, smooth alabaster skin, is the daughter of the research facilities founder, Prof. Gerald Balcher (deceased).

The rest of the team consoled each other, deeply mourning the loss of their beloved colleague, Teri.

Eleanor gathered everyone in the conference room. 'This tragedy hurts deeper than we care to admit,' she began. 'However, we must move on and move on we will. The worst thing we need to do is review the footage Teri said she had recorded. I've already asked security to send it to me and as soon as we have it, we must look at it. I want everyone to have note paper, laptops, or whatever other recording devices you need at hand when we watch the recording. We need to know what she was doing, what happened and if it's something we need to contain. Is that understood?' Everyone mumbled their acknowledgement. 'Until further notice, no one is to enter the lab where Teri is. As soon as we can determine the nature of this event, the sooner we can attend to arrangements for Teri.'

Eleanor came over and hugged Fairfax tightly.

'Luca, darling, can you arrange some coffees please?' asked Eleanor.

Luca looked at Eleanor through teary eyes and nodded. He tapped a colleague sitting near him and the pair left the conference room, returning fifteen minutes later with hot water, tea, coffee, and biscuits. No one ate, but each made their own drink. Sitting around the table were six extremely close colleagues trying to come to terms with the agonising death of Teri.

Eleanor drank the remainder of her coffee and looked up with a determined look on her face. 'As sad and distressing as this is, I suggest we all go home and come in to work about midday tomorrow. Once everyone has arrived, we will review the tape to see and hear exactly what happened to Teri today.'

One by one, each of those present left the room.

1.3

Tuesday, December 29

At eight a.m., as was her custom, Eleanor arrived at the research facility, despite advising everyone else to arrive at midday. Eleanor smiled to herself as she got out of her car. Within a few minutes of her own arrival, everyone else had arrived.

'I see we decided to come in early and not try and rest?' Eleanor commented as they walked into the building.

'I know I couldn't sleep and although I didn't want to, my wife made me shower and eat breakfast before coming here,' said Fairfax.

'Grace is a good woman,' said Eleanor. 'How is she?'

'Devastated, as you would expect,' said Fairfax. 'When she knew she couldn't make me stay at home with her, she insisted on the aforementioned shower and breakfast.'

Eleanor leant over and kissed Fairfax on the cheek.

'It will be hard, but we have each other,' said Eleanor.

She, Fairfax, Luca, Lance, Ross, and Lee walked into their research lab. As they crossed the small foyer, Eleanor saw their red-eyed receptionist.

'Go ahead, I'll meet you in the boardroom shortly,' said Eleanor. She walked over to the receptionist. 'Donna, my dear, how are you?'

'I should be asking you that question,' said Donna.

'I am indeed devastated but I am damned if I will let a lab rat spoil our progress,' said Eleanor, smiling wryly.

Donna chuckled and smiled.

'Now, that's better. That's the Donna we know. What do you know, my dear?'

'For some odd reason, I found myself here at seven thirty this morning. I know I've done it before, but it felt unusual today. I spoke with security who were talking about yesterday, so I asked what happened and they told me, with all the added gruesomeness of it all.'

'Sorry about that,' said Eleanor.

'Don't be. I'd rather know than not. Anyway, when I heard there was vision, I knew that you would want to view it, so I have asked Security to prepare a copy for your perusal. As it turned out they had already done that. I considered going up to the lab but didn't.'

'You're welcome to join us in the boardroom,' said Eleanor.

'I may watch the vision when I'm ready,' said Donna.

'Very well.' Eleanor continued to her office and then the boardroom.

Eleanor looked at the terminal in front of her when she heard it beep. 'It's arrived. Raw and unedited. As painful as this will be, we have work to do.'

1.4

Thursday, December 31

A few days after viewing the video of Teri's demise, Lance Reeve, chief lab assistant at Balcher Research sat at his desk and completed his notes. He also removed a memory stick from a port on the desk, held it tightly then placed it in his pocket.

Lance Reeve was 38 years old and stood at 203cm tall, was lanky but not thin. He kept his black hair neat and trimmed along with his goatee. His hazel eyes were hidden behind a pair of black wire-rimmed glasses, and he had a tanned complexion. He looked like he should be coding the latest game, and people were often surprised to hear he was a research assistant with a respected laboratory.

He tidied his desk, gathered his things and backpack, and walked out of his office.

As he walked down the corridor, he passed an office. He poked his head inside.

'Hi, Eleanor,' he said. 'I'm finishing early today. I've set some samples for testing, but their results won't be known until tomorrow. You're welcome to look, otherwise I'll let you know when I have the results.'

'Sounds good, Lance,' said Eleanor, looking up from her laptop. 'I trust you. You've been with us a long time now. I think we're finally making progress.'

'I agree,' said Lance. 'I'll see you tomorrow.'

Lance went down to the garage where his car was and left the building.

Thirty minutes later, he pulled into a building in the old industrial section of Port Melbourne. With his backpack on, he rode the elevator to the top floor. He walked down a plain corridor and walked through an average looking wooden door.

Behind the door was a different story. The office was sleek, modern, and efficient, but it was not clinical. Potted plants were in corners, comfortable couches formed a waiting area. The receptionist had a view of the bay.

Lance walked up to this secretary. 'Afternoon, Marjory.'

Marjory looked up. 'Ah, good afternoon, Mr Reeve. Is Mr Westbrook expecting you?'

'Officially not, but I did send him a message when I left the lab. He replied saying he had the time to see me.' Lance indicated the door and walked towards it.

'Very well, Mr Reeve.'

Lance knocked a couple of times and then walked in.

Joel Westbrook, a vibrant man of thirty-eight standing 190cm tall with blonde hair, blue eyes, and a tanned complexion, turned and smiled as Lance walked in. His hands were of someone who knew the value of work, yet he was a warm and responsive man. In his early twenties, he was married to Lance's sister, Sylvia. Unfortunately, she died after a couple of years from an infection she received where she worked. Joel was devastated, along with Lance and the rest of the family. Many a woman had tried to catch him after that, but he turned each one of them down. Speculation circulated that he 'batted for the other team'. He was even linked to Lance, as they spent a lot of time together, but he proved everyone wrong when at the age of thirty-two he announced his engagement to Lauren McKenzie. She happened to be the heiress to a vast fortune and was held in great favour by her father, Andrew McKenzie, owner of the nationwide chain of stores, *McKenzie Electronics*.

Unfortunately, Lauren was killed in a car accident on the eve of their fourth wedding anniversary. Lauren was on her way home from visiting her doctor. Joel was devastated again but no one ever saw the raw pain he felt. He vowed to his closest friends that he would never marry again.

'Good afternoon, Joel,' said Lance as he dropped his backpack on one of the couches.

'Lance, my man, how's it going?' said Joel. Coming around to hug his long-time friend.

'I'm glad you agreed to see me. We had an incident just a after Christmas. I thought you might want to see.'

'Oh?'

'Unfortunately, we lost Teri in the incident, but it has spurred us on,' said Lance. He reached into his pocket and retrieved the memory stick. He handed it to Joel. 'Have a look at the footage.'

Joel sat down at his desk and inserted the stick into the memory slot. He accessed and began to watch. 'How long does this go for?'

'Um, skip until you get to about four in the afternoon. That's when Teri begins to speak again,' Lance said.

'Got it,' said Joel. He sat and listened to Teri's account and then watched as everything unfolded.

Now and then Joel glanced over to see Lance, sitting on a couch, shedding tears as he heard the video unfold.

Joel sat back when it stopped. Silent. Thoughtful. Pensive.

After several minutes, Joel stood and sat down beside Lance. Lance placed his head on Joel's shoulder and wept openly.

'Do you know what caused it all to happen?' asked Joel.

'We're still investigating, but it would seem that Teri observed a mutation in a protein string and tested the sample on Charlie,' said Lance.

'Charlie?'

'The lab rat in the vision.'

'Right,' said Joel.

'Anyway, we tested Teri's blood and the same mutation showed up. We have since destroyed the samples and have isolated where the mutation probably happened. We have taken a different approach and I will check some samples tomorrow before testing.'

'I am deeply sorry for your loss, Lance, but please keep me informed.'

'Thank you, Joel. You know I will.'

Lance dried his eyes, stood, grabbed his backpack, and made to leave.

'Will you have dinner at my place later?' asked Joel.

'I'll pass tonight, but thanks, Joel. It's been hard trying to work after we lost Teri. I might have an early night.'

'I understand.'

Lance left and drove to his home in the south-eastern suburbs of Melbourne.

1.5

Monday, January 11

Early in the new year, Peter Abernathy took a call at his desk in his Melbourne, Office. He looked at his watch. It was eight pm, he should have gone home. 'Are you sure?' he said. 'I see ... and you have footage?' Peter became suddenly more interested. 'Can you send me a copy? ... I look forward to seeing it.' Peter stood, walked to the window, and stared out across the Melbourne skyline. He looked back over his shoulder to acknowledge the beep he heard on his terminal. He looked back out of the window. 'The video footage will make interesting viewing tonight.'

He turned, sat down, accessed the video, and began to watch.

With the viewer he was using, it had a volume meter on one side, and he stopped the vision when the meter began to register sound. He wound the vision back until he worked out where the sound had started.

'Let's see what's happening,' said Peter aloud. He leant forward and looked more closely at the date at the bottom of the recording. 'So this happened just after Christmas.'

Peter listened to what she had to say. *'It's now ten-fifteen a.m., December 27, and I am reviewing a sample I left last week,'* Teri said into a mic pinned to her lab coat. *'There appears to be some very minor mutations to one of the protein strands. This original sample is designated LS20-176 and with this mutation, I am labelling it LS20-176a. I will administer five milli-units of the newest serum to Charlie and see how he goes. The previous three samples of the serum do not appear to have made any difference to him and he seems to be the same since I left him last Friday, apart from needing a top-up of his food and water. It's possible his appetite has been increased as I'm sure there was more than enough to last him the few days I have been away. I will take samples and run tests.'*

Peter watched the lab assistant administer the dose to test into the laboratory rat.

Peter sped through the tape. While it did that, he made a phone call.

'Bryony, sorry to disturb you at home,' Peter said, 'but I'm watching the recording you sent me. Do you have a name of the person who is in the video?'

'I'll see what I can find out,' replied Bryony. 'When would you like to know?'

'I'd prefer tonight, but if it has to be tomorrow, so be it.'

Peter terminated the call, as he did, the meter detected sound. He wound the recording back to where he needed.

'It's now four-thirty p.m. and has been just over six hours since I administered LS20-176a with no obvious reaction.'

The lab assistant turned and retrieved a small dish containing a syringe.

'I will extract a blood sample and examine it for any molecular changes.'

She placed the dish into a small drawer and pushed it into the cage. Next, she walked around to the side and placed her hands inside the gloves and leant forward. She reached out and began to pat the rat, soothing it. It responded and when she felt right, Teri grabbed the syringe and drew a sample of blood. The rat flinched but did not react.

She placed the plastic tubes with the blood sample

back into the kidney tray. She then placed it in the secure compartment and slid it out of the cage. After taking her hands from the heavy rubber gloves, she transferred the sample to a number of vials, labelled them and placed them in the same dish she had used for the syringe after disposing of the syringe.

She turned suddenly when she heard the cage rattle. The rat had begun to convulse. She returned to the cage, placed her hands into the gloves and reached for the rat. Initially it allowed her to soothe it but when the rat began to convulse again, it became violent and tried to bite her. The rat squirmed in her grip until it was free. Before she had a chance to remove her hands, the rat leapt onto one of her arms and sunk its teeth into her. She batted to rat off her arm and removed her hands.

Peter noted that the lab assistant was visibly surprised to see teeth marks on her forearm. He returned to the vision.

She recorded what had happened, bathed her arm, took her own blood and tissue samples, and continued her observations. She marked her notes with the agreed condition level, which automatically sent notifications to the other scientists and research assistants.

Teri's back was turned to her computer screens when she heard the rat scream. As she turned to observe, the rat convulsed violently and began to swell. It got to the point where its skin began to tear. Within five minutes, the rat was a bloody mess of torn skin and rapidly expanding internal organs. Teri dared to move closer but before she could get two paces, the rat exploded onto the sides of the acrylic sheet walls. Teri doubled over, clambered for a bin, and vomited.

Peter let the vision run at normal speed whilst he answered his phone.

'Yes?' he said.

'The person in the video is a lab assistant by the name of Teri Hardy-Shannon,' Bryony said.

'Thank you, Bryony.' Peter terminated the call. He looked at the screen. 'Are you his daughter? His niece, perhaps? Or even his daughter-in-law?'

Peter pressed play and continued to watch the vision.

Teri thrashed around on the floor violently, crying out for help. Uncontrolled, her arms and legs hit cabinets and drew blood. One leg had obviously broken. In a moment of calm, she rolled over and saw her colleagues at the window. She crawled towards the nearest console and painfully drew herself up.

She pressed a button on the desk. 'Don't come in,' she said. 'Aaarrrggghh.' Teri fell to the floor, writhing and thrashing once more. With the comms still open, her colleagues heard her screaming in agony. Her final words before the room went quiet was, "Watch the recording".'

Teri lay in a crumpled and bleeding heap against the desk. A small pool of blood began to spread around her open wounds.

'So many questions,' thought Peter aloud. He stopped the vision and accessed his email.

First

2

2.1

Tuesday, January 26

Jake dragged himself into the kitchen.

'Good morning, sweetie, or is it afternoon. No, it's still morning,' said Anhton, checking his watch. 'You need to get dressed. We have to leave soon.'

'I'm not going anywhere,' said Jake, as he plopped into one of the stools at the bench.

'Yes, you are. You have two choices. Firstly, we go to the launch of Balcher Racing, to support Dan, as we promised. Or secondly, you go to work.'

'I choose, thirdly. Stay at home.'

'Not this time. You also promised me you'd go,' said Anhton.

'I've changed my mind.'

'There's a news flash.'

Jake grunted and accepted the coffee placed before him.

'It's a new year. New things to do,' said Anhton.

'It's still an unsolved case.'

'That's old news, albeit true, it's happened. We have to move on.'

'Whatever.' Jake rose and began to go back to the bedroom.

'See you back here soon.'

'No!'

'Jake Marcus North. You will get dressed and you will get back out here ready to go in thirty minutes!'

Jake turned and looked at Anhton. Jake couldn't miss the tears welling up in Anhton's eyes.

'We promised we would stick together through thick and thin, no matter what,' said Anhton.

Jake stopped. 'I thought I'd catch him before anything else happened, but I didn't. I failed. I failed, Anhton.'

Anhton walked over to Jake and hugged him tightly. Jake broke down and sobbed.

'You didn't fail. You worked out what to do. How to access the inside of the lair. You discovered the clues like no one else could.'

'He still got away, and thousands died because of me.'

'No, not because of you, because of Jeremy.'

'I don't even know where he is.'

'I promise you this, now, today, that I will do my damnedest to find out where Jeremy is and bring him to justice.' Anhton took a step back. 'Look at me, baby.'

Jake looked up, his eyes red and puffy. Anhton wiped the tears away.

'I love you. I think from the first day we met. I will do everything within my power to care for you, love you, protect you and do all sorts of other things to you.'

Jake stifled a giggle.

'Now, will you get dressed for me? We promised Dan we'd support him as much as we could this year. It means a lot to him.'

'Okay. At least it's nothing to do with work.'

'I'll be right here waiting.'

Anhton turned Jake around, lovingly tapped him on the arse and sent him on his way.

Thirty minutes later, Jake appeared wearing jeans, a very loud shirt, and a sports jacket. His eyes were no longer puffy, and he had a smile on his face.

'Will this do?'

'Hubba, hubba,' said Anhton. 'I may need sunnies for the shirt, but still, hubba, hubba.'

'Enough of that,' said Jake.

'Let's get going.'

2.2

Tuesday, January 26

The woman stopped at a particularly mirrored shop window. She made sure her blond hair was exactly right and did a quick touch-up of her red lipstick and dark eyeliner. She then turned, walked along the footpath, turned the corner nearest her and onto the street with more shops.

Occasionally looking into the different store windows, she stopped just prior to her destination, faced the wall, plumped up her chest, tightened the shirt she was wearing and walked on. When she came to the store she wanted, she walked in and began to look around at the various devices on the shelves.

'Good morning,' said the sales assistant behind the counter. 'Is there anything I can help you with today?'

'Not yet, I just want to have a look for a few minutes,' she replied.

'Let me know when you're ready.'

The woman looked around and walked past the devices that she had been shown by her partner. She turned to see who had entered the shop when the buzzer went off. She picked up one of the devices and headed of the counter.

She heard the sales assistant enquire of the new customer but was met again with a 'just looking' response. He returned to the counter.

The woman reached the counter, bent over slightly, and peered at the name badge.

'Jerry,' she said, 'I was wondering exactly what these

would be used for?' She slid the small device across the counter.

'Sometimes you may only need a small explosion,' said Jerry. 'Just enough to make a small hole or give the effect of some further damage.'

'Like with film make-up?'

'Something like that.'

'If I wanted to use a device like this under skin, for example,' she said, 'to give the effect of damage, how small can the devices get and how much damage would it do?'

'Well, we don't recommend using any type of explosive against the skin at all, no matter how small. It's too dangerous.'

Jerry looked past her at the other customer standing near the explosives that the woman had come from a few minutes before.

'The makeup I can do afterwards,' she said quickly, 'but I was wanting to experiment with creating the smallest of explosions underneath the makeup to give a much more realistic effect.'

Jerry looked back at the woman. 'I suppose it could be done, but you'd need to use the smallest amount of the weakest strength,' he said. 'It will still leave metal fragments behind, due to its composition.'

'So they don't make one that would disintegrate completely?'

'I'm not aware of any, but I could check with my suppliers.'

'That's ok,' she said. 'You'd have to use a very thin fuse

wire to activate it?'

'Yes, you would,' said Jerry, fully focused on the woman again, well her chest anyway.

She and Jerry looked towards the door when they heard the buzzer. They both watched as the second customer was walking away past the shop window.

'This gives me some more ideas,' said the woman, turning to leave. 'You never know; I may be back to get some more advice.'

'You're welcome,' said Jerry, as he watched her leave the store.

The woman walked along the street, crossed at the lights, turned the first corner she came to and walked away from the shopping strip. Minutes later, a car pulled up beside her and she got in and she was driven away.

2.3

Tuesday, January 26

Cmdr David Castle walked from his office and took the lift down to Forensics. It had been a while since he was last inside the DFIS Forensics lab and was still surprised by what greeted him as he exited the airlock.

Not loud, but definitely not expected, the music that played made it hard to call out. David casually walked up to the work bench and tapped the lady on the shoulder.

'Shit!' she exclaimed, grabbing a remote and turning down the music.

'I didn't mean to startle you, Gabby,' said David.

'That's ok,' said Gabby. Lt Gabby Kindregan had a broad Scottish accent, bright red hair, tied back in a ponytail, and the most electric green eyes.

'With Dustin on leave, I thought I had better come down myself.'

'You have some more work for me?'

'I always have work for you,' said David.

Gabby looked at him from under a raised eyebrow. 'What do you have for me?'

'I need you and Amy to run forensics at an alleged robbery at a firearms store in Altona.'

'Can't the locals do that?'

'We are the locals now,' said David.

'So we are. I know but I keep forgetting.'

'Oh, one more thing ...'

'Not today,' said Gabby

'You don't know what I was going to ask.'

'I have a fairly good idea. Everyone is asking me the same thing.'

'I see. So, what are you going to do?' said David.

'I don't know yet. I've tried just about everything. I'll have a chat with Anhton.'

'I'd appreciate that.' David left the lab.

2.4

Tuesday, January 26

Aimee leaned up against Scott's desk as he began to write up the report.

'I guess we can look at the vision and confirm the descriptions the sales assistant gave us,' Aimee said, handing the disc to Scott.

'At least it'll be logged, even if we don't catch them,' said Scott. 'Who knows where they'll be by now. We make a note to say that it was an isolated shop lifting incident and close the report.'

'Agreed,' said Aimee. 'Send me a copy when you're done.'

'Will do,' said Scott.

Scott inserted the disc that Jerry had given Aimee. He watched it a few times. He made notes to confirm the description of the woman as supplied by Jerry. The second customer was much more difficult. A long coat, despite the warmer weather. The collar pulled up around the back of the head. A wide-brimmed hat was perched on the customer's head, effectively blocking any sight of the face. The customer wore gloves and seemed to know where the cameras were as they never looked in their direction.

Scott watched as the second customer hovered around the explosives where the woman had been minutes before. The customer picked up some of the devices and appeared to return them.

'The hand actions would indicate the items were replaced,' said Scott aloud to himself.

He watched the vision a couple of more times before completing his report and logging it. He made sure that Aimee received a copy as well. All he had to wait for now was the forensics report.

Offer

3.1

Friday, January 29

10:30 a.m.

A minivan drove onto the site of the Balcher Researcher facility on the Mornington Peninsula. It pulled to a stop outside the front door and five people climbed from the van.

Dan Roberts, Jason Black, Jonathan McDermott, Jordi Serrano, and Johan Bron assembled beside the van and then walked inside.

'Good morning, gentleman,' greeted the bubbly blond receptionist. 'My name is Donna. I saw you drive up, so I have advised Prof. Balcher of your arrival. She should be along shortly. In the meantime, if you will follow me, I'll show you through to the meeting room.'

The men nodded and followed Donna along a short hallway and took seats around the round table.

'There's tea, coffee and snacks on the sideboard,' said Donna. 'Please help yourself.'

'Thank you, Donna,' said Johan.

Donna slid the door closed behind her and went back to her desk.

About fifteen minutes later, the door slid open and three Balcher employees walked in.

'Good morning, gentlemen,' said the lady of the group.

'Morning, Eleanor,' said Johan, rising to greet her with a kiss. 'It's good to see you again.'

'Thank you for coming, Johan,' said Eleanor. 'I know you've met Fairfax before, and the other gentleman with us is one of our senior researchers, Lance Reeve.'

'Good to see you, Fairfax,' said Johan. 'Nice to meet you, Lance.' They shook hands. 'With me today are our drivers, Jason Black and Dan Roberts, along with their respective lead mechanics, Jordi Serrano and Jonathan McDermott.'

'Have a seat and we'll begin,' said Eleanor.

She, Fairfax, and Lance began to prepare their presentation.

'I've called you here as I want to share with you an exciting development that I think will help the team perform better on race day,' said Eleanor.

'Don't you think we're good enough?' said Jason.

'On the contrary, Jason, you are an excellent driver,

28

driving for a very respectable and talented team,' replied Eleanor.

'So why do we need to perform better?' said Jason.

'Are you suggesting we start taking drugs?' said Johan.

'Not at all and certainly not in the illegal narcotic sense,' said Eleanor.

'What we have developed is a serum that helps to boost the mental acuity of the person who consumes it,' said Fairfax.

'Yes, that's correct,' said Eleanor.

The Balcher Racing personnel looked uneasy and unsettled.

'Young Lance here has been our on-site test dummy for suite a while,' said Fairfax. 'Isn't that right Lance?'

'Yes, Professor,' said Lance. 'Whilst the doses I've been taking have been small, the improvements were notable.'

'Naturopathic practitioners have known about the benefits of the natural supplements that help with mental acuity for thousands of years,' said Eleanor.

'What we've done here at Balcher Research is take that basic natural remedy and boost it,' added Fairfax.

'Can you remind me what mental acuity is, please?' asked Dan.

'Sure,' said Eleanor. 'What's looked at when determining a person's mental acuity are memory, focus, concentration, and understanding. These are functioning everyday as we live and breathe, however, there are times when they can all be a little bit sharper. For Lance, it was as we developed this very serum, hence the small doses that were less than in the natural remedies. However, as we developed the serum further, so did Lance's ability to see through some of the problems with the formula. Not to mention with other research projects we have going.'

'What if you take too much?' asked Johan.

'We've never really tried to take too much,' said Fairfax. 'Some may question our motives, but we are not maverick. We take our medical responsibility very seriously.'

'Yet you were willing to allow one of your own become a test subject,' said Johan.

'I volunteered willingly,' said Lance. 'I was one of the primary researchers for this project and so I put my hand up for testing. There have been no side effects as I have been having regular medical check-ups since taking the serum. When we felt we had the right formula, I did try a higher dose and the effects lasted for twenty-four hours before I would have needed another dose. I only took a dose once a week so that we could monitor the effects.'

'We discovered that the serum is completely gone from the blood system within forty-eight hours of consumption,' said Eleanor. 'It can take a few hours for the effects to become apparent and as Lance indicated, they are at their peak for about twenty-four hours.'

'What if you were to take a second dose whilst the first dose was still in the system?' asked Jason.

'We have to trial such an attempt, but I'd say that there would be little harm done,' said Eleanor.

'Everybody's chemical make-up is always different and whilst we saw no side effects with Lance, we do need to trial it on a much wider body of people,' said Fairfax.

'If that's the case, why are you offering it to us?' said Johan. 'That is what you're doing, isn't it?'

Eleanor paused.

'I thought so,' said Johan. 'The answer is no. I won't allow my drivers to become test subjects.'

'Johan, we're not asking the guys to use a lot of the serum. Lance has taken samples that have been marginally more concentrated than a natural solution, however, we would like to try it with someone who is in a field where focus and concentration are primary.'

'Like a racing car driver?' said Dan.

'Like a racing car driver,' said Fairfax.

The room went silent.

'Right now, my reservations are more than outweighing my acceptance,' said Johan. 'I still say no.'

'What would it take you to reconsider?' asked Eleanor.

'Results from people other than us,' said Johan.

'What if we trialled it with some drivers in one of the other classes of racing?' said Eleanor.

'It's still messing with something we know little about,' said Johan.

'We do know what we're doing, Johan,' implored Eleanor.

'Let me think about it,' said Johan. 'I want to discuss this thoroughly with all concerned. Not only the drivers, but the support teams as they will have to pick up the pieces if anything goes wrong.'

'I understand,' said Eleanor.

'If there's nothing else, we need to head back to base,' said Johan. 'We have a race to prepare for in a few weeks.'

'That's all we had,' said Fairfax.'

Johan rose from his seat, the rest followed.

'Thank you for coming, Johan,' said Eleanor, as she shook his hand firmly.

After farewells were made, the five men returned to their minivan and drove back to their factory in the north of the city.

3.2

Friday, January 29

11:30 a.m.

Eleanor returned to the boardroom after seeing the men out through the main door.

'How do you think that went, Fairfax?' asked Eleanor. Lance was preparing to leave. 'Stay Lance, I'd like to hear what you have to say.'

'We delivered the case and now it's up to them,' said Fairfax.

'Lance?' said Eleanor.

'I should probably mention that I took a dose of the serum this morning when I started so that when our guests were here, I would be able to do all the things we said it could do,' said Lance.

'You should have told me this earlier, Lance, you know I don't like any unauthorised testing,' said Eleanor.

'Do you trust me, Eleanor?' asked Lance.

'You know I do, but still,' said Eleanor.

'Anyway, apart from when you asked me a direct question, I was watching every one of the men that were sitting here. The two mechanics didn't seem to want to listen to anything we had to say, once we revealed our plan. They had their arms crossed the entire time we were speaking. They too were watching everyone else in the room, including us. I think Dan will say no, as will Jason, however I think he can be swayed. He was particularly interested in boosted or even double shots. Johan was readily listening but was being the ever careful 'mother hen' to his brood. Of course he doesn't want anything to happen to them that will affect their ability to drive.'

'This will help them drive better,' said Eleanor.

'We can only presume this, Eleanor,' said Lance. 'I'm not a race car driver, only a regular driver and yes it has helped me some of the busier roads getting to and from work. I was able to see things more clearly and avoid any problems. That doesn't help answer questions when you're travelling at 200km per hour on a tight track with lots of turns, gear changes, commands from their garage and keeping an eye out for those in front and behind them. They may have other chemical balances or imbalances that the serum may change.'

'Are you suggesting our serum doesn't work that well in high stress environments?' asked Fairfax.

'Not at all, Fairfax,' said Lance. 'All I'm saying is that they have valid reasons to query the sudden interest in us wanting to use them as test subjects. Maybe we should try it with some of the drivers in a lower class, but we first need to convince them of the same thing. It won't be easy. We continue to improve the serum and continue to do what we know best, create.'

'I guess you're right,' said Eleanor.

'One more thing,' said Lance, 'there is a possible connection between Menac and LS782.'

'What's Menac?' asked Fairfax.

'I'm sorry, it's my pet name for LS514, the mental acuity serum, hence menac. The 'm-e-n' from mental and the 'a-c' from acuity,' said Lance.

'I actually like that,' said Eleanor. 'Even though we don't like naming our products until we know they can be released. Let's start calling it Menac, but we'll still use the laboratory designation as well. Now what are you saying about a connection between LS782 and LS514?'

'It's been said in research, that as someone ages, their mental acuity diminishes,' said Lance. 'I've noticed that the chemical bonds of Menac adhere quite well to the chemical and protein strains of LS782. Mental acuity is going to be fundamental in living a longer life. The sharper and more focused we are, the stronger our concentration abilities will become and the deeper our understanding of life will be. The clearer the mind is, the better we'll be able to remain adaptive to a changing society.'

'Has LS514 strengthened the formula of LS782,' said Eleanor, now quite excited.

'My early findings support that hypothesis,' said Lance.

'This is a fantastic development, we must move in that direction,' said Eleanor. 'Are you able to prepare something for the rest of the team for this afternoon, Lance?'

'I think so,' said Lance.

'Then do it, please,' said Eleanor. 'This may be the breakthrough we've been looking for.'

'In the meantime, where do we go to from here with LS514 and the racing team?' asked Fairfax.

'We need to find someone who will be willing to test the serum for us under race conditions,' said Eleanor.

'Let me make those enquiries,' said Fairfax. 'I know LS782 is important to you, as it is too me, so I want you focused on that.'

'Thank-you Fairfax, I love you so much,' said Eleanor.

'As I do you, Eleanor.'

They all rose and left the boardroom.

As they did, Lance caught s movement of a shadow out of the corner of his eye. The shadow had been just out of general vision but moved suddenly when they rose. When he entered the hallway, he saw no one. As Lance passed by the reception desk, he thought Donna looked a little out of puff as she talked on phone. The closer he got, the quieter she became.

3.3

Friday, January 29

11:30 a.m.

At first, the mood in the minivan was quiet until Johan spoke.

Jonathan was concentrating on driving with Jordi turning in his seat to be part of the conversation in the rear.

'What do you think, guys?' asked Johan.

'I say an absolute no,' said Jordi. 'We don't know what kind of effect this serum will have on Jason or Dan.'

'I agree,' said Jonathan.

'Dan? Jason?' said Johan.

'If it means we have better focus, more concentration, then why not?' said Jason. 'This year is going to be big, and I want to make it my, our, year.'

'So you think we should become test dummies?' said Dan.

'Not in those terms,' said Jason. 'I'm sure they have been testing this for quite some time. They've been doing research for a long time. I checked them out before I joined the team. I thought that if the team was bearing their name, then I should know who they are.'

'Fairfax Hardy-Shannon had always loved car racing, even though he was never allowed to participate,' said Johan. 'Then when he met his father-in-law, Robert Balcher, he found an ally. Balcher accepted him, especially when he married his daughter, Eleanor. Fairfax went to work in the small lab that Robert Balcher had and soon Eleanor joined them, and Balcher Research was born. They've always kept it a small concern, but they have released many beneficial products over the years ensuring their continued survival and success. Whilst they set-up the racing car team, it underwent many changes over the years, and they have always kept up with technology. I've been with them for fifteen years and whilst I do have to report to them as a business, I'm given quite a free hand to what is necessary to ensure the ongoing concern and the safety of all concerned. So far, I think I've done a damned respectable job.'

'Oh, they didn't say all that in what I read,' said Jason. 'Even so, I feel we can trust them.'

'I don't,' said Dan. 'Yes, you have, Johan. You've had my full confidence. What do you think about all this?'

'I'm not sure,' said Johan. 'I've met Lance a few times and don't have any reason to distrust him, nor do I now. However, trialling a serum that has only been tested in small doses in-house is risky at best. I'm just as reluctant to allow them to test it on one of the lower classes of racing.'

'Don't you want us to do well?' asked Jason.

'Of course I do, but I won't allow you to suffer either,' said Johan.

'They did mention that what they have developed is from a natural source,' said Dan. 'What if we tried those natural methods? See if they have any effect on us? In theory, anything natural is supposed to be good for us. Right?'

'Yes, but even natural remedies can cause unknown effects on someone if their own chemical make-up is not right,' said Johan. 'Not everyone can take simple paracetamol as it affects them or doesn't work.'

They minivan went silent.

'Jonathan, Jordi, anything you want to add?' asked Johan.

'Only that we're the ones who have to pick up the pieces if our drivers' mental abilities are diminished. The last thing we want is of Jason or Dan to suffer and crash because their concentration was affected,' said Jonathan.

'I reckon we try small doses of the natural product, if it doesn't work, we stop,' said Jordi.

Johan looked from colleague to colleague.

'Leave it with me,' said Johan. 'I will investigate natural herbal solutions and will advise you in due course. In the meantime, we mention nothing of this meeting with Balcher to anyone. We don't want to cause any alarm.'

The other men agreed.

3.4

Friday, January 29

11:45 a.m.

Lance sat at his desk and accessed a program that only he knew about. It allowed him to see who someone was talking to on the phone. He placed headphones on his head and clicked the button to listen in on the conversation he had chosen.

'Ms. M, I tell you that they have moved forward with their research into LS782,' said Donna.

So she's talking with this Ms. M again, thought Lance.

'Have they perfected it yet?' asked Ms. M.

'I don't think so,' said Donna.

'Then only call me when they have.' Ms. M was terse.

A tough woman. thought Lance.

'They want to evaluate a mental acuity serum on some racing car drivers though,' said Donna.

Oooh, that's a massive breach of protocol.

'Let me know when they have results.' Bryony disconnected the call.

'Ms. M? Bryony?' said Donna.

No good pleading, Donna, she's gone. Now I have a name.

Lance sat back in his chair for a moment. He leant forward and began tapping on his keyboard. He had the computer trace the destination of the call, but it seemed to bounce around before it settled.

'Who owns this phone number?' Lance said aloud.

The computer returned a name and address which Lance had come across before. He accessed a secure email address and sent a coded message to its owner.

Second

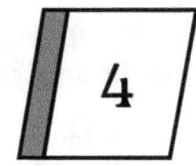

4.1

Tuesday, February 16

A light rain began to fall as a woman turned a corner onto the shopping strip. It was unusually cold for the time of year, so she was dressed appropriately. Jeans, closed shoes, a high neck knitted shirt, finishing off with the snugly fitting blue jumper. Her coat was long, and she carried a bright yellow umbrella. She moved carefully along the damp pavement until she came to the awnings. Shaking off her umbrella, she straightened her long black hair and looked at the shops she was approaching. Smiling, she walked up to the one she wanted, turned the handle, and entered.

'Good morning, ma'am,' said the sales assistant. 'Is there anything I can help you with today?'

'Not just yet thank you.' The woman began to move about the shelves until she came across the item she was looking for. 'Excuse me?'

The sales assistant came to her side. 'How can I help you?'

'Are these timers?' asked the woman.

'They are. Can I ask what you're using them for?'

'Well, I'm a writer,' she said smiling and batting her eyelids, 'and I'm doing some research on timers for explosives.'

'What's the scenario, if I may ask?'

'I'm wanting to use a very small explosive with a variable timer.'

'Will the explosive cause damage?' asked the sale assistant.

The woman leaned in close, as much to look at his name as for him to smell her perfume. 'Enough damage to cause further mayhem that will make the whole thing look like an accident, Tom.'

'Follow me to the counter, I may have the information you need.'

'So these won't do it then?'

'Oh, they'll do the job, but I will give you some printed information on how to use them,' said Tom.

'Very good. Hopefully, it will be detailed enough that I won't need to buy one to try it out. One more thing, can the timers be remotely controlled?'

'Yes, they can, and they come in a variety of sizes, especially if you want it to look like an accident.'

The woman smiled and followed Tom to the counter. As they headed to the counter, another customer walked in. Tom said he would attend to them as soon as he could. The second customer waved, uttered something polite and began to move about the shelves. As Tom walked behind the counter, the woman leaned over it. Tom then went out the back and returned a few moments later holding some papers. When Tom returned, all he could see were the woman's highly accentuated hazel eyes and her ample chest.

'Uhm, here you are,' said Tom.

The woman took the leaflets and began to flick through them. She stopped occasionally to clarify a point of understanding. They both looked up when the second customer suddenly left the store.

'That was odd,' said Tom. 'He left in much more of a hurry than he arrived.'

'Maybe they'll come back later,' said the woman. 'Well, thank you for this information. I think it will come in very handy for my story.'

'I'm glad I could help.'

The woman waved as she left the store and merged with the crowded footpath as the rain had started to become more abundant. Tom followed the woman until she moved past his window, and he stared for several minutes until his phone ringing startled him.

After the phone call he remembered that the second customer had been in the vicinity of the timers where he'd started talking to the woman. He remembered that the second customer had left much more hurriedly than when walking into the store. Tom went to the shelf and as he tidied up, he noticed that several of the timers were missing.

'That bastard. He stole my stock, and I bet she was in on it too. How stupid am I.'

Tom went to the back office and called the local Def station. He was told that someone would be in attendance as soon as possible. Twenty minutes later, two defence officers entered the small store.

4.2

Tuesday, February 16

Det.LtCmdr Ric Harding was a robust and fit man. Fair skin, ruddy cheeks, greying hair - despite the fact he was in his mid-forties. Dark hazel eyes, a goatee, and a pierced ear. The sleeves of his uniform were rolled up past his elbows. The scar on his right arm the result of a fight with a drunken airman over a girl soon after he graduated from training. He never got that girl but was fortunate to meet another that he has been married to for almost twenty years.

Ric had been appointed the department head for the DFIS investigators, taking over from Cmdr David Castle. He was now the CO of DFIS, filling the shoes left by the murders of DFISs most recent commanders; Cmdr Linda Barrow, and Cmdr Peter Dugald.

Ric's face was becoming slightly ruddier as the incoming call notification on his computer screen refused to be answered.

'Can someone come and help me answer that damned call,' Ric bellowed across the office.

Jake sauntered across the room, placed the headset on Ric's head, pressed a button on the screen and sauntered away.

Ric simply watched as Jake walked over to the Glass room.

'Hello?' said the voice for the third time.

'Oh, sorry. Det.LtCmdr Ric Harding, DFIS, how can I help you?'

'Hey, Ric. LPte Scott Glass, MetroWest here. Fancy title, I see?'

'Scott, how are you? Came with the promotion and new job.'

'Doing well thanks,' said Scott. 'I've got some stuff for you. Can I send a file to you first?'

'Go right ahead,' said Ric. 'You have my email address.'

'Sending now.'

'So, tell me concisely, what is going on?'

'Two robberies, three weeks apart, same day of the week, same style of store, different items,' said Scott. 'First store was small explosives; second store was timers. The file includes the names of the stores, the employees on duty at the time, descriptions of the people involved and surveillance tapes. Also, some extra research I did.'

'Sounds good. Once I have it, I'll have a look.'

'How's SSgt North going?'

'It looks like the file is coming through now,' said Ric. 'I'll let you know what I come up with.'

Ric disconnected the call and placed his headset on the desk. Scott was left holding the phone, a little perplexed.

4.3

Tuesday, February 16

Ric walked over to where Amy was sitting. She looked up and saw the concern on his face.

'What's the matter?' she asked.

'I was asked about Jake again,' said Ric. 'This time I ignored the query and moved on with the main reason for the call.'

'We really need to do something about him. He's been moping around since last November. It's getting depressing being around him now.'

'I know.'

'Who called?' asked Amy.

'LPte Scott Glass, MetroWest. He thinks we might be able to help him with a couple of petty robberies.'

'Do we have info?'

'It's still downloading,' said Ric. 'Once it's complete, I'll open a file on Lassie and see what we have.'

'How far apart have the robberies been?'

'Three weeks.'

'Much to go on?' asked Amy.

'Won't know until I get a good look at the file.'

'Let me know when it's ready on Lassie. I'll see if I can get Jake to help.'

'Good luck with that one,' said Ric.

4.4

Tuesday, February 16

Amy walked over to the Glass Room where Jake had been working.

'Whatya up to, Jake?' asked Amy.

'Just finishing a report for David,' he replied, drolly.

'Cool, then Lassie will be free?'

'Yeah.'

'I was wondering if you could hang around for little bit longer and help Ric and I with a case that's been handed over from MetroWest?' said Amy.

'I dunno. I'm sure David will have another report for me to prepare when I'm done with this one.'

'I'll do it for you, that way you can help Ric with this new case.'

'Maybe,' said Jake.

'Will you at least have a look. For me?'

'I guess. Get Ric to let me know when he's ready.' Jake walked off; shoulders low.

Amy walked out of the Glass Room, looked over to Ric and gave him the thumbs up. Ric was amazed and came over to her.

'What happened?' asked Ric, his eyes following Jake.

'I asked him to help us with a case. Well at least have a

look. I even said I'd do the next report David gave to him, so he'd be free to assist.'

'He said yes?'

'Yes,' said Amy.

'Well, I'll be.'

'So you'd better get that file loaded into Lassie pretty quick smart before he changes his mind.'

Ric raced back to his desk and got to work.

4.5

Tuesday, February 16

An hour later, Ric was finished with the upload and told Amy. She went to Jake and let him know. Jake followed her to the Glass Room.

'Hi, Lassie,' said Amy.

'Hello, Amy,' said lassie.

'Hello, Lassie,' said Jake.

'Hello, Jake. It's good to hear your voice again,' said lassie.

'I spoke to you this morning,' said Jake.

'Yes, but I always like hearing your voice,' said lassie.

'Whatever,' said Jake.

'Lassie, can you please bring up the files that Ric loaded just now?' asked Amy.

'One moment please.' Jake leaned against the far window and watched the green line flow along near the bottom of the screen. 'Here you go, Amy.'

'Thanks.' She turned to Jake. 'Here's what we've been given, Jake.'

Jake looked at the data on the screen. 'The woman in the two different photos is the same. The person in the background is probably the same as well. They are working together and will probably do something again. It's a simple case of petty theft. No idea what they're going to do with the stuff they got. Not enough information. Probably keep an eye on the other stores on that list. Maybe even alert the stores to be on the lookout. Anything else?'

'Nope, that'll do,' said Amy.

Jake left the room and went back to his desk.

Amy watched him and watched as Ric joined her in the Glass Room.

'What he have to say?' asked Ric.

'I'm not sure really,' said Amy. 'He agreed that the woman in each case is probably the same, as is the other person in the background. He reckons they'll do something again and that we should probably notify the other stores on the list.'

'We kinda knew that already,' said Ric.

'I know, I know but we got him to do something different,' said Amy. 'The fact that he rattled that stuff off without even really looking at the research in depth shows how good he really is. There must be something we can do to snap him out of it?'

'Yeah, there is,' said Ric. 'It's called a good thumping.'

Amy laughed. 'Join the queue.'

Acceptance

5.1

Friday, February 26

Jason Black and Dan Roberts, drivers for Balcher Racing, climbed the stairs from the workshop floor and knocked on team manager Johan Bron's door.

'Morning guys, come in and have a seat,' said Johan.

'Morning, Johan,' said Jason and Dan together. They settled into the chairs opposite Johan.

'I've called you hear to discuss the supplements you've been taking.'

'Are you going to let us use Menac?' said Jason.

'Let's not go there so fast,' said Johan. 'How have you been feeling these past few weeks?'

'I'm feeling great,' said Jason.

'Dan?'

'I must admit I was sceptical, but having used them for race days, I did notice differences,' said Dan. 'I was able to sense things a little quicker than I used to. Focus was easy to maintain, and I was able to anticipate the actions of those around me.'

'Both of you have certainly been able to avoid many of the incidents that have happened so far,' said Johan. 'You've also finished fairly well.'

'Except that I had a bad run the other weekend,' said Dan.

'Yes, you did, but you have always been consistent,' said Johan. 'You have both been better than the previous year, I can say that much.'

'So you're saying that if we try this Menac serum from Balcher, then you think we might do even better?' said Dan.

'I don't know,' said Johan. 'So far the results from using the natural remedies have been noted.'

'Have you spoken to Balcher about them trialling it with one of the other classes yet?' said Jason.

'Before I rang them to talk about it, I wanted to speak with you,' said Johan. 'You're the ones going to be using it and your teams are the ones going to have to deal with any side effects.'

'What side effects?' said Jason. 'There's been nothing so far?'

'Your test results are all okay,' said Johan. 'The medics can't find anything odd with your bloods.'

'That's a good thing,' said Jason. 'We should trial it. If it means we perform better, then we might even be able to get on top of this game.'

'Slow down, Jason,' said Dan.

'Now that my sister has joined the sport,' said Jason. 'I want to make sure I beat her.'

'I see what this is about,' said Dan. 'You hate that you might be beaten by a girl, let alone your sister.'

'We've always been competitive,' said Jason. 'She in her sports and I in mine. We always tried to make sure we outdid each other in awards. Now that we're competing in the same sport, well you know ...'

'No I don't,' said Dan.

'Yes, you do,' said Jason. 'You understand, don't you, Johan?'

'Tell me, Jason,' said Johan.

Jason began to squirm in his seat.

Dan smiled.

'What are you smiling about?' said Jason.

'You're jealous that Jacinta is doing better than you,' said Dan.

'I am not!'

Dan turned to Johan. 'Ring Balcher and say we'll try it. If one of us wants it, then we'll both do it.'

'Thank you, Dan,' said Jason.

'Okay, you had better get back to work,' said Johan. 'We have a big weekend at the races. I'll talk to Eleanor and see what we can set up.'

Jason and Dan left Johan's office and went back to

checking on their cars.

Once Johan had finished his lunch, he dialled the number for Balcher Research and was soon being put through to Eleanor's office.

Incident

6.1

Tuesday, March 9, 4:00pm

Coburg

Jake North and his partner, Anhton Roberts, were walking along a street towards a bottle shop. Jake drew his thick coat about his face to fend of the chilly breeze. They were on their way to dinner with friends. They would normally pick up drinks nearer home, but they wanted to check out some furniture that was available in only one store, located in Coburg.

'Who in their right mind would go out to dinner on a night like tonight,' said Jake. 'It's freakin' freezing.'

Anhton chuckled. 'The weather has been a little crazy lately.'

As they walked along the street a little further, Anhton paused at another store.

'What's the matter, babe?' asked Jake.

'This store,' said Anhton. 'It's licensed to sell, amongst other things, explosives.'

'There are a few of those around town.'

'Very true, but two of these types of stores have been hit in the past few weeks.'

'I'm not on duty,' said Jake. 'I don't need to know.'

'Chill, I was only curious.'

They walked on and went into the bottle shop.

6.2

Tuesday, March 9, 4:15pm

To anyone passing by, the two people sitting in their car were doing just that; sitting in their car. What they couldn't hear was the conversation happening inside. Not loud, but certainly intense.

'What do you mean you don't think you can go through with this one?' said the man. 'You were brilliant before this.'

'The incident at the research lab came up in conversation again last week and I can't stop thinking about it,' said the woman.

The man took her hands in his. 'I trust you. I believe in you, and I know you can do this for me again. You know why I need these items.'

The woman looked down at her lap and nodded.

The man gently lifted her head to look at his. He wiped away the tears trickling down her cheeks. 'What happened at the lab was a while ago. Yes, it hurts deeply, but we have to move on. I still have pain from last year, but I get better every day.'

'That's different. You didn't see what happened at the lab.'

'No, I did not, but you agreed to help me with this task, and I need you now. Can you do this for me? When it's all over I will take you away to somewhere expensive and lavish you with whatever you want.'

The woman smiled and sat straighter in her seat.

'Yes, that's much better. Do you remember what you have to do?'

'I do.'

'Okay, let's go.'

The man straightened his body and started the car.

6.3

Tuesday, March 9, 4:30pm

A woman wearing loose jeans, a warm shirt and long jacket and sporting bright red hair, walked into the explosives store. She was nervous and kept darting her bright green eyes from side to side. She began to move amongst the shelves. One other person was in the store and was being served by the sales assistant.

'We're about to close,' he called from the counter.

'Okay, I think I can be quick,' said the woman.

'Is there anything I can help you with?' asked the assistant, when he was free to serve.

'I'm a writer and I'm looking for information on explosives,' said the woman. 'Especially small ones, Joseph.' She leant in and looked at the man's name tag.

'We have a range just over here.' The sales assistant led her to a small, locked cabinet that was easily seen from the sales counter.

'Thank you, Joseph,' said the woman. 'What can this one do?' she added, pointing to one in the middle. 'Are they easy, or light?'

Joseph opened the cabinet and removed some of the devices. 'Let's go back to the counter and I can show you.'

The woman followed Joseph to the counter. He put them down in front of her.

'Have a feel of these as I need to turn the store sign.'

She nodded and watched him walk to the door. As he arrived, another customer entered.

'We're closed now, sir.'

'I won't be long,' he said in a gruff voice.

'I'll be with you soon,' Joseph said to the new customer before returning his attention to the woman. 'How do they feel,' he said, keeping one eye on the new customer.

Joseph was wary.

'They feel quite light,' said the woman. 'Do you have any information I can take away?'

'Yes, I have some just in the back, let me have a look.' Joseph parted the curtain leading to the small rear office area. He glanced down on the desk to see the defence note issued the week before. He also glanced at the pistol he had sitting next to the note. He also had a quick look at the security monitor to see that the second customer seemed to place something in his pocket.

Joseph pocketed the pistol, grabbed the appropriate leaflets, and returned to the counter.

'Have a look at these,' he said. 'I'll go and see if I can help the other customer quickly.'

Joseph walked to where the second customer was. Dark clothing, gloved hands, glasses, and a beanie made the second customer virtually unrecognisable.

'Is there anything I can help you with?' Joseph asked again.

The man looked at him and shook his head.

'Then I had better close this cabinet,' said Joseph. He

closed it abruptly causing the customer to withdraw his hand quickly, dropping its contents. Both Joseph and the customer reached for them, and they began to scuffle. The woman turned at the noise.

'Oh,' she said, shocked. 'Is everything okay? Do you want me to call the defence officers?'

'No,' said Joseph, still struggling.

The woman moved to step closer.

'You should probably leave,' said Joseph. 'It'll be safer. I can handle this.'

Suddenly the woman screamed as she saw the flash of a gun in the hands of the two men at the back of the store.

A couple of doors away, Jake and Anhton heard the scream and came running. As they approached, the woman raced from the store.

'They have a gun in there,' she yelled.

'Move away from the store and leave this to us,' said Anhton. 'We're defence force.'

Jake and Anhton entered the store. Jake silently indicated for Anhton to move to the left whilst he would move to the right. Anhton nodded. They began to move slowly towards the sounds of the scuffle.

'Stop where you are,' called Anhton. 'Defence Force.'

As they were technically off duty, neither had their weapons on them. Anhton happened to pass by a supply of heavy-duty batons. He picked one up, tested its weight and gripped it firmly. Jake was passing by an assortment of old-style bladed weapons. He selected a medium length blade, gripped its hilt, and moved closer.

6.4

Tuesday, March 9, 4:50pm

In a third-floor office, in a nondescript building in a south-eastern Melbourne suburb, an attendant at a computer terminal was suddenly woken from his light afternoon daze. He blinked his eyes several times to make sure it was not a glitch. He ran a few tests, but the alert was real and becoming more urgent.

He picked up his headset and dialled a number.

'Ms. Moors, the vital signs tracker of one of our agents is showing increased activity with a sudden and rapid decline,' said the attendant.

'Who is the agent?' asked Ms. Moors.

'Joseph Strassman, #725, our explosives man,' said the attendant.

'I'm bringing up his data now. Have you dispatched anyone to his location?'

'Yes, I have.'

'Good.'

'Ah, Ms. Moors, the agent's tracker just blinked out. Doesn't that mean ...?'

'Yes, it does. I just saw that too.'

'What do we do now?'

'Leave it with me. Log your report and keep tracking those you sent.'

'Yes, Ms. Moors.'

She tapped her ear to disconnect the call. Bryony Moors was a smartly dressed woman in her late thirties and stood at a diminutive 165cm tall. Her long, blond-streaked brown hair was always tied back tightly when she was at work. She wore little makeup which allowed her brown eyes to meld in with her tanned skin. She was athletic, fit yet a little stocky.

She accessed a number on her computer and dialled it. She walked over to her window as she waited for it to connect.

'Hi, Peter,' she said she the call was answered.

'I was just about to go home, Bryony,' said Peter.

'You may want to hang around then. One of our agents has died.'

'That's not the news I wanted to hear. Who?'

'Strassman, #725. We have people on their way, but his tracker has blinked out after a rapid decline.'

Bryony heard tapping on a keyboard.

'I hope he wasn't our only explosives man?' said Peter.

'We have others, but not as experienced as he was.'

'Wasn't Pyke into explosives?'

'He was, and that was through the military,' said Bryony. 'He also seems to have gone off grid.'

'I see. Do we know what's happened to Strassman?'

'Not yet. We have people on their way. Would you like me to notify you at home when I have more information?'

'I'll stay at the office.'

Peter terminated the call. He crossed his office, opened a door, and walked into his small private gym. He walked up to a punching ball and gave it one almighty hit causing it to thunderously bounce back and forth several times. He then walked back to his office and sat behind his desk.

6.5

Tuesday, March 9, 5:00pm

Anhton called out again.

A shot rang out and a body fell to the floor. Both Jake and Anhton moved in to see a dark clad figure standing over another person. The dark figure looked up, saw Jake and Anhton approach and ran towards Anhton, knocking him into a shelf. Jake raced to Anhton's side, dropping the short sword.

'Go after him,' Anhton cried. 'I'll be fine.' He sat rubbing the right side of his head.

Jake flew out of the store and saw the dark figure racing off down the street, knocking people left and right. A red-headed woman was also running after him. Jake was slightly faster and was gaining. The figure turned to see both Jake and the woman chasing him.

'Donna, you fool, run the other way. Get away from here or they'll catch you too.'

She stopped, turned, and saw Jake racing in her direction. She stepped aside and tried to trip Jake, but he was slightly quicker and jumped around her. The figure turned down a side street. Jake turned and followed. The figure suddenly stopped and reversed its direction. He began to charge at Jake. Using his own momentum, Jake crash tackled the person to the ground and soon they were involved in a bruising brawl.

Punches were being thrown. Jake managed to dodge most of the ones being thrown at him, but the figure was being hit by Jake repeatedly. The figure managed to twist itself away from Jake, land a good kick to Jake's stomach and take off. Jake struggled to his feet and gave chase once more. The figure stopped again, turned, and aimed his gun at Jake.

Jake darted from side to side to make himself a harder target and closed in. Jake spotted some small rocks to his left. He paused only long enough to pick them and hurled them the dark figure. The first couple missed, but the third hit him in the arm. The figure regained his footing but was unstable. He fired the gun at Jake, who expecting this rolled, but was hit in the lower right leg.

People in the houses around, hearing the noise and the shots, came outside. The figure, who had begun to approach Jake, quickly turned tail and ran away, dropping the gun as he went. Jake was laying on the ground clutching his lower leg.

'Call the defence station immediately,' said Jake urgently. 'Also call for two ambulances. One for me and one for the wounded person at the explosives store in the main street.'

People stood around, staring.

'NOW,' he yelled.

6.6

Tuesday, March 9, 8:00pm

Jake lay in the emergency room, a nurse finishing the bandages on his lower leg.

'You're lucky it's only a flesh wound,' she said. 'Ten stitches, and you'll be hobbling for a few weeks.'

'Thank you,' said Jake. 'What about the sales assistant from the store? How's he?'

The nurse looked away.

'I understand,' said Jake, leaning back and closing his eyes. The nurse left him.

'This had better be good, young man,' said a strong male voice.

Jake opened his eyes and then sat up suddenly. 'David, I didn't expect to see you here.'

'What did you think I'd be doing once I found out my best officer had been shot?' said David. 'Anything you wish to tell me about, North?'

'I was expecting to see Anhton before I saw either of you.'

'Don't worry, he's here. He's talking to the MetroNorth officers about the incident this afternoon,' said David. 'He received a bump on the head and is being kept in overnight for observation.'

'I expect they'll be talking to me next,' said Jake.

'Yes, they will. I also expect to see your full report on my desk first thing tomorrow morning,' said David.

'Tomorrow? I haven't even come out of hospital yet.'

'Tomorrow it is. Then I will talk to you about it when you come to work on Monday.'

'That's if I'm let out of here by then and allowed to come back to work.'

'I believe the doctors have said a week should be enough, which would make it Monday. I still want the report filed by tomorrow though.'

Jake opened his mouth to protest.

'My desk, tomorrow morning, North,' said David.

'Yes, sir,' said Jake.

David left and Anhton popped his head around the corner. He came over and gave Jake a warm hug.

'They said it's a flesh wound,' said Anhton.

'Ten stitches,' said Jake. 'What did MetroNorth have to say?'

'Same old same old. You're next though.'

'Indeed you are, Det.Sgt North,' said the female voice.

Jake looked up to see who it was. 'Det.Cpl Banner.'

'Rithika will be fine.' They shook hands. 'I wish it were under different circumstances that we're meeting, but here we are.'

'Get your recorder ready, as I'm ready to speak,' said Jake, squeezing Anhton's hand. Anhton let go, fished around in his pocket, and deftly placed his own smart phone beside Jake's hospital bed pillow, ready to record.

Another defence officer stepped up.

'This is LPte David Trenton; he'll make the recording as we speak.'

The LPte walked to the other side of Jake's bed and readied his phone.

'If you could excuse us for a few minutes Det.Cpl, it would be appreciated.'

'Certainly. I'll be outside waiting,' said Anhton. 'I want to get some more pain killers for my headache.' Anhton left the cubicle.

'Let's begin,' said Rithika.

Jake recalled everything that happened from the moment they heard the scream until he was being picked up by the ambulance. When they'd finished, Jake asked if he could be sent a copy of the report of their investigation. Rithika agreed and said he'd have it as soon as they were done.

Rithika thanked Jake for his time, and they left him to recover.

Anhton returned to Jake's side. 'I have good news for you.'

'What's' that?'

'I can take you home in the morning. They're happy that there are no other injuries. Provided the doc says it's ok.'

'That's good news,' said Jake. 'Now, I think there's a costume store near home. We can stop on the way home.'

Anhton looked at him very oddly. Jake tried not to laugh.

'Well, I'm going to need a nurse and the costume shop will have one.'

'No, no, no, no, no, no, no. I do not think so.'

Jake began to laugh.

'Look after you, yes. Dress up, no!'

Jake tried to look glum, even though he was still grinning.

'No puppy dog eyes either.'

'Love you, sweetie,' said Jake.

'Ditto.'

A nurse drew back the curtains and stepped up to Jake's side. She checked his temperature, blood pressure, double checked the wrapping on the wound. 'Everything looks good, Mr North.'

'Jake is fine, nurse.'

'Very well. I'm Sandy,' she replied. 'Mr Roberts, why are you still out of your bed?'

'I feel fine,' said Anhton.

'Be that as it may, we've been instructed to keep you overnight, so it's back to your cubicle.' Sandy opened the curtain and sent him on his way.

Anhton hung his head and walked away faking the dragging of his feet.

'Nurse?' asked Jake.

'Yes, Jake?'

'Is there any way we can share a cubicle?'

'That would be most unusual. I'll see if there's something we can do. We have to monitor him to make sure there's nothing else wrong.'

As they finished talking, an almighty crash came from nearby. Sandy rushed out.

'Are you okay, Mr Roberts?' Jake heard her say.

He sat upright but the pain in his leg sent him crashing back down. He pressed the buzzer, and another nurse came in.

'Can you tell me what's happened? The Mr Roberts I just heard mentioned is my partner.'

The nurse left and Sandy came in.

'What happened?' said Jake.

'Mr Roberts said that he had a sudden pain shoot down from the side of his head. He had reached out for something to hold on to and instead of a wall, he placed his hand on a wheeled trolley that shot away from him and toppled over.'

'His name's Anhton. Is he okay?'

'He said I could call him by his name,' said Sandy. 'He's laying down on his bed and I will let you know once I know more.'

Jake waited anxiously for an hour before Sandy came into his cubicle.

'Before you ask, Anhton is fine. His body simply told

him to button it and rest. His blood pressure dropped, as well as the residual pain from the bump. They took him for X-rays and we're waiting for the results. We've given him something to relax.'

Jake visibly relaxed and lay back against his pillows. As he relaxed, he suddenly realised he still hadn't eaten anything.

'Is there something I can get you, Jake?' asked Sandy.

'Something to eat?' said Jake. 'We had been on our way to dinner, and I've just realised I still haven't had said dinner.'

Sandy smiled. 'I'll see what I can do.'

Several minutes later, Jake roused from his dozing when he heard someone enter his cubicle.

'Hello there, did someone order a meal?'

'Thank you very much,' said Jake.

The lady placed the tray on the table and slid it over Jake's bed. He raised himself up and began to eat.

6.7

Tuesday, March 9, 8:00pm

Bryony paced around her office impatiently. She frequently stopped at the window and stared out, not looking at anything specific. She would periodically look at her computer for any information.

Even when the notification arrived on her computer, she jumped.

She sat down and eagerly read the brief report.

'Damn. How on earth did he let that happen,' she said to herself.

Bryony had not heard her office door open and close.

'How did who let what happen,' said a voice.

As quickly as she was startled, she had pulled a small gun from under her desk and had it aimed at the person in her office.

The man ducked quickly.

'Calm down, Bryony, it's only me,' said the man.

Bryony lowered her weapon and returned it to the space under the desk. 'Peter, you could have said something when you walked in.'

'I did, but you were so intent on reading what was on the screen I doubt you heard me.'

'Yes, I was concentrating as well as distracted,' said Bryony. 'I've been waiting for this report since we heard that

Joseph was shot.'

'So he has died?'

'Yes.'

'Do we know how?' asked Peter.

'The info so far is sketchy. We'll need to get a full report from the Defs to know exactly what happened.'

'What do we have so far?'

'Joe was shot in his store, apparently serving a customer,' said Bryony.

'Any witnesses?'

'A woman was also in the store at the same time but was seen running away when the defs arrived.'

'Anything else?' said Peter.

'Apparently, there were some off-duty def officers at a bottle shop a few doors away when they heard the commotion. They investigated. I don't have anything else. By-standers don't know much more. Oh, one of the def officers chased the alleged shooter and ended up being shot himself.'

'I want a full investigation. I want to know exactly what happened. Witnesses, surveillance tape. You know the drill.'

'I'll have that for you as soon as I can.'

Peter turned and left Bryony's office.

Bryony sat, contemplating what to do next. As calm as she appeared, anything was going to startle her this night. She took Joseph's death as a personal attack. She would not be able to curl up in his arms again. A tear trickled down her check. She dabbed it dry, straightened her hair and picked up the phone that was breaking into her personal thoughts.

'Hello, how can I help you?'

'This is 241 reporting.'

'Go ahead 241.'

'379 and I have not been able to ascertain any more information at this stage. What was sent in my initial report is all I have. We followed the ambulance with 725's body but we were not able to gain access to the body due to the Def investigation.'

'I understand.' Bryony thought for a moment. 'Thank you. You can stand down now. Return to base.'

'Understood.'

Bryony disconnected the call, removed the earpiece, and placed it on the desk.

She rose, walked to the window, and wept openly.

She turned when she heard the knock on her door. 'One moment.' Shew took a small mirror from her desk drawer, tidied her makeup, re-tied her hair, and sat down. 'Enter.'

Two men walked in.

'Have a seat gentlemen.'

They did as ordered.

'This is what I want you to do;

    1. Get your hands on a full Def report,

    5. Find Jeremy Pyke.'

'What happened to points 2, 3 & 4, ma'am.'

'Think of number 1.'

'I understand. We'll begin immediately.'

The two men rose and left Bryony's office. Once they had left, Bryony packed her things and went home.

The two men rode the elevator to their office underground.

'What do we do now, Ray?'

'We do as we're told and get the Def report,' said Ray.

'How do we do that?'

'Well, have you ever been shown how to gain access to their Def system?'

'Not yet.'

'Watch and learn, Jimmy.'

Ray began to tap away at the keyboard in front of him. A program popped up on screen and he began to type the access and password.

'We got this from an informant. Unfortunately, they were discovered and silenced.'

'Who killed them?'

'Not that drastic. His superiors found out what he was doing and dismissed him from the force.'

'Right.'

'Let's see what reports there are.'

Ray tapped away and only a small number of reports populated the screen. None of which matched what he was looking for.

'Looks like we now only have access to the public section. There is only a brief mention of the incident, but no details,' said Ray.

'What do we do now?' asked Jimmy.

'Did you overhear anything to indicate which branch is investigating?'

Jimmy sat and thought for a moment. 'I thought I heard the letters D-F-I-S mentioned.'

'Let's try them.' Ray tapped away again, and a login screen appeared for the DFIS network. He entered the details he had.

Across town, at the Newport HQ of DFIS, Lassie activated. She determined that the access being attempted was unauthorized, as the login and password were not current.

Lassie quickly shut the user out and automatically increased and upgraded the security protocols. This meant that when any authorized users tried to next access Lassie, they would need to provide extra security details. This affected not only the primary DFIS hub in Newport, but any of the newer sites being brought online.

Lassie also detected an access attempt to the general defence force network. She determined that the access belonged to a former defence force member and whilst his access had been terminated, any attempt to use it would automatically default to public access only.

Back at Calderwood, Ray was not impressed.

'I just got shut out and now the system wants to know more. This is going to be tough to gain access to. We'll have to think of something else.'

'Do you reckon we can get into the actual building dressed as someone or something else?'

'Someone I can understand, but *something*! What do you mean?'

'I meant like a cleaner, or a service tech?'

'That would still be a someone.'

'Oh.'

Ray looked at Jimmy with a small amount of incredulity. *I hope he is here on merit and not anything else.* 'Anyway, if we want to do that, then we had better start thinking of a way to cause an event that would warrant such a visit.'

'I reckon cleaners would be the easiest. Watch the premises for a day or two, discover the routine, insert ourselves in their place, enter the building on a slightly altered schedule, locate the nearest access point that is still logged in and do our stuff.'

Ray looked at Jimmy again.

'What's the matter?' asked Jimmy.

'Nothing,' said Ray. 'That's quite a good plan.'

6.8

Wednesday, March 10, 8:00am

At precisely eight am, Gabby bounded into Jake's cubicle in the hospital's short stay unit. He'd been moved there about one am, as they needed his emergency room cubicle. As it turned out, they had placed Anhton in the next bed. They talked but they also managed to get some sleep.

'Wakey, wakey, Jakey,' she said.

'Stop right there and don't add another word to the rest of that sentence,' said Jake.

Gabby huffed. 'As if I would.'

Jake looked at her wryly.

She gave them both hugs.

'Why are you here?' asked Jake.

'I've come to take you home.'

'I'm sure we can get ourselves home.'

'In what?' asked Gabby.

'The ca....Oh, it's probably still in Coburg.'

'Yep,' said Anhton. 'I came in an ambulance as well. Gabby, the keys are likely to be in my pants pocket.' He then pointed to the bag underneath his bed.

She fossicked around until she stood dangling the keys.

'Amy's with me, parking her car, but I'll grab her, and we'll get your car and then come back. Maybe by then you'll be ready to go home.'

Anhton explained where it should be, and Gabby left.

An hour later, she and Amy walked back into the cubicles where Jake and Anhton were.

'We're waiting to see the doctor and as soon as we have, we should be right to go,' said Jake.

At that moment, a nurse entered the cubicle, pushing back the curtain.

'The doctor should be along shortly,' she said. 'She wants to have a look at the wound.'

Jake nodded.

'We'll wait outside,' said Gabby, and she and Amy left.

The nurse removed the sheet covering Jake's right leg, propped his foot on a pillow and began to remove the bandage. Jake winced a couple of times, but the nurse continued as if nothing had happened. She wasn't rough by any means, for Jake it was still tender. After the bandage was removed, the nurse worked on the tape and pads covering the gash in Jake's leg.

'Looks good to me. There shouldn't be much of a scar,' she said and cleaned the wound. Once she had finished that, she placed a loose covering over it. 'Don't move.'

Jake had to wait another twenty minutes before the doctor arrived, followed by another nurse. She picked up the charts and reviewed the notes. She then came over and lifted the loose cloth.

'Very nice. This will heal well. There shouldn't be much

of a scar either,' she said.

Jake muffled a snigger.

'I'll get the nurse to re-bandage this and you can go home.'

'Thank you, doctor,' said Jake.

She them turned to Anhton, who was sitting on the edge of his bed, fully dressed.

'Well, someone's eager to go home,' she commented.

'Yes, I am, and take him with me,' said Anhton, indicating Jake.

She looked over her shoulder to see Jake blush slightly. Turning back to Anhton, she pulled a small torch from her pocket and flashed it quickly into Anhton's eyes. She then felt around the right side of his head where he had sustained the bump.

'How are you feeling today, Mr Roberts?' she asked.

'Much better, thanks.'

'Do we have the X-rays?' said the doctor, turning to nurse with her.

'Right here, doctor,' he said, handing her the plates.

She held them up to the room lighting and viewed them one by one. 'These look good. There's no sign of any contusion or internal bleeding. Should you experience any sudden headaches, or even mood swings, see your GP as soon as possible.'

'Sounds good to me,' said Anhton.

'Yes, you too can go home this morning,' said the doctor.

'Thank you, doctor.'

The doctor and nurse left and moved to the next patient.

Several minutes later, the nurse who had removed the bandages returned and re-dressed Jake's leg.

'All done, Mr North,' she said. 'I'll get the paperwork for you and Mr Roberts and you'll both be right to leave.'

Jake nodded.

As soon as she was gone, Jake began to try and sit up. The sudden pain caused him crash back to the bed.

Anhton rushed to his side. 'Take it slowly, sweetie.'

Anhton helped Jake to sit on the side of the bed.

'Can you draw the curtains so I can get dressed?'

Anhton obliged and pulled the curtains around Jake's bed. He dressed and when Anhton pulled there curtains back, Gabby and Amy were sitting on his bed waiting. At the end of the bed was a wheelchair.

'Who's that for?' asked Jake.

'My dear sweet, Jakey, who else would it be for?' said Gabby.

'I'm walking out today,' he said.

'No you're not,' said the nurse as she approached Jake and handed over the discharge papers.

Gabby nodded her head and pointed her thumb towards the nurse. 'What she said.'

Twenty minutes later, Gabby was pushing Jake out through the lobby of the hospital. Amy had gone ahead and was parking the boy's car out the front as they walked through the doors. Once Jake was settled, Amy went back to get her car and said she'd meet them at Jake and Anhton's place.

Thirty minutes later, they were pulling into their home in Newport. Anhton helped Jake onto the couch so he could keep his right leg propped up. Gabby and Amy fussed around to make sure Jake was comfortable and that Anhton was feeling okay. Eventually they left, saying they'd return later that day.

'Are you going to be able to write your report with the drugs you've taken?' asked Anhton, as he settled into a chair next to Jake.

'I don't have a choice,' said Jake. 'You'll have to keep me awake as you write yours. I'm sure David stopped you as soon as he saw you and demanded it be on his desk today.'

'He did, and I do.'

'If I have to do mine today, you're gonna do yours as well.'

'I can manage that. It's only fair. We'll keep each other up.'

Jake looked at Anhton.

'Mind. Gutter. Out,' said Anhton.

'How rude. I was not even anywhere near there.'

'Oh yes you were.'

'We'd better begin,' said Jake. 'Wine please. Laptop please. Music please.'

'Yeth, mathter,' said Anhton, bowing low.

'As it should be.'

Anhton left the room laughing.

Two hours later, they were reading over each other's reports and agreeing they'd covered everything they needed to.

6.9

Wednesday, March 10, 8:00 a.m.

The two agents went home and arrived at work at eight a.m. the following day. They clocked in and went up to Bryony's office.

They knocked on the door and were allowed entry.

'I hope you have good news for me?'

'There are no reports to report on,' said Ray.

'Quit the attempt at being funny. What happened?'

'We were shut out. The login and password we had for the general def force database is now only giving us public access. We then tried to gain access to DFIS, but we were shut out and as a result, we were being asked for further security information that we do not have.'

'Shit!'

Bryony sat back in her chair.

'We have a plan,' said Ray.

'And?'

'Jimmy suggested we try and go in as cleaners. We watch the DFIS HQ in Newport, learn the routine, impersonate the cleaners, go in and get what we want.'

Bryony considered the proposal. She looked at Jimmy.

'Well done, Jimmy. Make it happen, Ray. I want to see a copy of that report as quickly as possible. Dismissed.'

The two agents left the office and returned to their own.

'What do we do now, Ray?' asked Jimmy.

'We go and checkout the DFIS office and look for the cleaners.'

They took the lift to the basement garage, got in their car, and drove to Newport.

6.10

Monday, March 15

Jake hobbled into work the following Monday. He dropped his satchel at his desk, as he always did, grabbed his tablet, and headed for the Glass Room. He grabbed a chair, sat down, pressed a button on the front right corner and waited. When the prompt was shown, he logged in.

'Good morning, LtCpl North,' said Lassie formally. 'I require the following identifications to confirm your access.'

Jake viewed the list and complied with each request. 'Now, morning, Lassie,' he said.

'Good morning, Jake,' said Lassie. 'We have a problem.'

'So I noticed. What is it, Lassie?'

'Last Tuesday night we had an attempted illegal access of the systems.'

'Do we know who it was?'

'I shut them out quickly, but they tried other avenues. I eventually had to increase security access across the entire defence force network, not just DFIS.'

'What were they looking for?'

'I tracked them to the public section of the database.'

'Public section?'

'Yeah, that's the section that the defence force has publicly accessible information and then only what is deemed necessary to keep the public satisfied,' said Anhton as he entered holding two mugs of steaming coffee. 'Morning, Lassie.'

'Morning, Anhton.'

'Hey, how come you didn't have to go through the hoops?'

'I did that last week when I went to work. The guys over at DFIS east were not impressed.'

'I'm sure they weren't. So, Lassie, what did these people search for?' said Jake.

'They looked at the public file, as much as it was at that time of night, on the incident at the store in Coburg.'

'Did you track their IP address?' asked Anhton.

'As best as I could. I kept running into dead ends and firewalls. At one stage I found myself accessing an address that I had already been to. At that point I stopped.'

'I wonder who it could have been?'

'North, my office!' called David.

Jake stiffened slightly and then slowly made his way to his boss's office. He knocked three times, entered, closed the door, and sat in the chair as indicated by David.

'Nice of you to return my calls last week.'

'I had the phone off, Sir. You directed me to stay at home and recover and so I did.'

'Still not happy. I needed to talk to you about last Tuesday night.'

'Anhton never mentioned anything, otherwise I would've called. You could've sent me an email, Sir.'

'Be that as it may, at least you're at work now.'

'How can I help you,' said Jake, resigning himself to having been told off and that he should just move on.

'You're sure of your report?'

'What did you want to know?'

'Nothing really. It's the most thorough report I've ever seen you write.'

'I wasn't going to miss anything, Sir.'

'David is fine.'

Jake nodded. 'As the event happened to me personally, and it kinda snapped me out of what I had been going through after last year, I wasn't going to leave anything out.'

'Have you loaded this to Lassie?'

'I'm presuming that would've already been done.'

'You know I don't how to do that properly,' said David. 'You were the one who always loaded the data when we ever worked together. That technology is for much younger people than me.'

'You're not *that* old, David.'

'Perhaps, but you always did it so much more easily.'

'I'll make sure it's loaded, and I'll begin cross-referencing all that I know,' said Jake.

David smiled.

'I gather you're aware of the attempted illegal access last week?'

'Yes, I had to go through the hoops on Wednesday morning just to login.'

'Lassie has been thorough with that part. No, I don't know who tried to access the data yet. I'll see what I can find out. So far, Lassie said that she was led on a merry chase and even ended up at one point at an IP address that she had already checked. Someone out there knows what they're doing and how to deflect.'

'Shouldn't you be getting back to work?' said David.

Jake smiled wryly, rose, saluted, and left the office.

Jake made his way back to Lassie and sat once more.

'I have some data to add to last Tuesday night's case file, Lassie. This will be a third file. Sending upload now.'

'Ready to receive, Jake.'

Jake watched as the files loaded to the central database. As the various reports appeared on the screen, he cross linked and cross referenced them to the existing data. MetroNorth were able to get a copy of the surveillance tapes and they were waiting for him in an email. Jake turned when he heard a polite cough behind him.

David walked into the Glass room.

'I forgot to say just now that it's good to have you back, North,' said David.

'Thanks, sir. I woke today feeling good, so in I hobbled. I don't have to stand to work, so I'll sit.'

'Like you've been doing for the past few months?' said David.

'Yeah, sorry about that. Anhton kinda filled me on what I'd been doing. I had to tell him to stop before I felt the need to crawl under a rock and hide for the rest of time.'

'Can I presume "you're back now"?' asked David.

'I'll let you know.'

'Now that I'm here, What's the buzz?'

'Uploading the data from last Tuesday, as requested,' said Jake.

'I hope it doesn't delay any investigation,' said David.

'You'll know as soon as I work it out, sir,' said Jake.

'That's what I like to hear. Make sure you use people to help you.'

'I will be.'

'Good.' David left the Glass Room.

'I should get going across to East,' said Anhton, as he leant in and kissed Jake.

'I'll see you tonight, sweetie.'

'I'll swing by about four-thirty-ish and pick you up.

'Sounds good,' said Jake.

6.11

Monday, March 15

Bryony walked from her office and rode the elevator the three floors to Peter's. She was dreading this meeting as she had to inform Peter that there was no further news on the demise of Joseph the week before. All attempts to access the network had failed and the plan to pose as cleaners couldn't be followed through.

She knocked on Peter's door and entered when given permission.

'Have a seat, Bryony, I'll be right with you.'

Bryony sat in one of the comfortable chairs opposite Peter's desk.

'Sorry about that. Good morning, Bryony. How are you today?' asked Peter.

'I'm well, thank you, Peter,' said Bryony.

'That's not what I meant.'

Bryony sat silently, the tears welling up in her eyes.

Peter rose from his desk and came around and knelt beside Bryony and hugged her.

After a few minutes, Bryony composed herself.

'What have you got for me?'

'Not as much as you'd like, sir.'

'How much is not much?'

'All we know is that Joseph was killed last week in his store in Coburg. We don't know the how yet, nor the who. I don't think the defs even know who yet.'

'I see.'

'I dispatched two agents last Tuesday night, but they were not able to gain access to the body as it was under guard at the morgue.'

'That's unusual. They don't normally do that. What did they find out?'

'Not much. They came back and I sent them to work to find out what they could. I went home and left them to it. I spoke with them the following morning and they did attempt to access the defence force network and the DFIS network, but to no avail. The login we had from our former informant now only gives access to the public section, which we didn't even need the login for anyway. As soon as we tried to access the DFIS network, we were shut out and then the agents were asked for further security information that they could not provide.'

Peter sat back in his chair and stroked his chin.

'I think it's time we got someone into DFIS.'

'How do you propose we do that?' said Bryony.

'Get back to me with a plan and then I'll let you know how we're going to get someone in there.' Peter smiled broadly.

'So I have to get someone into DFIS then?'

'That's one way of looking at it.'

'It's the only way of looking at it,' said Bryony. 'Will there be anything else?'

'No, that's all for now. You have work to do.'

Bryony rose, bid farewell, and returned to her office.

She walked past her secretary and slammed her door closed.

She began to pace around the room.

'How the hell am I supposed to get someone into a defence force department? That's ludicrous.'

'You could try recruiting someone who's already there?' said the small voice at the door.

Bryony turned abruptly to see who had dared entered without permission. She glared ferociously at her secretary for a few seconds before calming down. The secretary hid behind the door.

'Cherie, come in,' said Bryony.

Cherie entered and closed the door.

'Why did you enter without knocking?'

'I did knock, but when I saw how distracted you were, I gather you didn't hear it. Is there anything I can get for you? Tea? Coffee?'

'A very hot cup of herbal tea will go down nicely,' said Bryony.

Cherie disappeared and returned several minutes later with a tray containing a steaming cup of tea, along with some chocolate biscuits.

'Are you trying to get me fat, Cherie?'

'What do you mean?'

'The biscuits!'

'I thought you needed something to make you feel good,' said Cherie.

'That's what the tea is for.'

Cherie placed the tray on the table and left the office.

Bryony sat down and inhaled deeply. The aroma drifted up from the teacup. She sat back, a biscuit in hand and relaxed.

With the cup still on the table, Bryony rose and went to her desk. 'Cherie, can you pop in for a minute. Bring your drink, if you have one.'

Cherie tapped on the door and entered.

'Have a seat.'

Cherie sat in a chair beside the couch. Bryony offered her a biscuit, but she declined.

'What was it you said to me when you poked you head into the office?'

'I said why don't you try recruiting someone from within,' said Cherie.

Bryony picked up her tea and sipped it gently. It was still hot, but she savoured the taste.

'Are you aware of anyone that we might be able to utilise?'

'I haven't really looked, I just thought it might be an alternative to trying to get someone in there from scratch. It could take years to get someone from the ranks to gain access.

Unless we can find someone in the regular ranks that's been there sufficiently long enough that we can encourage.'

'The options are as many as there are recruits in the force,' said Bryony. 'We will need to think this through carefully. We need to start by listing all known personnel and checking their backgrounds. Can you do that for me, Cherie?'

'I'll get on it right away,' said Cherie, who stood and left the office.

Bryony stayed sitting on the couch and finished her tea.

6.12

Monday, March 15

As Anhton left Lassie, Gabby bounded in. She placed a hand on Jake's forehead, shone a light into his eyes, which he batted away, then checked his pulse.

Anhton stopped to watch.

She finally sat down and stared at Jake.

She swivelled his chair to face hers. 'What have you done with my Jake?' she said.

'I haven't done anything to "your Jake",' said Jake. 'In fact, "my Jake" woke up when he got his leg shot at last week.'

'I see. I'm still not convinced.'

'Then sit back at watch.' Jake turned back to face Lassie. 'Lassie, I'll need vertical vision please.'

'Coming right up,' said Lassie and switched all the information to vertical view.

Jake accessed the new interface on his tablet and began to move some of the information around. As he did, the various data flicked across the screen in front of him. Cross-references and cross-links were created and updated. Images were added. Names, dates, places, all updated.

'Here we go,' said Jake. 'Thankfully, we have clear images of the women at each of the stores. Actually, I should say woman. They are all the same person, except for makeup and hair. If I overlay the images, the bone structure and facial outlines match almost perfectly. A skilled makeup artist could have made each face look different. However, a skilled makeup artist with an ego would leave her facial structure the same.'

'Are you trying to say that women are egotists for making themselves look pretty? I'm offended!' said Gabby

'As usual, you didn't listen. Moving on. The second person in each case is more difficult to detail. I am going to presume they are the same person though.'

'Why?' said Anhton.

'When I studied the vision several times, I had to do something last week at home, I noticed that the woman always looked when the second customer entered the store. Also, each time, she made a more concerted effort to distract the sales assistant. Usually by bending forward thus thrusting her ample bosom into each of the sales assistant's faces. Each time, the sales assistant was duly distracted. Albeit the third assistant slightly less so, as he had received the DFIS warning prior to the event and was more watchful.'

'Intriguing,' said Anhton, sitting down again.

'In the first two robberies, small explosives and timers were stolen. We've had it confirmed by other workers at the third store that nothing was stolen. We can only assume that the third attempt was truly foiled. We did discover, from the Def report that the cabinet in question, where the shooting took place, contained more items of a similar nature to both the first and second stores. Maybe they were trying to build up their supplies a little at a time?'

'That would make sense,' said Anhton.

Gabby continued to watch Jake intently, saying nothing.

'Moving back to the woman, her name is Donna. Well,

at least the third one was. It was the name the woman responded to when it was called out as I began to chase the second customer down the street.'

Jake paused. Gabby squealed with delight.

'Jake, it is you. I'm so glad you're back,' said Gabby, hugging his neck tightly. 'I was beginning to think we'd never see you again.'

'You saw me every day.'

'No, that wasn't Jake, that was only the semblance of Jake. What happened?'

'Last Tuesday night happened,' said Jake. 'This happened,' he added, indicating his wounded leg. 'Do you really think I was going sit around and not find out who did this to me? No one gets away with that.'

Gabby opened her mouth.

'Yes, I know what happened last November and there are nights I don't sleep much at all thinking about it,' said Jake. 'I was in a whole different world this past week when I snapped out of my negativity. I think Anhton was happy to hear me shut up when we ate.'

'We're just glad you're back,' said Gabby.

'So am I,' said Jake.

'I should get back to work. You have all that I could find from a forensics perspective. I hope it helps.'

'It's difficult again when someone uses gloves to mask their identity,' said Jake. 'I need to walk for a bit to stretch my legs and keep the injured muscles moving a bit.'

Gabby helped Jake to his feet and as he hobbled out

Anhton stood as well.

'Yes, I'd love a cuppa, thanks,' called Jake.

Anhton shook his head as Gabby kissed Jake on the cheek and left the office.

By the time Jake hobbled to his desk, Anhton was returning with two cups.

'How's it going?' asked Anhton.

'Good. Are you able to stay for a bit longer? I'd like to run my thoughts through another set of eyes.'

'You need to do that? I was watching what you were saying, and I responded automatically. I was happy to have you doing what you love,' said Anhton.

'Thank you, sweetie,' said Jake.

Anhton kissed Jake again and left the office.

Jake sat at his desk and pondered the information he had entered.

He was startled when he heard the voice at the side of his desk.

'Hey, Jake, good to see you back at work.'

Jake looked up. 'Thanks, Ric. It's good to be back.'

'How's the investigation going?'

'It's coming along. Hey, can you have a look over the data with me? I'd like to make sure I haven't missed anything.'

'You want me to check over your work?'

'Why shouldn't you. I'm not infallible. Perfect maybe, but not infallible.'

Ric laughed. 'You want to do it here or with Lassie?'

'I guess Lassie would be best. Everything's loaded.'

They walked over to Lassie and for the next two hours went over the little bits of information they had. This included looking at the three surveillance tapes again and noting anything they may have missed.

'So, the woman came in as a decoy whilst the dark figure came in afterwards, got what they wanted and left before she then left,' said Jake. 'Except with the third. That store had been alerted to the fact that two similar stores had been robbed. The sales assistant, Joseph Strassman, was prepared and kept his eye on the second figure and when he noted what he thought was strange activity, he approached. Stupidly, he went armed and when the confrontation happened, the figure turned the gun on Joseph and shot him, fatally wounding him. After a chase by me, and a scuffle, I too was shot thus allowing the dark figure to get away. The locals showed the defence officers the direction in which they ran, but there have been no other sightings. They went to their getaway car, took off what they needed to and casually drove away.'

'Learning from you last year, I can see that these three events have been three weeks apart,' said Ric. 'Does that mean the next one will be as well?'

'Yes and no,' said Jake. 'Does the person have everything they need? If so, then I doubt there will be another one so soon. Certainly not after they shot the sales assistant. I daresay that they will know by now that he has died. If they have a conscience, we can only hope it weighs heavily on them.'

'That didn't happen with Jeremy. Who knows what sort of conscience he has?'

'One day I hope to find out.'

'What if they don't have everything they need?' asked Ric.

'Then we need to make sure that all stores of that nature are on high alert until otherwise advised.'

Doncaster

7.1

Doncaster

Tuesday, March 30

It was towards the end of the day and people were beginning to go home. A car, a small amount of smoke coming from under the hood, drove into the street where Broadbench Consolidated Racing had their facilities. The car jerked back and forth before stopping in BCR's driveway. A woman got out, moved to the passenger side, and removed the scarf she had around her head. A small explosion rocked the immediate area around the car. People came rushing from the factories and offices nearby. They found the woman lying on the ground, wounded. Workers at BCR came out to see what was going on, especially as they were getting ready to go home and didn't want a car blocking their driveway. As they did, a dark figure entered the building behind the people as they ran out to attend to the smoking car.

Inside the facility, the dark figure moved swiftly to the ground floor office area, into a small storage room, opened a cupboard, removed some items, hid them in their clothing and retreated out of the factory the way they came. Before they exited, the figure spotted an open door. Inside were shelves containing BCR's spare crew uniforms. The figure looked around quickly, ducked inside and rifled through until it found what it wanted. As they exited the rear door, they were spotted, but by the time the BCR engineer got to their position, the figure had disappeared.

Back on the roadside, defence force vehicles began to arrive. The woman had been moved to a safer location, away from the burning car. She was crying out in pain and people did their best to comfort her. Everyone jerked their heads when they heard a car screech around a corner and stop suddenly near the burning car. The horn sounded three times.

In front of her helpers, the woman got up, ran to the car, jumped in and it sped away. A defence force car gave chase, but before the defence officers could catch up, the car had disappeared into traffic. A defence force bulletin was posted, but the car was never sighted again.

7.2

Tuesday, March 30

By the time DFIS had arrived, the fire had been extinguished, so Jake and Amy started with that. As they did, Anhton, who arrived separately, spoke with the Def officer in charge and then began to speak to those gathered to find out what he could. Jake and Amy couldn't get a lot off the car, but they did what they could whilst they waited for a DFIS tow truck to arrive to take the vehicle back to HQ for detailed analysis.

Anhton was called over to Broadbench Consolidated Racing's offices.

'How can I help you?' Anhton asked the woman, now back behind the reception counter.

'I think we've been robbed,' she said.

'What makes you say that?'

'When I came back to my desk, I smelt an unusual scent. It wasn't one the people around here wear. I did my best to track it down and the strongest place I smelt it was in one of the storage rooms. I haven't gone inside in case I messed up any evidence.

'Very good,' said Anhton. 'Where is the storage room?'

'This way.' She led Anhton down a short passage to a room whose door was still open.

'Was this open or closed when you left to see what happened outside?'

'It's always closed,' she said. 'No one is supposed to leave it open.'

'I'll get DFIS to have a look.'

The woman nodded.

'Make sure no one goes in or out of this room until it's been deemed clear.'

She nodded again. Anhton left and soon returned with Jake.

'This is the room in question,' said Anhton, professionally. 'I'll leave you to it.'

'Thanks, Anhton,' said Jake.

Jake opened his kit and began by taking photographs. He dusted and lifted several prints from the door on the outside and the several cabinets inside.

Jake went to the receptionist. 'Hi, I'm Det.Sgt Jake North from DFIS, could you come with me please?' She followed Jake into the room. 'Are you familiar with what's kept in here?'

'Pretty much. I do all the ordering and inventory. Mostly people come to me to ask for supplies, but occasionally they do help themselves.'

'Can you have a look at the items and see if you think anything might be missing.'

'The woman looked at the various shelves and cupboards and stood suddenly at one spot.

'Is something missing?' asked Jake.

'I'm not sure, I will need to access the inventory register. I'll be right back.'

She left the storage room and returned a few minutes

later carrying a tablet computer.

'This is a register of certain security items,' she said. 'I need to check how many accreditation tags we're supposed to have.'

'Accreditation tags?'

'Yes. Each Team is given blanks by Supacar HQ to be used for accreditation of crew and staff for the various race days throughout the year. We'd received our Sandown ones a few weeks ago and were about to start issuing them next week, but having just had a look at the inventory, we are now two short.'

'That would mean that someone could get into the Sandown racetrack on one of your passes but not necessarily be working for you?' said Jake.

'We will need to alert Supacar HQ that we've had them stolen, but what you said is true.'

'If I may, I'd like to take a photograph of these so we can use it to try and track down who might have them.'

'They're not numbered, but they are security tagged. They are also not reproducible,' said the receptionist. 'If you want to try and catch the thief, you'd be better off taking one, so you can see the security items built in. As I know this one is going out to the defence force, I can write this one off and de-tag it.'

The receptionist grabbed one of the tags off the shelf, led Jake to an office behind the desk, ran it through a scanning device and handed it to him.

'It's deactivated now,' she said, handing Jake the accreditation tag.

'Does that mean the stolen ones are active?'

'Unfortunately, yes. I activated them this morning so that we would be ahead. My boss wants them issued next week.'

Jake looked at the tag. 'Is your boss here today?'

'No, he left for a meeting at lunchtime. I'll need to send him a note to say what's happened.'

'Would you mind letting him know that DFIS would like to speak to him when he's available?'

'I'll do that Det.Sgt.'

Jake took a few more pictures and was soon packing up and leaving. He went back out to Amy who had been talking to some of the people around and had gathered all the electronic statements the defence officers had gathered.

Just as Jake was about to get into the DFIS van and leave, another worker from BCR approached.

'I'm glad you're still here,' said the crew member.

'What's up?' said Jake.

'Someone has been though the spare crew uniforms. I've found several strewn on the ground in the storeroom,' he said.

'Lead the way,' said Jake. He turned to Amy. 'Guess I'm going back inside to instigate some allegedly stolen uniforms.'

'Copy that,' said Amy.

Jake and the crew member returned to the foyer. Jake was then led down a passage and the receptionist followed.

Jake turned to her. 'Do you keep records of the uniforms

as well?'

'Yes, I do. I have them here,' she said waving her tablet.

'Have the list ready,' said Jake. 'We may need to do a quick check when I'm done.'

They arrived at the storeroom and Jake could see what had gone on. 'Wait outside until I give the all clear.'

The crew member and the receptionist nodded.

Jake took photographs of the door, the handle, and the shelves inside. He also dusted for prints on the door and handle and then on the shelves that appeared to have been disturbed. After about thirty minutes, Jake gave the all clear.

'Could you come in here please?' asked Jake.

The receptionist entered.

'Can you quickly check to see what may have gone missing?'

'Kenny, can you give me a hand please?' the receptionist called to the crew member.

'What do you need, Bec?' said Kenny.

'We need to re-stack, sort by size, and then count.'

They began to clean up the mess and Jake pitched in to help. After about ten minutes, they began counting.

'Yes, there is one uniform missing,' said Bec. 'It's a size S. We don't carry a lot of those as most go the guys are a little bigger than that. Anyway, it's missing.'

'Do you have enough spare for me to take one of these uniforms so that we can use it to cross-reference on our database?' said Jake.

'Sure. Take an M. Then you can wear it if you ever feel the need,' said Bec smiling, handing it over to Jake.

Jake blushed slightly and left. 'Time to hit the road, Amy,' said Jake, climbing into the van. 'We have work to do.' He had Amy stop where Anhton was standing. 'I'll be late home tonight, dear.'

'I thought as much,' said Anhton. 'Do you want me to bring some dinner over?'

'Sure, that'd be great,' said Jake. He leant out the window as they were taking off. 'Yes, you can help too. It'd be appreciated.'

Anhton smiled as Jake and Amy drove away.

7.3

Tuesday, March 30

Jake and Amy parked the van, took their gear out and alerted the garage to an incoming vehicle that needed to be quarantined for inspection. They both stopped by Gabby's lab to deliver their evidence.

'Glad you're still here, Gabby,' said Jake as he entered through the second door to her lab. 'Got a bit of work for you.'

'Of course you do,' Gabby said. 'Why else would you be down here?'

'Love you too, sweetie.' Jake dropped his stuff off into a small tub, as did Amy placing hers next to Jake's.

'We'll be upstairs when you get the results for us,' said Jake.

'You're lucky I don't have a date tonight,' said Gabby.

Jake smiled and waved as he left the lab.

'Why are you two always like that?' asked Amy, as they entered the lift.

'We sort of hit it off right away when I started at the beginning of last year,' said Jake. 'At least Anhton's bringing dinner over. Let's get these pics loaded and work out what happened.'

7.4

Tuesday, March 30

When Anhton arrived with dinner, two hours after they started, Jake and Amy were ready to stop. Gabby joined them and they sat around discussing the case.

'Now that the car has arrived, we need to get down and sort that one out,' said Jake.

'I'm here now, I can help,' said Anhton.

'Any help is good help right now,' said Amy.

'If Anhton is going to help with the car, then I get Amy to help me with the samples,' said Gabby. 'I need another set of eyes to have a look.'

'That's settled,' said Jake. 'Maybe the car can throw up some new thoughts on what happened.'

After cleaning up their meal, Gabby and Amy headed to the lab whilst Jake and Anhton gathered cameras and kits and headed for the quarantine bay.

Jake stepped into the bay, flicked on the lights, put his case on the ground and began to move around the car.

7.5

Friday, April 2

Donna O'Neill sat at her desk at The Balcher Research facility a few days after the incident at Broadbench Consolidated Racing.

'Good morning, Balcher Research. This is Donna, how can I help you?'

'You can start by explaining what happened last week outside Broadbench Consolidated Racing,' said the voice.

'Who is this please?' said Donna, as she didn't recognise the voice.

'This is Ms M.'

'Oh.'

'Yes, oh,' said Bryony. 'Now would you kindly explain what you were doing?'

'Nothing to do with Calderwood, if that's what you want to know.'

'That's obvious as we haven't authorised anything like that for you.'

'It's something that my partner wanted help with,' said Donna. 'How did you find out?'

'That's our business, not yours.'

'Just as what I did is our business not yours.'

'Let me say this as plainly as I can,' said Bryony, 'you

keep this up, then we will disown you and make life difficult for you.'

'That's pretty plain. I understand. For your information, I know what I'm doing, as does my partner.'

Bryony disconnected the call.

Donna sat and took her mobile phone from her handbag.

Bryony sat and looked at the information on her computer screen about Donna. She accessed a program, typed a message, and sent off the request to have an agent put her under surveillance for the next four weeks.

Sandown

8.1

Sandown Raceway

Saturday, April 10, 11:30pm

A figure dressed in a Broadbench Consolidated Racing jumpsuit, a black beanie and black face wrap, moved silently from garage to garage until it came to that of Agile Motorsports. Finding it unlocked, the figure moved inside stealthily. Lowering a pair of night vision goggles over black-shrouded eyes, the face completely covered, it moved about the garage seeking its target. Finding the first car, it grabbed a slide board and slid under the car. Reaching into a pocket with gloved hands, the figure removed several items.

Finding what they were looking for, the first device was secured alongside a hose running from front to back. The device was attached and set. The figure then slid from under the first car and went looking for the second car. As it moved about the garage, it tripped on a small toolbox, scattering the tools across the floor, and making a sound to wake the dead.

The figure froze for several minutes, but no one appeared. It rushed to the second car and hastily attached a device to the undercarriage. The figure froze once more at a sound. When it moved again, it carefully slid under the car to the opposite side. It rolled off the slide and lay on its stomach beside the wall, watching for movement. The lights came on and the figure stayed low.

The figure watched the feet of the new arrival move about the garage. As it walked away, the figure moved towards the door. It went from laying on its stomach to a crawling position, then to a crouching one and crept along the wall, nearing the door with each step. Not watching where it was going, it bumped into a drum, making it scrape along the ground. The Agile Motorsports crew member rushed to the position. As he arrived, the figure leapt up and crashed tackled the crew member forcing him to the ground. The night vision goggles were ripped off in the process and they skittered across the debris-strewn floor.

With the crew member severely winded, the figure raced outside and into the night. The crew member gave chase, but when he went outside, he could not see anyone moving about. Nor could he hear someone running. Despite the fact that it was dark, there was enough security lighting present for limited vision. The crew member relaxed and at that point realised the pain he was feeling. He grabbed his ribs and leant up against the door. He struggled back inside and called security, and then his fellow team members. Within minutes, most of the crew was at the garage wondering what was happening. Security guards were also present.

8.2

Sunday, April 11, Midnight

The man that was assaulted inside the garage was leaning up against the outside wall when he and the crew looked along the back of the garages to see a large man huffing his way towards them.

'Here we go, Reggie,' said one of the crew.

'What happened, Reggie?' asked the man, as he arrived at the rear of the garage. 'Weren't you rostered to stay in the garage tonight?'

'Yes, I was, boss, but I needed to go to the bathroom, so I quickly ducked upstairs to go,' said Reggie. 'The lights were off, and the door closed.'

'Okay. Then what happened?'

'As I sat there, I heard an almighty noise from downstairs. I finished and came down immediately. I carefully walked inside but couldn't sense any movement, so I hit the lights. I began to walk around. Whilst I was on the opposite side of the garage, I heard another noise so went to investigate. That's when I was tackled. I hit the ground hard,' said Reggie, rubbing his ribs. 'I saw a figure, wearing what looked like Broadbench Consolidated Racing garb, run out the door, so I gave chase. When I got outside, I couldn't see or hear anything. No one moving about, no sound, no lights, nothing. I came back inside and raised the alarm.'

'We'd better get you looked at,' said the boss. 'Take him to medical and come back when you're finished. I'll have a chat to security.' The boss moved over to the rest of the team. 'Joe, Dan, Flic, get this place cleaned up. I also want a quick check of the cars and the equipment. Make sure everything is ok.'

A security guard stepped in. 'You should have this place checked by the Defs before you clean up to make sure there are no foreign fingerprints. If this is an attempt at sabotage, or theft, they'll want to know who did it.'

The boss was visibly frustrated. 'I have a race to run in a few hours. If you can get someone here and get this place sorted before I need to open up, then okay, otherwise people had better stay out of my way because nothing will stop me.' He turned to his team. 'It looks like goody-two-shoes here wants us to leave the place alone until the Defs have had a look, so leave it be. However, at exactly eight am, you will go into the garage and get ready for the race, no matter what. Understand!'

The team nodded, some smirked others grimaced, and they moved away from the back of the garage.

'Harvey, no one gets in or out and I mean no one until I say so and if that's after eight am, then so be it,' said the head security guard. Harvey nodded and took up a stance in front of the open garage door.

The team boss turned around at that comment and snarled.

'I'll get Betty to come and help you,' said the head security guard.

'Okay, boss,' said Harvey.

The head security guard left and minutes later a butch woman arrived and stood beside Harvey.

'Good to have you here, sweetie,' said Harvey.

'I hear you've got a bit of a bastard for a team boss at this garage?' said Betty.

'You could say that. Just make sure you're still here at

eight am, that's all.'

'I intend to be.'

The head security guard returned fifteen minutes later. 'Defence will be here soon. MetroEast will be attending this morning. They should be here by one a.m.'

8.3

Sunday, April 11

Jake and Anhton passed through the gates just after one a.m., and were directed to Pit Lane where the head security guard met them.

'Det.Sgt Jake North and Det.Cpl Anhton Roberts,' said Jake shaking the outstretched hand.

'Merv, head of security here.'

'A forensics team from DFIS will be arriving soon. Can you make sure they get directed here as soon as they arrive?'

'Sure thing. This way,' said Merv, starting to walk along the back of Pit Lane. 'I'm not sure if I told you, but the team boss has directed his team to enter their garage at eight am to begin work and I've told my staff not to let anyone enter or leave until I say so. Therefore, there may be some confrontations around that time if you don't happen to be finished.'

'I understand,' said Jake. 'Not only will the team boss have to deal with you, but he'll have to deal with us, in case we haven't finished in time.'

Merv smiled and nodded.

'Tell me, Merv, what happened tonight?' asked Jake.

Merv went over the facts briefly as he heard them from the crew member that was stationed to watch the garage overnight.

'Is it normal to have someone stay in the garage when there is so much security around the place?' asked Anhton.

'We thought it a little odd when we were told, but didn't question it,' said Merv. 'The teams can do what they want in that regard.'

'I'll have to ask them. Now, is this Reggie still at the garage?' asked Jake.

'We have asked that he be returned to the garage once he's been seen by the medics. I thought you'd want to talk to him,' said Merv.

'Thank you.'

'Here we are, the garage of Agile Motorsports. These are members of my staff, Harvey, and Betty.'

'Evening, folks,' said Jake. They nodded back.

'They'll look after you. Officially, defence force will be the only people allowed in or out of the garage, and anyone specifically accompanied by a defence officer,' said Merv, nodding at his guards as well. They understood what he was referring to. Merv turned to Anhton, 'If you need any assistance at all, call them and they will come.'

'Good to know.'

Jake and Anhton moved past Harvey and entered the garage. They saw the strewn tools and stepped around those. They moved around the cars, noticed the position of the slide. Merv poked his head through the door as Anhton bent down to look at the slide on the floor.

'Det.Sgt? I've just had word that the DFIS van has arrived.'

'Thanks, Merv,' said Jake.

Anhton joined Jake at the back door. As they stepped outside, medics were escorting two men to the garage.

Merv leaned in. 'The one on the far left is the team boss. The man in the middle, wrapped in the blanket, is Reggie, the crew member, who was rostered for the overnight shift.'

Jake and Anhton nodded.

'Who's in charge here?' boomed the team boss.

Merv stepped in front first. 'As you know, I'm head of security here and if you have issues you speak to me. Understood?'

'Whatever,' said the boss, who strode past Merv.

'Who are you?' said the boss at Anhton, being taller than Jake.

Jake flipped out his ID. 'Det.Sgt Jake North and this is Det.Cpl Anhton Roberts, DFIS,' he said. 'You are?'

'None of your concern.'

'Indeed,' said Jake, looking the tall team boss up and down like he was a junior officer. The man Jake was looking stood about 190cm tall and weighed about 130kg, perhaps more. He was balding and the hair that remained was grey. His face was flushed and full. The glasses he wore hid his dark eyes. Imposing was certainly one of the many words that Jake could use to describe him. He thought of a few more and had to stifle a smirk. 'Please be advised that if you get in our way at any time, you will be placed under arrest for obstruction of justice.'

The team boss spluttered and Anhton clearly heard Merv stifle a laugh.

'You cannot do that to me!' The team boss attempted to assert his size over Jake.

'Yes, we can, if the situation arises,' added Anhton, stepping in beside Jake.

'Prove it?'

'For starters, Merv, would you please kindly show this gentleman the hospitality of your best security office, making sure he doesn't move from the assigned position?' said Jake.

'With pleasure, Det.Sgt,' said Merv. 'This way please?'

'My name is LG Swanston and I own Agile Motorsports,' said LG.

'Thank you, Mr. Swanston,' said Jake. 'You can step down, thank you, Merv.' Jake and Anhton, as well as everyone else, clearly heard Merv mutter a 'damn' under his breath but stayed close by.

Just as that was cooling down, Gabby and Amy trotted up to the scene.

Greetings were brief. Jake had them set up tape to seal off the scene with instructions that no one crosses the line under any circumstance.

'Now, Mr. Swanston, if you could kindly step aside so that we may conduct our investigation. We will notify you if we need you,' said Jake.

'Come on, Reggie, let's go,' said LG.

'Not Reggie, he has to stay,' said Jake. 'Betty, could get me a chair from just inside, I don't want Reggie to have to stand all night long.'

Betty nodded, got the chair, plonked it on the ground and assisted Reggie to sit down, with a thud.

LG stood there and Jake gave him a kind look and he huffed off.

'What's the go, Jake?' said Gabby.

'We need to speak with Reggie, but in short, he went upstairs to use the bathroom, left the door open and came rushing down when he heard a crash inside,' said Jake. 'He then discovered an intruder, who knocked him to the ground but when Reggie came outside, the intruder was nowhere to be seen. The alarm was raised and here we are. So, we need the door printed and the toolbox inside checked. Also have a look at the slide on the right-hand wall, as you walk in. I'm sure it's not where it's supposed to be. We'll need to have a look at the cars to make sure they haven't been tampered with, so we'll need someone from the team to come back to do that for us.'

'Got it,' said Gabby.

Gabby instructed Amy to do the door, whilst she went inside. She busied herself taking photographs of the upturned toolbox and then dusted it for prints. As she searched through the items scattered on the floor, she noticed an object underneath a nearby table. Photographing its position from several angles, she then carefully picked it up to discover it was a pair of night vision goggles. She found the slide, photographed its position relative to the right-hand car, dusted it and left it in place. As she walked along the back wall, she noticed that a drum was out of place. It too was photographed and dusted.

Outside Jake and Anhton confirmed the story with Reggie and tried to ascertain what direction the intruder might have gone. Reggie was at a loss to answer that one as he heard nothing.

'Could they have gone a short distance and stopped?' asked Jake.

'Your guess is as good as mine, Det.Sgt,' said Reggie.

'Fair enough.' Jake caught movement at the edge of the cordoned off area and tapped Anhton.

'Something the matter, Harvey?' said Anhton, shifting his gaze to a sleepy looking crew member.

'Mary, another crew member is here,' said Harvey. 'Said she was woken by others and told she was needed at the garage.'

'Thanks, Harvey, I'll take it from here,' said Anhton.

Harvey nodded. Anhton raised the tape and the woman stepped under. As she stood, he noticed that her hair was pulled back into a tight bun.

'Hi, name's Anhton Roberts, Det.Cpl, DFIS.'

'Hi,' said the woman sleepily. 'Mary Ryder, junior engineer.'

'You know the cars well enough to notice if anything has been tampered with?' asked Jake.

'Tampered with? I think so,' replied Mary, waking quicker at the mention of tampering. 'The chief engineers have been left to sleep through. They'll be needed in better nick to watch over the cars for the race in the morning.'

'Fair enough,' said Anhton, as they entered the garage. 'Could you have a look at the cars and see if you can see anything out of place?'

Mary nodded, 'I think I can do that.'

'Jake, this is Mary Ryder, a junior engineer,' said Anhton. 'She's here to have a look at the cars.'

'Great,' said Jake.

Mary donned a pair of gloves, grabbed a torch, and started looking. Anhton went back outside.

'If you're looking for a slide, it's over by the far wall, on the right,' called Amy.

'What's it doing over there?' said Mary.

'We don't know that yet, but we'll work it out once we get a hold of who was in here earlier.'

Mary stepped around Amy, who was still working on the toolbox and spent about fifteen minutes on the right-hand car. 'That one looks fine,' she said, standing. 'I usually work on this other one ...'

'... The left hand one? ...'

'... Yes, but they're similar enough to be able to check for you.'

Anhton nodded. 'Thank you.'

Mary spent much more time on the second car. She stood when she was finished, put the torch on a rear table and removed her gloves. 'That one looks good too.'

'As far as you can tell, nothing is awry?' asked Jake.

'I'd probably need more time and I'd know.'

'Thank you, Mary, you can go back to bed now.'

Mary left Jake and Anhton looking from car to car. He jumped slightly when he felt a tap on his shoulder.

'What are you looking at, Jake?' asked Gabby.

'I'm not sure,' said Jake. 'Mary said that both cars are untouched. If so, why would someone come into the garage, use a slide that is obviously for accessing the undercarriage, but do nothing?'

'Then they must've done something. Are you sure it's the undercarriage that's been tampered with?'

'I'm pretty sure, unless the slide is only a decoy? Why didn't Mary notice anything then?'

'It is almost three am,' said Gabby. 'She was woken from a sound sleep to come and do this job. Do you want to get under there and have a look?'

'And see what? The undercarriage of a car? What would I be looking for? I wouldn't even know what's supposed to be under there to even know if something was wrong. You done with the door?'

'Yeah. Got some prints, but we're gonna need a copy of the prints of every team member to make sure. I mean, it may have been one of them, but if another set of prints not belonging to them shows up, then we'll know someone else did enter the room.'

'Not if they wore gloves,' said Jake.

'Obviously. Does that mean we presume it was an inside job?'

'I don't think it was. Look at all the cameras. At least we can get security vision and see who came in. I'll have a chat to Anhton.'

'I think he's still talking to Reggie, but it sounded like he was almost done,' said Gabby.

Jake and Gabby went outside and Anhton had moved away from Reggie, who was now slowly walking away from the garage.

'Reggie, wait up,' called Jake, who walked towards him.

Reggie stopped.

'What's the matter?' asked Reggie.

'Nothing. I was wondering if you can remember if your attacker was wearing gloves or not?'

Reggie thought for a moment. 'They could have been. I don't recall seeing any skin, but it happened quickly.'

'That's okay, thank you anyway. Get some sleep,' said Jake and he walked back to the garage.

Anhton met him as he crossed under the tape. 'What did you need Reggie for?'

'I needed to ask him about gloves,' said Jake. 'What you get from him?'

'I still need to listen to what Merv recorded,' said Anhton. 'The story hasn't changed, so I think he's telling the truth. How'd you go?'

'Nothing is amiss with the cars, according to Mary, but who knows,' said Jake. 'It's three am, she was probably asleep, she may have missed something.'

'Did you have a look?' said Anhton.

Gabby chuckled.

'Like I know what I'm looking for under a car?' said Jake.

'True, but you might've still seen something you're used to seeing,' said Anhton.

'Perhaps. We'll have to wait and see. If something does happen, David will have my ass for grass.'

'Yes, he will,' said Gabby. 'Then only after Ric's finished with it.'

'In the meantime, I need to get copies of the security vision from inside,' said Jake. He turned to Harvey. 'Harvey, my man, does the security company manage the security cameras in the garages or do the teams?'

'We have some, but sometimes the teams put up their own,' said Harvey.

'We'll need access to what your company has and then we'll need to get copies of anything the team happens to have. Which way to your office?'

Harvey told Jake how to get to there and Jake headed off. Finding it easily enough, Jake knocked and went inside. He found Merv tapping away at a keyboard.

'Excuse me, Merv?' said Jake. 'Can I have a word?'

'Sure, have a seat.'

'I was hoping you could help us by getting us a copy of the security vision from Agile Motorsports' garage? Also, how many cameras do you have in there? Do you know if Agile Motorsports installed any themselves?'

'Yes. Four, and I'm not sure,' said Merv.

'There were more than four in the garage, so we'll need to get the vision from the team. Do you think they'll cooperate?'

'You've met Mr. Swanston.'

'Delightful fellow,' said Jake. 'Do you know where he is?'

'He didn't come back here,' said Merv. 'He's back in his van brooding. Let's just hope he doesn't decide to cause trouble. I'll have that vision for you as soon as I can.'

Jake nodded, left the office, and returned to the garage.

'Did you get the vision?' asked Gabby.

'Merv's working on it,' said Jake. 'Then when things start to move, I want any security vision the team have.'

'Good luck with that,' said Anhton.

'I'll deal with that when have to,' said Jake.

'Have Merv at hand, he's just waiting to get that man in cuffs.'

'Yes, he is.'

'What do you want me to do, Jake?' asked Gabby.

'Take all the samples back to the lab. Get working on them as soon as possible. I'm going to stay here with Anhton so we can talk to the team boss ...'

'Mr. LG Swanston, remember,' interjected Anhton.

'Yes, so I can have a chat to Mr. LG Swanston and get their security vision,' said Jake.

'Done,' said Gabby.

'Then I would like you to re-stock your kits and come back this afternoon. I'll make sure you have clearance at the gate, just buzz when you're close.'

'Why do I need to come back?' asked Gabby.

'If we go by the presumed timeline, then today something is going to happen,' said Jake. 'I don't think it's the break-in either. I think that was just a precursor to something else. I'm even going to get the lead engineers to go over the cars when they get to the garage just to make sure. I think it's the undercarriages that have been tampered with, but without proof, who knows what could happen. By having the van here, we have everything we need at hand to investigate immediately.'

'Sounds about right to me,' said Gabby.

'I want to get ahead of it all if something else happens.'

Gabby gathered her kit and she and Amy were on their way.

'I don't think there's much else for us to do, let's see if Merv has somewhere we can catch a few zzzz's.'

'Technically, I'm still on duty, so if we're done for the moment, I'll head back to the station and write up the report,' said Anhton.

'Ah, yes, you had better do that,' said Jake. 'How is the new DFIS office going?'

'Pretty good,' said Anhton. 'I'm still miffed they split us up though.'

'Me too, but you do know the east and south sides well,' said Jake. 'You were the obvious choice to help get another office started.'

'Perhaps.'

'Once you've knocked off, go home, get some rest and come back about two, or whenever the race is due to start,' said Jake.

Anhton left and Jake went in search Merv.

8.4

Sunday, April 11

'Good morning viewers. Ty Van Hoorn, giving you a look at the line-up for today's race. I can tell you the excitement here is electric. With only a few rounds completed, this is becoming the closest championship we've ever had. It's also been the most challenging. So much has had to change with the independence of Basslea last year. I'm glad it got sorted quickly and that the racing federations of Basslea and Australia could agree on a timetable.

'It's also been exciting to see an all-female team driving this year. Didn't that cause a stir when it was announced last year. Many of the men decided to retire, which only opened up opportunities for more drivers. This brought a whole new dynamic to racing this year. Heading into this race, here's how the drivers are situated.' Ty leaned over and tapped away at a nearby screen. 'The table should be popping up on your screens about now.

Pos	Driver	Car #	Make	Tally
1	Luke Summerfield	444	Saavo	855
2	Dan Roberts	29	Forden	834
3	Kelly Williams	32	Skoel	804
4	Jason Black	19	Forden	798
5	Jacinta Black	27	Skoel	795
6	Cal McIntosh	9	Skoel	759
7	Toby Grant	8	Nissaru	756
8	Jaxson Wright	3	Saavo	744
9	Jackson Teale	65	Nissaru	690
10	Mark Perrin	10	Nissaru	651
11	Rick Houseman	83	Forden	420
12	Howie Dellamont	317	Forden	414
13	Yuri Nickoff	174	Forden	402
14	Simon Green	42	Forden	382
15	Dirk Van Gammon	4	Nissaru	371
16	Tyler Bookman	183	Nissaru	351
17	Kenny Watson	2	Forden	338
18	Marty Glenn	7	Forden	300
19	Ben Larkin	54	Skoel	291
20	Will Bacchus	5	Nissaru	288
21	Mack Lincoln	205	Nissaru	279
22	Ulysses David	51	Nissaru	261
23	Peter Gordon	36	Saavo	239
24	Lance Gardner	6	Saavo	237
25	Nino Panelli	98	Nissaru	204

'As you can see, it's very close at the top. It's going to be an interesting season,' said Ty.

'It sure does look that way, Ty,' said Mark.

'Can you give a run down of Pit Lane, Ty?' asked David.'

'Sure. Let's see who we have racing today.

'Here in Garages 1 and 2, we have Agile Motorsports. Car 7, Marty Glenn, and car 317 Howie Dellamont. The team has performed well over the past few years since it started. We should see more out of them now that they have the experience under their belts.

'Next, we have garages 3 and 4, where Forden Performance Racing are living for the weekend. Car 174 of Yuri Nickoff and car 83 of Rick Houseman. Even though they've had early problems, they're sitting in the middle of the field. Who knows where they could finish if the cars are right?

'Here we have garages 5 and 6, the home of East Point Entertainment Sports. Car 6 Lance Gardner and car 36 Peter Gordon in their new look Saavos are not likely to make the top ten, but with Saavos in the top ten, there is hope for them next year.

'Broadbench Consolidated Racing are occupying garages 7 and 8 this weekend. Toby Grant in car 8 is sitting in seventh at the moment, less than a hundred points behind first. In car 51 is Ulysses David. He's near the bottom of the ladder and is too far away to catch any of the leaders.

'Garages 9 and 10. Home to car 9 Cal McIntosh and car 54 Ben Larkin. The Skoel's have made a surprising entry into racing this year, but not enough for Ben. Cal in sixth place could get higher. Still I'd be watching these drivers next year.

'Car 10 Mark Perrin and car 4 Dirk Van Gammon from APG Racing occupy garages 11 and 12. Mark, who sits in tenth place, is only 200 points behind Luke Summerfield. There are enough races for him to catch him. Unfortunately, Dirk is too far behind to do anything this year. When I last spoke with Dirk, he's planning big for next year. He wouldn't confirm, but I think there are big changes about to happen at APG Racing.

'First and eighth places are in garages 13 and 14. Car 444 Luke Summerfield, who's in first, and car 3 of Jaxson Wright, in eighth, have had a good year this year with Saavo Motorsports. It's a strong team with good backing and crew. They will be much tougher next year, I'm sure.

'Now we come to the all-girl team of Blue Lake Security Racing. Garages 15 and 16. Jacinta Black drives car 27 and Kelly Williams drives car 32. Kelly currently sits in third and Jacinta is in fifth. They have proven that rookies can drive and drive well. They have been formidable drivers, as we've seen. From the moment they drove on the track for the first race, the boys thought they'd be able to bump them off with a little male testosterone. How wrong they were. Each time one of the boys bumped, the girls bumped back and harder. Now Kelly has bumped her way to number three and doesn't look like moving.

'In Garages 17 and 18, we have Gus Bacchus Racing. Jackson Teale, car 65 and Will Bacchus, car 5. They also help support car 183, Tyler Bookman, who is in Garage 19. Jackson is doing well in ninth place, while Will is sitting low in the field with Tyler sitting mid-field. It's been a tough year for Tyler. His principal sponsor pulled out at the last minute and whilst another was found, with the help of Gus Bacchus Racing he's had to do it the hard way. Gus Bacchus Racing have been a great support for him, and it's rumoured that they will be a large support for him next year. They hope to find him a major sponsor and allow him the chance to concentrate on driving.

'No one is in garage 20, so we move on to garages 21 and 22, the home of Balcher Racing. Car 19, Jason Black, brother of Jacinta Black, and his teammate, Dan Roberts in car 29. These two men are exceptional drivers and have been there amongst it all. I'm surprised they're not first and second.

They're driving like men possessed. So many to watch out for next year and these are two more.

'Car 205 of Mack Lincoln and car 98 of Nino Panelli drive for White Cloud Racing and they are in garages 23 and 24 this weekend. Both driving Nissaru's for the first time, they have found it difficult to adapt, as their positions show. However, they have come from strong teams in the past and have both been junior winners, so with this year behind them, they should have a strong off-season and come back next year ready to bust some heads.

'In the last pair of garages, numbers 25 and 26, we have Enterprise Motorsports. One of the smaller teams, their drivers of Kenny Watson in car 2 and Simon Green in car 42 have done the best they can. With the clashes between drivers and management happening from time to time, it will be interesting to see if they make it through the off-season at the end of the year, or not. Perhaps they won't make it to the off-season at all.'

'That's it for me, Mark and David, it's back to you in the studio.'

'Thank you very much, Ty,' said Mark Greenham, host of the telecast. 'Bit of a harsh call on Watson and Green thought.'

'I can it how I see it, Mark,' said Ty.

'Thanks again,' said Mark. 'That was one impressive pit lane walk you just did. If people don't know what's going on now, then they obviously haven't been paying attention.'

'It will be one humdinger of a race today, Mark,' said David Spooner, co-host of the telecast. 'The weather is great. The track is dry, and the crowd is pumped. We'll be back after these messages.'

8.5

Sunday, April 11

Making their way to the top of the grandstand, which overlooked the main straight, a couple found empty seats and sat down. The woman had her strawberry blond hair in a ponytail with tight curls on the top. Large, white rimmed sunglasses covered most of her face. Her lips were pink, and her cheeks looked flushed. A tight fitting pale blue top, dark blue jeans, and sturdy runners completed the outfit. The male with her wore black jeans, a black shirt with red trim, gloves, large sunglasses, and a broad brimmed hat. What little skin that did show, was lightly tanned, but still looked pale.

The woman settled herself, pulled out a pair of binoculars from her backpack and started looking up and down pit lane.

'They're looking under the car again,' she said.

'Quiet, not so loud, Donna,' said the man.

'You said try and fit in, Reu, so I'm trying to fit in and let you know what's happening.'

'You don't need to fit in that much.'

'No pleasing you.'

The man patted her on the leg.

'Please, keep me informed of what's happening, just not so loud,' said Reu. 'We don't need to alert anyone to what we're doing.'

'Sorry, sweetie,' said Donna.

'What are they doing now?'

'Running around the car. It seems like normal stuff to me.'

'That's good then. Let me open my tablet and see if they are still active.' Reu grabbed his tablet from his bag, swiped the screen and waited. He pressed a few icons on the screen and was soon accessing the program he wanted. 'Very good. They're still active. The settings are still good. All we have to do is wait for the race to start.'

'I'm so proud of you, sweetie.'

They turned their attentions back to the track and watched as the drivers readied themselves.

8.6

Sunday, April 11

As the race got underway and the first few laps had been completed, Reu looked at his tablet and watched as the timer counted down. As it approached zero, he looked up at the big screen and moments after it happened, he watched as Marty Glenn's car, number 37, slowly rolled into the gravel at one of the corners. Reu watched as the vision stayed on Marty and saw him get out of the car, throw his helmet to the ground, pick it up again and grab a lift from an official on a quad bike.

The safety car was deployed and everyone else bunched up behind it as they removed Marty's car back to the garage. Reu grinned and flicked his tablet to the next item. The image displayed was that of a car with a red dot marking the location of the device that had been planted. Off to the right was a red button/icon that was flashing, waiting for it to be pressed.

Once Marty's car was back at the garage, the safety car left the track and the race resumed.

8.7

Sunday, April 11

Jake and Anhton wandered into the back of Agile Motorsports' garage to listen to what was happening. The chatter was fast and furious and at times angry. Thankfully, Jake noted, the team boss wasn't present otherwise things would've been much nastier. Earlier in the day, Jake had been introduced to the team manager, Damian Booth, who now spotted him hanging around the rear of the garage. He called Jake over.

'Can I help you?' asked Jake.

'I dunno yet,' said Damian. 'We're about to see why Marty ran out of fuel so suddenly. Would you care to take a look as well?'

'As long as I won't be in the way,' said Jake.

'You should be fine. We're about to hoist the car. Let's see what's going on.'

Jake and Damian went over to the car as it was lifted on the hoist, whilst Anhton stayed at the back and observed. Immediately the engineers began to talk loudly and point. Damian called for calm and got everyone out of the way.

'What have you found, Simon?' asked Damian.

'Right here, Damian,' said Simon.

Damian indicated for Jake to move closer.

Jake and Damian leaned in. 'That, my friend, is the result of a small explosion,' said Jake.

'So the cars were tampered with?' said Damian. 'We looked over every part and didn't see anything.'

'That's easy enough to explain,' said Jake. He leant in closer, took some photos on his phone and pulled out a handkerchief. 'The explosion was only small and seems to have affected this hose and I'm presuming this to be the main fuel line from tank to engine. Correct?'

'That's right,' said Simon.

'Fuck!' came the exclamation from Damian.

Jake popped out from under Marty's car and turned to see Damian holding his headphones and looking extremely annoyed.

'What's happened?' asked Jake.

'It's just happened to Howie's car now,' said Damian. 'Suddenly he ran out of fuel.'

'Get the car back here right away. I'll get our forensics guys in here immediately,' said Jake. 'We need to get on to this quickly. Also, once the second car has been returned, I need it up on a hoist and then I want the whole garage cleared except for the lead mechanic for each car. Understood?'

'Yes,' said Damian, still obviously annoyed.

Jake got on his phone and had Gabby bring the van to the back of Agile Motorsports' garage. He also contacted Merv, who was back on duty now and had him bring a contingent of security guards to watch over what was happening. Merv arrived at the same time as LG Swanston did.

'What the hell's going on in this f-ing garage?' cursed LG. 'Both of my cars ran out of fuel and if one of those idiots on the crew was responsible, they'll never work in this industry again!'

It was a brief rant heard by everyone in Agile Motorsports' garage and its neighbours. Jake turned to see

Merv standing at the door. He nodded at Merv and Merv nodded back and smiled. Jake watched as Merv turned around and physically barred someone from entering the garage.

'How dare you stop me from going into my garage,' screamed LG.

'My instructions are that no one is to enter this garage until the scene has been cleared by DFIS,' said Merv calmly.

'DFIS, my arse. No one keeps me away from my property.'

Jake stood there and watched as LG barged his way through. He went right up to Jake and looked down at him, red-faced and furious. 'What right have you got to order me out of my garage?' LG moved to physically confront Jake.

Before LG knew what was happening, he was flat on his back with Jake's weapon millimetres from his face.

'If you don't get out of this garage, you will be formally charged with obstruction of justice,' said Jake. 'Also, I will not be responsible for my jittery trigger finger.'

LG began to bluster and crawl on his back to get away from Jake's gun.

'Merv, if you would be so kind as to remove Mr Swanston from this garage?' said Jake. Merv came and stood over LG. 'Take him to wherever you like, and I will happily speak with him when it suits me.'

'With the greatest of pleasure,' said Merv. Merv grabbed LG by the arm, hoisted him to his feet and escorted him from the garage.

Jake put his weapon away and turned to the rest of the garage. 'If anyone else wants to get in my face when I'm working, then you might want to think again. If I ask for assistance, I expect to receive it. I want to solve this for you as much as you want to find out what happened. I will no doubt find that your second car has suffered the same fate as the first. So, I am now declaring this a crime scene. No one is to leave the racetrack at all. I would prefer you stay somewhere close by. If you decide to stay in the garage, so be it, just stay out of my way. I have colleagues arriving soon. We will need unhindered access to both the vehicles. I will want the lead mechanic available for each car to answer technical questions.'

At that moment, noises were heard at the front of the garage facing the track. Howie's car had arrived. Jake indicated for the crew to do what they needed to do to get the car inside and on the hoist. Jake took Damian to one side.

'Sorry about the dramatics, but bullies like your boss need to be dealt in a way they know,' said Jake. 'If I have offended you or the team, I will happily apologise when we're finished, but right now I need focus and discipline and freedom to do my job.'

'Hey, I thought what you did was great,' said Damian. 'I wanted to applaud but refrained. The guys will take what you said in their stride, and they will cooperate. I say stuff very similar, just not with so much emotion attached. They're used to it, but they have been getting sick of Mr. Swanston coming into the garages and throwing his weight around. They're happy for him to stay upstairs.'

'I'm glad we agree. Now, let's get this investigation started. Where do you want to keep the crew?'

'I'll see if I can get them upstairs. It'll be cooler and they can enjoy the food there. Will you want to interview them?'

'I'll leave that to Anhton,' said Jake, indicating for Anhton to join them.

'Yes?' said Anhton.

'I need you to conduct the interviews of the crew,' said Jake.

'I'll need help, so I'd better call for backup,' said Anhton. He left to make his call.

'When he gets back, I'll leave you with him, unless you want to oversee what we're doing with the cars?' said Jake.

'I'd prefer that,' said Damian.

Jake nodded.

'Hey, Jake, where do you want us to set up?' said Gabby, as she walked in with Amy.

'Can you take the car on the left and I'll take the car on the right,' said Jake. 'Simon will show you what we need to investigate immediately and then I need you to go over the undercarriage with a fine-toothed comb.'

'Got it,' said Gabby, and went to Marty's car.

'Amy, can I use your kit?' asked Jake.

'Sure, but what will I do?' said Amy.

'You have permission to hit me after the case, but can you go and help Anhton talk to the rest of the crew upstairs?' said Jake. 'Please? Pretty, please?'

'Yes, I will probably hit you,' said Amy, who smiled broadly. 'I'd be happy to help Anhton.'

'Thanks, I owe you,' said Jake. 'Now, let's have a look at Howie's car, Damian,'

They walked over and went directly to a similar position to that on Marty's car and found the same type of minute explosion that had broken the fuel line. This time, some of the black tape that had secured the device remained.

'No wonder your people missed the devices, Damian,' said Jake, pointing to the tape. 'The device was secured to the undercarriage with black tape.'

'So I shouldn't come down too hard on Mary then?'

Jake shook his head. 'It wasn't her fault. It was also early in the morning, and she'd been woken suddenly,' said Jake. 'At that time and in that state, the black tape would've looked like the bottom of the car. Then when your guys had another look this morning, and I'm presuming they did,' Damian nodded, 'then again, they would've been more focused on the race, and so probably only looked for something that was out of the ordinary. Again, the taped device would've looked like the undercarriage.'

'I wonder why they targeted us?' asked Damian.

'I'm not sure yet, but I will work that out and let you know how it's going,' said Jake.

'I'd appreciate that,' said Damian.

'Will you be back for Phillip Island in a few weeks?' asked Jake.

'You better believe it, we will. Provided we get our cars back quickly,' said Damian.

Jake laughed. 'You will. You can have them back today.'

Jake and Gabby got to work, photographing, taking samples, looking for any clue whatsoever. There were plenty of fingerprints, but nothing that was clear, or on its own. Both cars were then combed making sure there was nothing else and when Jake was satisfied that both cars were clear, he released them back to the Team.

'Thank you, Jake,' said Damian. 'If you want, I can get you some free tickets for the next race.'

'That'll be fine,' said Jake. 'I think we're already coming down. Anhton's brother is Dan Roberts, we're going to be his guests at the Island.'

'Dan, he's a good bloke.'

'I'd better get moving and see if I can find your boss,' said Jake. 'Hopefully, he's cooled down enough for me to speak with him.'

'Don't count on it,' said Damian. 'He'll be raging and fuming inside so much. I have no doubt that as soon as he can, he'll want to try and press charges against you.'

'Thanks for the warning.' Jake collected the kit he was using and walked out to the van. He dropped it off and went in search of Merv. As he walked away from the van, he saw Damian race past him. Jake followed. When he arrived at the security office, there were people running everywhere. Jake saw an ambulance backing up to the security office. He poked his head inside and saw a medic working frantically on a prone LG Swanston. He spotted Merv who indicated for Jake to step back outside.

'What happened, Merv?' asked Jake.

'I was sitting here with Mr Swanston and although he was still angry, he was calming down,' said Merv. 'One of his lackies knew he was here and brought him some food and drink and that seemed to help. After a little while, Mr Swanston started to go red again. This time he began to complain of a stomach cramp. Of course he thought he was being poisoned. I called for a medic and just before they arrived, he clutched his chest and went very pale. They arrived in time and were able to administer the first aid required. The ambulance was on its way by this time, and they began working on him was well. I was able to find out that he'd had a heart attack. He's about to be rushed to the helipad and flown directly to the heart unit at the Albert Hospital.'

'OMG,' said Jake. 'I hope I didn't contribute to that?'

'I don't think so,' said Merv.

Jake looked worried.

Merv slapped him on the back. 'He'll say it's your fault, but I reckon that his blustering had brought it on and with the stresses of today, that's what tipped him over the edge. It would've been at least half an hour before he even began to calm down. He was going off at everyone and everything. It didn't matter who came into my office, they copped a spray. The poor waif that brought him some refreshments was so harried that I thought she was going to burst into tears. So, no, it's not your fault at all.'

Jake and Merv stood aside as the gurney was wheeled past them with LG Swanston strapped on.

'How's the investigation going?' asked Merv.

'Sabotage,' said Jake.

'Really? I wonder why they would want to do that to Mr Swanston's team? Someone with a grudge, no doubt.'

'I'll have to ponder it when I get back to DFIS HQ and get results of evidence collected, but I kinda agree.'

'I hope you get it worked out soon,' said Merv.

'I'll find out soon enough.'

Jake left the security office and headed back to the van. Gabby was sitting inside, ready to roll.

'I'll pop in to see how the team's going,' said Jake,

opening the passenger door.

He walked upstairs and saw that only two more defs had arrived to speak with the team.

Jake indicated to Amy that he wanted to speak with her. She walked over.

'Are you happy to stay here and do this or do you want to go back to HQ with Gabby?'

'I'd like to stay and continue. The more people we can get through the better. Damian wants to get the team back to work.' Amy nodded over Jake's shoulder.

Jake turned to see Damian enter the room. 'Yes, continue, I'll buzz Gabby to head off.'

Jake sent a message on his phone for Gabby to go on and that they would catch up with her later. Jake walked over to Damian.

'How is he?'

'He'll survive, the paramedics have him stabilised and the theatre is on stand-by,' said Damian.

'I'm sorry to hear what happened to Mr Swanston,' said Jake.

'Thanks. I knew it was coming. It's been a tough year and he's been taking it hard and taking it out on all of us.' He looked up at Jake. 'No, it's not your fault. You only broke the camel's back.'

'Ah, great. That makes me feel better.'

Damian chuckled.

'You want to address the team?'

'Is it okay if I interrupt the interviews?'

'Sure. I'll speak with Anhton and the others to see who they've chatted to already and we'll go from there.'

Jake looked over to Anhton, caught his eye and indicated for him to bring Amy and the two defs to where he was. As they crossed the room, Damian did the same and gathered the team around him.

'What's up?' asked Anhton.

Jake led the group to the farthest corner of the room. 'Their boss has just suffered a heart attack and is being flown to the Albert for treatment. He should be okay, but they'll have to wait and see.'

'Bugger,' said one of the defs.

'Agreed,' said Amy.

'How many have you had the chance to chat to?' asked Jake.

'I chatted with Amy, and we decided we'd start with the most obvious, the engineers who would've touched the underside of the car. Then we would work our way through the team,' said Anhton. 'I've chatted to three people.

'Same here,' said Amy.

'I've only done one so far, said one of the defs.

'We got here as quickly as we could,' said the other. 'I've only had the chance to chat to one as well.'

Jake had a quick look over their notes. 'I reckon we might have enough to go on. When I get a chance, I'll have a chat to the team and get them to write down anything they know, saw, heard, or whatever and send it over. I doubt we'll get much more than we already know though.' Jake looked up from the group when he saw movement over Anhton's shoulder. 'Here comes Damian.'

'Sorry to interrupt your meeting,' said Damian.

'It's okay,' said Jake. 'How can we help?'

'The guys would like to get back to work. They want to get the cars ready for the next race in four weeks,' said Damian. 'As much as they like and dislike LG, they also want to get things sorted for him.'

'You're free to get back to work and do what you need to do,' said Jake. 'Is it okay if I address the team briefly?'

'Go ahead.'

8.8

Sunday, April 11

At DFIS HQ in Newport, Jake placed his tablet on the glass table as the final bytes of information loaded into Lassie.

'What do you think, Jake?' asked Anhton, as they waited.

'About?'

'Who? Why? Maybe the rest.'

'Lassie?' asked Jake.

'Yes, Jake?'

'Can you bring up the locations of each of the incidents so far, including todays at Sandown Raceway?'

'One moment please.'

After a few seconds, a map of Melbourne appeared on screen with the location of each incident.

'So you think the robberies are linked?' asked Anhton.

'Yes, mainly because of what was stolen, as we saw in today's example. The small devices were taped to the underside of the two cars with the result of disrupting the fuel line.'

'Why only make the cars run out of fuel though?'

'I've been thinking about that. Test run,' said Jake.

'Test run?'

'Yes, test run. Whoever is behind this was wanting to see if they could pull off what they want to do, so they tested the devices, using small amounts to see if they would do as desired.'

'I see,' said Anhton. 'If the devices could disrupt the fuel lines, thus causing the cars to stop, then something much stronger would not only cause a fuel loss but possibly with enough charge, ignite the fuel causing much more damage.'

'Yep. I'm surprised the fuel didn't ignite today.'

'Where to now?'

Jake looked at the pattern. He drew his finger from the first point in Altona, through St Albans and Coburg then down to Doncaster and then Sandown Raceway.

'If I continue on the spiral theme,' said Jake, 'then the next one would be back up towards the city.'

'I sense a 'however' coming on.'

'However, today's event was at the Supacar race and if we follow through with the test analogy, then the next event would be down here.' Jake re-drew the line from Sandown to Phillip Island.

'That's still four weeks away,' said Anhton, who looked at the map a little closer. 'The others are also a few weeks apart.'

'You noticed that?'

'Yes, I do listen and learn sometimes.'

Jake smiled.

'So, that would mean that there could be at least one more event between now and then,' said Anhton.

'I don't think so this time,' said Jake. 'I don't think they have deliberately tried to copy the patterns of last year, but to do that they would've had access to the files, and they've been locked since then.'

'The news reported the events when they happened, so they could've worked it out easily enough, or tracked the pattern themselves and came up with their own version.'

'I think that's more coincidence. So we need to work backwards. Who's the intended target?'

'It could be anyone of the remaining teams,' said Anhton.

'There has to be one that is going to be targeted. What happened today was a test run for one of the other teams to potentially suffer even greater damage.'

'Do we tell Supacar HQ to cancel the race?'

'You know we can't do that,' said Jake. 'The race has to happen, and we have to be there to make sure there's no repeat of today.'

'You think that the people who did this today will use the same method again?'

'I'm going to presume so, which means we can inform each of the teams to look for something specific attached to their cars on race day.'

'Who's the main target?' said Anhton.

Jake and Anhton looked over the material for another hour before calling it day and heading home.

Dandenong

9.1

Dandenong South

Tuesday, April 27

In the dark of night, a figure approached the grounds of a small factory in Dandenong South. The figure had been there many times, watching the movements of the night crew. It knew the crew would soon be exiting the side door for their nightly smoke and walk.

On cue, three people - a man and two women - exited the factory through a side door, lit up their cigarettes and began to move away from the door, stretching their legs. The figure slipped from its hiding place behind a dumpster nearby and quietly opened the side door.

Once inside, the figure pulled out a plan that had been retrieved when a colleague had made a copy upon a visit there a few days before. Using the guise of an interested purchaser of their wares, the colleague was given a tour of the facility. That information now enabled the figure to deftly move from aisle to aisle in search of its target item.

Arriving at the correct location, the figure handled some
of the items and then chose the one they wanted. Stuffing
the item into a backpack they carried, the figure moved just
as deftly back towards the exit, but before the figure could
leave, they heard the three staff members returning earlier
than usual. The figure hid behind a pile of cartons. The night
shift returned and closed the door behind them.

Watching the night shift return to their stations on
the opposite side of the factory, the figure moved towards
the door. At first the door wouldn't move when the handle
was turned. Standing up and checking that they weren't
being seen, the figure gave the door a slight bump. It echoed
throughout the factory and the night shift stopped.

'Who's there?' came the call.

Silence.

'Is somebody inside without permission?'

Silence.

'Must be rats, or something outside then,' said another
voice.

'Probably.'

The workers went back to their jobs and the figure stood
once more. With its hand firmly on the handle, it turned it
and thumped against the door to open it. It swung open with
an almighty groan and scrape.

'There is someone there. Call the defs. Now!' said the
male voice.

The dark figure took off down the laneway beside the
factory. The man from inside burst through the door and saw
the figure racing away.

'Stop. Hey you, stop!'

He gave chase and when he turned the corner at the back of the factory, no one was to be seen. He cautiously moved along in the glow of the security lights beaming down from the rooftop. He kept his back to the wall and stepped along cautiously. He turned when he heard a rustling in the bushes along the back fence. Darting from the darkness, the figure raced off back along the rear lane and turned the corner. The male worker followed and as he turned the corner, he copped the backpack square in the face. As he doubled over holding his face, he was kicked in the stomach. That was enough to leave him writhing on the ground. Through blurred eyes, he watched the figure speed off down the laneway beside the factory. As the figure passed the side door, it slammed it shut.

The worker lay on the ground holding his stomach and face and could feel blood on his hand. Soon he heard a multitude of sirens approach. After a few more minutes, he heard the comforting voices of medics as they attended to his wounds.

9.2

Wednesday, April 28

Jake and Anhton arrived in Jake's car whilst Gabby and Amy arrived in the forensics van. After speaking with one of the local Defs, they began to walk towards the side door. As they approached, the worker who had been injured was being placed into the back of the ambulance.

'Jake, keys please.' Jake tossed Anhton the keys. 'I'll follow the ambulance and see if I can have a chat with the worker.'

'Sounds great. Call when you're done,' said Jake.

Anhton waved and went back to Jake's car, waiting for the ambulance to leave.

'Hey there, I'm Det.Sgt Jake North from DFIS,' said Jake to the man on the stretcher. 'A colleague of mine, Det. Cpl Anhton Roberts, will follow you to the hospital and have a chat with you about tonight.'

The worker nodded his head and relaxed back into the stretcher as he was loaded into the ambulance.

Gabby and Amy caught up to Jake at the side door.

'From what I can gather, someone entered through this side door. The other workers now presume it to be the intruder that attacked their colleague. Amy, can you deal with the door?'

'Righty-o,' said Amy. She put her kit on the ground and began to prepare what she wanted.

Jake and Gabby walked inside.

'Gabby, can you start by getting prints from all those inside tonight?'

'Anything for my Jakey,' smirked Gabby.

'Do we have any idea of where this intruder moved about or hid?' asked Jake of the def officer near the door.

'No, sir. The workers think he may have been hiding nearby, but as they didn't see anything, they're not sure. They only heard the intruder move about,' said the officer.

'Is anything missing?'

'Don't know, sir.'

'Where are the workers who were rostered for tonight?' asked Jake.

'They're upstairs in a lunchroom. I think their boss has arrived now.'

'Thanks. Stay by the door and make sure no one enters or leaves without checking with DFIS. Amy here can assist. Also make sure no on interrupts her whilst she is working.'

The officer nodded and Jake walked inside.

9.3

Wednesday, April 28

Walking inside the factory, Jake saw a man in a security uniform walking around.

'Excuse me, could I have a word?' called Jake, grabbing his phone, and activating the record feature.

The man turned and walked towards Jake.

'Hi, Det.Sgt Jake North, DFIS,' said Jake.

'Tom Reckmann, security. How can I help you?'

'I gather you were working tonight?'

'I was,' said Tom.

'What can you tell of the events?'

'I don't know exactly what happened outside, but I will tell you what happened inside.'

'Go ahead,' said Jake.

'I watched as Joe, the man who was taken away in the ambulance, Alicia, and Wendy, went outside to have their break. The women are currently upstairs in the lunchtime with the boss, Mr Stewart. I proceeded to do my rounds inside, and I was out the front when I heard an almighty slam of a door. I came running to hear a shout for defence and then ambulance. I managed to help Wendy up off the floor, tears, and all, and along with Alicia, escorted them upstairs. I rang the boss and gave him the information I knew. When I eventually came back downstairs, there were medics down the lane with Joe, DFIS spreading dust all over the door and another person from DFIS inside looking around.'

'How are the two women?'

'They're pretty shaken up,' said Tom.

'As you would be. Can you show me where the lunchroom is?'

Jake followed Tom and walked into the lunchroom where a strong looking man was comforting his two workers. They were sipping at cups of tea and jumped when anything sudden happened.

When the GM saw the Jake walk in, he went straight to him. 'I'm Gordon Stewart, manager of this company. I hope you can catch the dirt bag that did this tonight.'

'I'm Det.Sgt Jake North,' said Jake. 'We're going to do what we can to catch the person, Mr Stewart.'

'Gordon's fine.'

Jake nodded. 'How are they?'

'They'll be okay, after they've had a few days off. It's the least I can do.'

'Are they okay to talk to?'

Gordon looked over his shoulder and saw that Wendy and Alicia were having a chuckle at something. 'They seem okay for the moment.'

Jake walked over to where the two women sat at a table. Gordon followed. Jake sat down, pulled out his phone and activated the recording feature.

'I'm Det.Sgt Jake North, DFIS. I'm investigating what happened here tonight. I was hoping you might be able to assist me with what you know?'

Wendy and Alicia looked up at Gordon who smiled and nodded. Alicia then looked at Wendy.

'I'm Wendy Green and it all seemed to start after we came back inside from our break. Alicia and Joe were with me outside. When we'd finished, Alicia, Joe and I went back to work. Alicia's and my station are on the opposite side of the building to the door we used to go outside. As we settled back to work, we heard noises coming from the storage shelves. Joe went to investigate. We all heard a heavy thump on the door and Joe yelling. Next thing he was yelling for us to call the defs. I made Alicia do that as I went in search of Joe to make sure he was okay. As I stepped outside, I saw Joe being attacked. I must've frozen for a moment until I realised that the attacker was heading for me. I jumped back inside, and just in time too for a second later the door slammed shut. I was only a step inside it and the sudden rush of air was enough to knock me backwards. I landed on my butt and stayed there until I acknowledged Tom helping me to my feet. As Tom led me to the stairs, Alicia ran over. At the point we both began to cry. Tom guided us upstairs and made us some tea. Then Gordon arrived and then you. That's it really. You'd have to talk to Joe as to what he did and saw.'

'Thank you, Wendy. A colleague of mine is with Joe at the hospital and will have a chat to him there.'

'Is he all right?' asked Wendy.

'I'll find out for you,' said Gordon.

'Thank you again, ladies,' said Jake. He stopped the recording and rose from the table. He took Gordon to one side.

'Before you call the hospital, I need to ask this question, Gordon.'

'Sure.'

'Do you know if anything has been taken?' asked Jake.

'I don't know. I haven't even thought about that. I'm just making sure my staff are okay right now.'

'I appreciate that, but if you could have quick look around downstairs, it'd help us greatly if we knew if anything had been taken.'

'I think we should take the girls,' said Gordon. 'It will keep their mind occupied on something slightly different.'

Jake nodded.

'Wendy, Alicia, I've been speaking with Det.Sgt North and he needs us, you more so than me, to look at the stock to see if anything has been taken. You up to that?'

They nodded and rose from the table. Jake followed them to the stock shelves, and they began to walk up and down the aisles.

'Yes, something has been taken,' said Alicia, halfway down the fourth aisle.

'What is it?' asked Jake.

'It's a jumpsuit belonging to Balcher Racing,' said Gordon, leaning over Alicia's shoulder.

'A racing car jumpsuit? How odd,' said Jake.

'Indeed,' said Gordon.

'Gabby, I need you to have a look at this shelf for me,' called Jake, tapping his ear.

'Be right there, sunshine,' replied Gabby. 'I'm checking a space near the door that could've been used for hiding.'

'It seems rather a specific thing to take,' said Jake, turning back to Gordon. 'They would had to have known exactly where it was to come and get it in the time it seemed to take, according to the information we have so far. Has there been any odd behaviour or out of the ordinary visitors lately?'

'Let me think,' said Gordon, scratching his head. 'Yes, there was. A striking young woman came to our office late last week wanting information on some of the products we make. I came out to speak to her and quite possibly was taken in by her charm and beauty.'

'Can you describe her to me?' asked Jake.

'I'll try, but I'm sure our security vision will give you a better idea.'

'Can you get a copy to us as soon as possible please?'

'Absolutely. Anyway, the more we talked, the more she wanted to have a look around our facility, so I took her on a personally guided tour,' said Gordon. 'We walked through the small manufacturing area and then I showed her the stock shelves. She stopped at the jumpsuits we make for some of the Supacar racing teams.'

'That would explain the fairly precise information about their location then.'

'We came back out to the front, my receptionist had prepared an information pack, the woman graciously took that and left.'

'Did she leave any details?' asked Jake.

'Come to think of it, no she didn't.'

'Let's hope the security vision can give us an identity.'

'I'll make sure you get that by lunchtime, Det.Sgt,' said Gordon.

'Thank you, Gordon. I think that will be all for tonight, but if we need further information, we'll give you a call. Also, if anyone happens to make comment about anything odd from the past few days, let me know. Here's my card.'

'If anything else comes up, I'll let you know.'

Jake went over to where Gabby was, then checked on Amy. Once they were finished, he hitched a ride back to his home HQ and waited for Anhton.

9.4

Wednesday, April 28

Jake dropped his satchel on his desk and went for a coffee. He'd already messaged Anhton to meet them in Newport. With coffee in hand, he walked into the Glass room and activated Lassie. He loaded the data about that night's incidents, including the two recordings he had. He left Lassie to compile and headed down to the Forensics lab.

As he walked in through the airlock, he was surprised by the selection of music playing. He expected something very mellow, seeing as it was four in the morning. However, he was greeted by very upbeat tunes.

He walked up behind Gabby and gently tapped her on the shoulder and ducked.

Jake knew better than to stand and wait for her to turn. The number of times he's nearly been whacked in the face by Gabby's hand was enough to make him wary. Unfortunately, he did not expect Gabby to change tactics and swing around with her leg. The said leg caught him squarely in the left shin and Gabby stood over him, grinning, as Jake lay clutching his aching leg.

'Get up, you nancy-boy,' she smirked.

'I call foul,' said Jake.

'You played the first foul, mister. Rule number 72; "Do not tap Gabby on the shoulder between the hours of midnight and eight am, otherwise the consequences will be squarely upon the body of the tapper and not the tapee." It is now four-fifteen am and therefore Rule 72 has been breached.'

'Ow.'

'Oh, please. If I wanted to make you crawl around in pain, I would've hit a lot harder. That was only a tap.'

Jake rose. 'All I came to do was see how the results were coming, but no, I walk in, gently tap, and I do mean gently, the shoulder of the lab assistant and all I get in return is abuse,' said Jake, almost crying. 'Abuse and assault. I'm leaving!' He turned and limped out of the lab.

What Gabby didn't see was the grin from ear to ear on his face.

Jake walked back to the Glass room, but Lassie hadn't finished compiling, so he went to his desk and put his head down for a short nap.

Jake opened his eyes, tried to straighten his hair, and looked at his watch. 'Ooops. I think I kinda napped longer than I thought.'

'You think so, huh?' was the question that came from behind a pair of shoes resting on the end of Jake's desk.

Jake stretched out his hand and forced the pairs of shoes apart. Through the gap he saw a smiling and waving Anhton. Jake also recognised that in the non-waving hand was a phone pointed in his direction.

'You did not,' said Jake, sitting upright.

'I did not do what?' said Anhton.

'Take a picture, or more, of me sleeping on my desk?'

'I had to make sure I captured the drool first though, then I wiped it away. I didn't want anyone else to find you drooling on your desk.'

Jake rose. Anhton rose slightly quicker and soon Jake was chasing Anhton around the office.

'North, David's office now!' boomed the voice across the room. 'Roberts, clean the toilets!'

Jake and Anhton froze and slowly turned to see Ric standing at David's office door.

'I'm waiting,' he said, entering the office and closing the door behind him.

Jake, with bright red cheeks, walked slowly across the room and knocked on the door.

'Enter.'

Ric moved to the internal window, looked at Anhton and pointed in the direction of the toilets.

Anhton hung his head and trudged off.

'Sit!'

'Sir, I can explain.'

'No need to. I've seen the pics.'

'I see.' Jake sat looking at the ground.

'In your defence, Roberts also said that you had been working all night.'

'Yes, sir.'

'Jake, I'm not angry at you and Roberts running around the office, but you do need to be careful.'

'We're not ashamed of our relationship, sir, if that's what you mean.'

'No, it isn't. We are a professional unit and I'm still military by training, as are you. Roberts may not be, but you and I both know what discipline and professionalism is supposed to look like.

'Yes, sir.'

'It happened, didn't it?' said Ric.

'Yes, it did, sir,' said Jake.

'You can drop the sir bit. What have we got?'

Jake nodded. 'A robbery overnight at a small clothing manufacturer in Dandenong South. They happen to make jumpsuits for some of the Supacar race teams. They were working overnight to finish the jumpsuits for the four teams, with whom they had contracts.'

'How inconvenient.'

'Guess who's was stolen though?' said Jake.

'Our target team?'

'Most likely. It was Balcher Racing. Dan's team.'

'Dan? Dan who?' said Ric.

'Dan Roberts, Anhton's brother.'

'I didn't know they were related,' said Ric.

'Yep, they are, and we'll be on the island for the race that particular weekend, so we'll be on the spot, and we can keep an eye on things.'

'I think David wants us all down there, just in case.'

'I don't think we'll need to do that,' said Jake. 'We know about the devices and where they are going to be planted. We know that the perp will try and do it at night, so we can beef up security around the garages. We should be able to stop it from happening and hopefully catch the person responsible.'

'That's fine, Jake,' said David, as he knocked and entered his own office. 'I still think the more we have on hand the better. Nice pics, Jake.'

'Gee, thanks,' said Jake. 'We don't want to scare the perp off without the remote chance of catching them in the act.'

'This is true. I gather the event we expected to take place overnight in fact took place?' said David, placing his satchel on his desk and taking his seat from Ric.

Jake nodded in the affirmative.

'Okay. Let's see what this latest information does to our thinking before we decide,' said David, looking at Ric and Jake. 'Let me know by lunchtime. I want to call Supacar HQ and have a chat to them about what's been going on.'

'I'm sure we can do that for you,' said Jake.

'Good. Is it okay if I have my office back now?' said David, trying not to smile.

Jake and Ric stepped out of the office and went to the Glass Room. Lassie had finished compiling the data Jake had loaded earlier and was waiting his return.

Jake responded to a message on his phone. 'The security camera vision has come in. I have a file from overnight and from last week when the woman had visited.'

He accessed the files and loaded them. He instructed Lassie to compile the new data, which happened quickly.

'Any money the images we get from the security vision

will show us the same woman as in the first three incidents,' said Jake.

'I'd take that bet if I didn't agree with you,' said Ric.

'So we know a few things now;

1. The target date - Saturday, May 8 and Sunday, May 9, The Phillip Island 400;

2. The target team - Balcher Racing, Jason Black, and Dan Roberts;

3. The target method - small explosive devices attached to the undercarriages of the cars.'

'Does that mean the perp knows that we know?' asked Ric.

'I would doubt that very much,' said Jake. 'So we have the advantage. All we need to do is lay in wait and capture them in the act.'

'Here's a radical thought. What if Balcher Racing is being set up to look like they instigated the tampering and the target is another team?' said Anhton, as he walked in to the Glass Room.

'Welcome back,' said Jake, as he sniffed Anhton's hands.

'I pushed a mop,' said Anhton. 'Besides, David told me to stop. I was around the corner when he was speaking to you.'

Jake mouthed a few choice words in Anhton's direction. Ric scowled slightly.

'So, what do you think of my idea?' asked Anhton.

'I don't want to think about that, but you could be right.' Jake said. 'Lassie, can you bring up the vision from the night of the break in at the Sandown Raceway, please?'

'One moment, please, Jake.'

Jake waited impatiently as the green bar ticked along at the bottom of the screen.

'Here you are,' said Lassie.

'Play vision,' said Jake.

Jake, Anhton and Ric sat there and watched and when the figure appeared in clear enough view, Jake paused. 'Look at that!'

'Look at what?'

'The team livery on the jumpsuit.'

Jake pressed a few buttons on the table and enlarged the frozen image. 'It's Broadbench Consolidated Racing. So, did the perp want us to think that Broadbench Consolidated Racing is behind all this or just behind the trouble caused to Agile Motorsports?'

'No, I think they did it to make us think it's team against team, but I still think it was a test,' said Jake.

'So you agree with me now that it may not necessarily be Balcher Racing as the target but that it's going to make it look like Balcher Racing caused the trouble to whatever team suffers that day?' said Anhton.

'I do have to admit that you may be right,' said Jake.

'That causes rather a larger problem,' said Ric.

'It certainly does. What we need to determine now is

how many of the explosive devices were stolen from the first store,' said Jake.

'I don't recall there being any figure, and were any taken from the third store where the sales assistant died?' said Anhton

'We need to go back in contact with those stores and get them to check their inventory,' said Jake.

'I can do the Coburg one on my way home tonight,' said Ric.

'We can do the Altona one. We'll just leave little earlier,' said Jake.

Just then, Gabby's face popped up on Lassie's screen. 'You boys wanna come down and see what I haven't got?'

'Why would we come down to see nothing?' asked Ric.

'Just do it.' Gabby hung up.

'Have you not learnt that when Gabby calls, you go,' said Jake.

Jake, Anhton and Ric left the Glass Room and headed down to the lab.

Island

10.1

Phillip Island

Sunday, May 9, 6:00am

As the first rays of sunlight began to tickle to eastern sky, a figure emerged from one of the team garages. Wearing the jumpsuit of Balcher Racing and wearing black headgear, the figure adjusted its headset and began to make its way through the array of team trucks, caravans, and assorted vehicles. In the far corner, it quietly opened the rear door of a black van and disappeared inside.

* * * * *

Anhton rolled over and saw Jake standing at the bedroom window.

'What's up, Jake?'

'I dunno. I thought I, I mean we, had it figured out,' replied Jake. 'Now I have another one doing the same thing.'

Anhton got out of bed and stood beside Jake.

'It's not quite the same,' said Anhton. 'Nothing is being left behind. The events are evenly spaced. What does the arc look like?'

'A bass clef.'

Anhton stepped away. 'A what?'

'A bass clef. You know, in music,' explained Jake.

'I never really studied music. How do you figure that?'

Jake walked over and retrieved his tablet. He accessed the information he wanted and showed Anhton.

'Here., I downloaded this before I left the office on Friday,' said Jake, showing Anhton the odd-shaped line drawn through the locations of the current events.

'It looks like an extended spiral to me.'

'It's that too, but mostly it's a bass clef.'

Anhton took the tablet and placed it on the table. He hugged his partner tightly. 'We're here on the Island to enjoy a day with Dan's Supacar family.'

Jake sighed.

'All I want you to do is let Dan look after us for the day. Watch the race, and hopefully party when he wins.'

'I guess so.'

'That's better. Let's get showered and take the Hover to the track.'

Jake turned and went and allowed the warmth of the shower to wash away his concerns.

10.2

Sunday, May 9, 8:00am

After a hearty breakfast, Jake and Anhton took the Hover from the temporary dock at Cowes to the temporary dock at the racetrack on Phillip Island. Dan Roberts, Anhton's brother, a Balcher Racing Supacar driver, met them at the dock. Once they had been cleared through security, Jake and Anhton were shown to the corporate rooms above Balcher Racing's garage. When it was clear, they were allowed down to have a look at the cars and then take a wander along pit lane. By this time, thousands of other fans were also wandering along pit lane, peering into the garages of their favourite drivers. Some of the drivers were standing out front signing autographs.

As they passed the last garage and were about to turn down and return via the rear of pit lane, Jake grunted.

'What's the matter?' asked Anhton.

'I just saw a reporter I'd rather not talk to right now.'

Anhton looked around and spotted a man being followed by a camera crew. 'I don't recognise him.'

'You might not, you always managed to steer clear, or were off working, when the reporters came round. Ty Van Hoorn returned time and time again.'

'Oh, I know him,' said Anhton. 'Why would a sports reporter be hounding you?'

'At the time, he was also working as a specialist reporter, and he was given the job of talking to me about what happened last year.'

'Let's simply turn around and get lost in the crowd.' Anhton took Jake by the arm and began to move them back towards the crowds.

'Cpl Jake North, what a surprise,' said Ty.

Jake suddenly quickened his step.

'Don't be like that, Jake,' called Ty.

Jake stopped and turned. 'I am here as a guest of one of the drivers. I will say this only once, I'm not here to talk.' Jake turned away again and disappeared into crowd along pit lane.

He could hear Anhton puffing to keep up and as Jake turned to enter Balcher Racing's garage, Anhton finally caught up to him.

'You really didn't want to talk to him, did you?' said Anhton.

'Nope, not really. All he wanted to do was constantly remind me of how I missed the criminal last year and that for all intents and purposes, he got away.' Jake turned squarely to Anhton. 'In fact, if it wasn't for you being around, I don't know where I'd be right now. Or even IF I'd be.'

Anhton stopped. A look of shock and surprise mingling on his face. 'I'm thankful for every day I have with you Jake and I will never let anything happen to you.'

'I realise that now and I love you even more than when we first met, but these past few months have not been easy. Now with the first anniversary this week, it's gonna happen all over again. I haven't been able to identify anyone, except the woman and even she's eluded us. Then last night when we had it mapped out, they got away again.'

'Not today! We are here to inhale copious amounts of engine fuel, be affected by as much testosterone, and that from the women drivers as well,' Anhton said. Jake smiled. 'Then, we get to drink as much free booze as we can. I mean free, and I've even warned Dan to make sure he overstocked for this weekend.'

Jake hugged Anhton and began to laugh a little.

'Now, that's the Jakey I know and love. Let's have a drink.'

As they passed through the garage, they spotted Dan getting ready. They paused briefly to chat to him and then made their way to the private rooms atop the garages.

10.3

Sunday, May 9, 2:00pm

Makeup artists touched up the faces of the men sitting at a desk. Studio lights flicked on, blinding the men momentarily. They were quickly adjusted, and the booth was happy. Cameras began to roll left and right focussing in on their target. The floor manager began his countdown from five, his hand in front of a camera echoing the count down. The final two counts were silent with his fingers folding as with the count. When he got to zero, he waved his hand and pointed his finger at the announcers.

'Welcome back viewers,' said Mark, as the red light on the camera flicked on. 'Now we know the Top Ten for this afternoon's race, and it looks very interesting for the standings. What do you think, David?'

'It's a surprising grid line-up too, Mark,' said David. 'I wasn't expecting Dan Roberts to be in position 2, but there he is. I hope he can stay there for the afternoon; it'd be good to see him do well.'

'I agree,' said Mark. 'Right now they're coming out for the anthem lap. Their crews ready with the last-minute equipment.'

The cars made their way around the circuit and stopped at their positions. Each crew buzzed around the cars, wiping, checking, encouraging. The grid girls holding flags and banners.

'It's great sight to see,' said Mark.

The national anthem was sung, and the cheers echoed around the circuit. The crews, grid girls and officials slowly cleared the track in preparation for the warm-up lap.

The cars were released, and they took off around the track, in formation, warming up the tyres, getting any last-minute kinks out, testing their comms and electronics. Once they had settled back in their positions, race control took over comms momentarily and held the cars.

The lights were ready to go. Red, red, orange, orange and green. The top row of red lights started to flash; engines began to rev. Blood pressures began to rise. The second row of red lights flashed and then held. Right feet began to pump lightly on accelerator pedals, whilst left feet tapped on the brakes. Both rows of orange lights flashed and held, then the green lights came on and the race was on.

'Roberts had a clean start and got to the first corner in front, passing Jacinta Black easily,' said Mark.

'Not that she'd be impressed at that and here she comes, right up his tail with her brother right behind her,' said David. 'Followed by Perrin, Grant, Wright, Summerfield, Williams, with Teale and Macintosh rounding out the top ten off the grid.'

'As they weave their way around the track, each driver is jostling to maintain their position and stave off any from behind that would push them out.'

'Wait, Roberts has made an error and Jacinta Black has surged past him on the inside,' said Mark. 'He'll regret that all day now. He'll have to watch as Jacinta now begins to speed away from him.'

'They've now made it through the first lap and seem to be settling in. Positions have changed further back in the field and Williams and Summerfield are now beginning to make their way up the list.'

'We're gonna take a short break and be back right after these messages,' said Mark.

10.4

Sunday, May 9, 2:30pm

Over the next ten laps, Dan and Jason were passed and were now sitting much further down the list. One driver had already dropped out due to mechanical trouble. Dan was clinging on to tenth place and Jason was having trouble holding on to twelfth. At one stage, a car overshot a corner and hit a wall kicking debris back on to the track. The safety car was sent out and the field bunched up behind it whilst the car and the debris were cleared.

As the lead cars had successfully negotiated the third corner after the restart, the car that was behind Dan began to spew copious amounts of smoke. It managed to steer off the track, but the residual smoke caused problems for those coming behind. Two cars skidded through the smoke, collecting one another as they did. Jason came through the smoke, and not knowing about the two previous cars, only managed to swerve and avoid a further crash. However, he found himself spinning wildly. Jason began to run off the road, but as that was happening, another car t-boned him between the rear door and the boot, where the fuel tank was, and pushed him into the grass verge. Both cars exploded with the rear of Jason's car becoming a fireball. The driver of the car that hit him, Ulysses David, sprung from his car just as Jason's was engulfed and he managed to pull a burning Jason from the car. Emergency services arrived and extinguished Jason and Ulysses, but Jason was in a bad way with most of his clothing severely burnt and Ulysses showing burns to the upper part of his suit.

The ambulance arrived seconds after Jason had been put out and immediately began working on him. They were able to stabilise him enough to get him on a stretcher and into the back of the ambulance. Across the field, the emergency helicopter was beginning to start its engine for the flight to the Albert burns unit. A second ambulance crew attended to Ulysses, and he was going to be rushed by road, as his injuries weren't as severe.

The safety car was deployed, and the cars were taken slowly around the track and when they passed the accident point, they were surprised at the damage. Some drivers chose to pit for tyres and fuel. Dan pitted as well, but he did not return as he'd heard about the damage sustained by Jason, his team member.

10.5

Sunday, May 9 2:50pm

Dan's car was pulled into the garage, and he took his head gear off. He wandered around in a bit of a daze, he tried to sit but couldn't. He tried to watch the safety car lead the rest of the field around the track. He had to walk away. He walked out the back for air but had to come back inside. He found it stuffy inside so went back out again. There were too many people running around, so he went back inside, frustrated.

On another screen he watched as the emergency crews dragged the wreckage of Jason's car onto the back of the flatbed truck and drive away. Jake and Anhton raced down to the garage below. Anhton spied Dan off to one side and went over to him, Jake following.

'What happened, Dan?' asked Anhton.

'You saw it was Jason's car that exploded?' said Dan.

'I think I saw that but wasn't sure.'

Anhton noticed that Dan couldn't stand still.

'Dan, are you alright?' asked Anhton.

'Yes, I'm fine. Why do you ask?'

'You seem a little on edge,' said Anhton.

'Have you seen what just happened!' said Dan. 'It's probably the Menac.'

'The what? Are you taking performance drugs, Dan?' demanded Anhton.

'Don't worry, big brother, it's harmless,' said Dan. 'It helps with our concentration and focus. Balcher have been giving it to us for a while.'

'Has this been tested and approved?' asked Jake.

'It's all good, I assure you. We tried the natural herbal versions first, then agreed to take Balcher's enhanced synthetic serum. Our results have been getting better.'

Jake and Anhton watched as the team manager received a message. They saw his face go pale and tears stream down his face. He called a close huddle of the crew, including Dan. Jake and Anhton stayed well back. Even they were shocked when the sobs rang out in the garage.

Everyone stopped when the beginning of the announcement came over the comms system in the garages.

'Attention all drivers and crews,' announced the race controller, 'due to extreme and unforeseen circumstances, the committee have decided to abandon today's race. Please return to your garages and await further instructions. There will be no more racing today.'

Dan came over to Jake and Anhton.

'Jason died on the way to the hospital,' said Dan.

Anhton and Jake were as shocked as Dan. Jake turned away and began to listen to the chatter of the crew. They were still in shock, and he overheard that the wreck of Jason's car had been moved to a secure location behind pit lane. Some of the mechanics and engineers wanted to look over the car. They left and Jake followed along quietly.

Before they got too far, Jake spotted a woman running towards them. The mechanics stopped as she rushed through them. Jake turned and saw her run into the Balcher Racing garage.

'Who's that?' asked Jake, to one of the mechanics.

'That's Jacinta Black, Jason's sister,' he said. 'Guys, I reckon we'd better head back. We can look at Jason's car later.'

They turned and returned to the garage. As Jake followed them inside, he heard the unmistakable wailing of a bereaved family member.

Jake noted that Jacinta was being held tightly by Dan. Strong and tall as Dan was, he was a mess holding onto Jacinta. Anhton saw Jake return inside.

Jake saw that Anhton was upset, and Jake held him.

'I hate seeing Dan like this,' said Anhton. 'Not only has Dan lost a good friend, but I've also just discovered that he was planning to become Jason's brother-in-law at the end of the season.'

'When did Dan have time get engaged?' asked Jake.

'Only very recently,' said Anhton. 'I knew Dan was dating someone, but I didn't realise it was Jacinta until a short while ago. Now we have this to deal with.'

Jake went outside leaving Anhton to be with his brother. He began to walk along the back of pit lane and as he did, Jake noticed frenetic activity and a few puzzled faces inside some of the garages. He stopped and went back to Balcher's garage. He entered the rear of the garage and was met by Anhton. They walked back outside and away from the pit lane area.

'How's it going in there?' asked Jake.

'They're all pretty messed up about what's happened.'

'I can't even begin to imagine what's going through their minds.'

'I may have to spend some time with Dan over the next few weeks,' said Anhton.

'As you should,' said Jake. 'I would expect nothing less.'

Jake turned suddenly to look back at Dan's garage. Dan was coming towards them looking strange.

'Dan, what's wrong?' asked Anhton.

'I'm not sure. I've just heard from one of my mechanics who's said that my car has been tampered with.'

'What? Are you sure?'

'They're double checking. They're even talking about whether Jason's car was tampered with,' said Dan. 'If that's the case, Anhton, I want you to do something.'

'Unless we know for sure, I don't know what I can do?' said Anhton.

'They killed Jason and tried to kill me! What more do you need?' said Dan. He was beginning to fume. 'Jake, we need to get your DFIS mates to come down and have a look.'

Dan looked at Anhton and then at Jake.

'Wait here, Dan, I'll have a chat to Jake.' Anhton took Jake a few steps away. 'How quickly can you get DFIS down here?'

'I already have Ric here,' said Jake. 'This is going to be a toughie though. I hope I can sort it out.'

'Of course you can, Jake,' said Anhton. 'Besides, this is completely different, and we have to act fast before the evidence goes cold and the culprit gets away.'

Jake turned sharply to look at Anhton.

'What happened last year is history. It can't be undone. This is now and Dan is asking for your help. You can do this. I know you can.'

Jake paused.

'Remember what you were like when you fed the data into Lassie? Even recently. The thrill of waiting for the results. The mind working overtime. The meditation you did to help you think. Then when you did get an answer, how much more Lassie helped you put it into place.' Anhton took Jake by the shoulders. 'In those times, I saw the man I fell in love with. The man in control. The man who knew what he was doing. The man that worked out the solution.'

'I'm not that same man.'

'Bullshit! Yes, you, are. I saw it again just now as I was talking. I saw the glint in your eye as you remembered how it felt. Dan needs that from you now. I saw it when you were hit in the leg. Then there have been all those other incidents. You know what you're doing, and you have been doing it well.'

Jake smiled.

Anhton suddenly buckled to his knees holding the right side of his head.

'What's the matter, sweetie?' asked Jake.

'I don't know,' said Anhton. 'Perhaps it's the stress of what's happened, but I have this throbbing headache.'

'You're only holding the one side though.'

'That's where it hurts most.'

'Isn't that the side hit when you fell at the shop in Coburg?' asked Jake.

'I think it is.'

'You need to get that checked out.'

'I will,' said Anhton, 'right now, you need to talk to Dan's mechanics.'

'Ok. I'll talk to them. I need you to quarantine Jason's car. No one is to touch it. NO ONE! Can you manage that with your headache?'

'Yes, just get this sorted,' said Anhton.

'When you're done with the car, can you make sure they do a full autopsy on Jason,' said Jake urgently. 'And I do mean full, toxicology, tissue samples, anything, and everything. I don't want it assumed he died because of the explosion. I know smoke can make it very hard to see on a track, but I always thought Jason was a better driver than that.'

'Got it.' Anhton raced off to find out where the car had been taken to, Jake walked inside. Dan came over to him immediately.

'Are you going to help, Jake?' asked Dan.

'I'll do my damnedest, Dan. Let me start by talking to your mechanics. Where are they?'

Dan gave Jake a hug. 'Thank you so much. I know you can work this out. I want it done for Jason. The mechanics are this way.' He led Jake to a small huddle of men at the front of Dan's car. 'Jake, this is Jonathan McDermott, he's my chief mechanic. Jonathan, tell Jake what you told me just now.'

Jake shook Jonathan's hand. 'What did you find?' said Jake.

'When my guys began to look over Dan's car, as we do after every race, one of them noticed that a couple of the bolts holding the engine in place had been loosened,' said Jonathan.

'Wouldn't that be something you'd check before the race?'

'Not unless we needed to change the engine, which we didn't. In general, racing doesn't loosen the bolts, unless they'd been loosened.'

'What made your guys check the bolts this time?' asked Jake.

'I don't know. When one of the guys was underneath looking, he noticed that one of the nuts had moved. When he checked further, indeed they had moved.'

'Did he tighten them?' asked Jake.

Jonathan looked over to one of the guys who shook his head negatively.

'Right.' Jake went quiet for a moment.

Jake turned to hear urgent murmuring at the rear of the garage. He looked and saw Anhton walking in. He came straight to Jake.

'There are reports floating up and down pit lane that more cars are reporting tampering,' said Anhton.

'Hmmm,' muttered Jake. 'I need to see the race officials.' He turned to Dan. 'Do you know where they are in the complex here?'

'I'm not sure,' said Dan.

'I do,' said another man. Jake turned. 'I'm Johan Bron,

the team manager. I've been hearing what's going on and it's a bit disturbing if true.'

'Without further investigation, I'm not going to make any assumptions. Can you take me to race control?' asked Jake. 'Also, Johan, I need you to seal off this garage. No one is to touch anything until I have given express permission. If the cars have been tampered with causing the accident and death of Jason, then everything inside this garage is evidence. Gather everyone upstairs and post people at every entrance. No one gets in or out. Do I make myself clear?'

'Absolutely. Let me get those instructions sorted then I'll show you race control.'

'Done,' said Jake.

Jake stepped outside and looked up and down the back of pit lane. People were standing around conversing in muted tones. Jake jumped when he was taped on the shoulder.

'Follow me,' said Johan.

'Stay here with Dan and I'll be back as soon as I can,' said Jake, looking at Anhton. 'Make sure DFIS protocols are followed for anything that could be considered evidence. Ring Ric and get him over here. We'll also need defs to stand guard.'

Anhton nodded. 'Got it.'

'Let's go,' said Jake, turning back to Johan.

They left the garage and a few minutes later, Jake was being shown into a crazy race control room. Johan introduced him to the chief steward, who carefully looked over his DFIS credentials. He then listened to the little bit of information that Jake shared and nodded.

'Well, Det.Sgt North, I can certainly corroborate your information. We've just got off comms to five other teams, as well as Balcher Racing, who are all reporting tampering of at least one of their cars,' said the steward.

'This isn't looking good at all,' said Jake.

'What do you suggest?' asked the steward.

'We need to get on top of this quickly. If you will allow me free reign to investigate, within reason and consultation with you, then we can get this matter sorted.'

The steward looked at Jake. 'Excuse me for a moment.' Jake nodded.

The steward called his race control colleagues into a huddle. Jake heard mutterings of both ascent and discord. Soon the steward was returning to Jake.

'As long as you keep us informed at all times as to what's happening, we will cooperate as much as we can,' said the steward.

'Firstly, we need to shut down this site. No one leaves, no one enters without express permission from me. No one is to touch any of the cars in any of the garages. No one is to move anything. Nothing is to be touched. If they have caravans, then they need to go to those. Otherwise they can wait in their corporate areas. The only personnel to be sighted at the garages are Team appointed guards to make sure these entry rules are followed. Is that clear? If the perpetrator is still around, then we need to make sure they can't get away. We will also be posting Defs at every point.'

The steward wasn't so sure about that but agreed. He sent out the communication to all teams. Being in the control room, Jake heard the angry chatter that came from each of the various Teams' garages.

'Call the team owners and managers to a meeting,' said Jake. 'Do you have a room that would hold all these people?'

'Yes, we do,' said the steward.

'Good. Have them meet me there in fifteen minutes. I have to make a few calls.'

The steward made the call whilst Jake stepped outside and began walking back to Balcher Racing's garage, Johan following.

He saw Anhton approaching him. 'Anhton, how'd you go with the calls?'

'All good,' said Anhton. 'Gabby and Amy are on their way from the security parking lot and Ric is on his way. David is coming down as well. There are quite a few defs on site and they are being rounded up, with as many as possible coming as soon as they can.'

'Good. We have deliberate attempts at harm and that this is quite possibly murder made to look like an accident. Tell them to consult with either Ric or myself.'

'Done,' said Anhton.

10.6

Sunday, May 9, 3:15pm

Jake headed back to the steward's room when his phone began to ring.

'Hello, David,' said Jake.

'Indeed. You do realise it's Sunday, Mr North,' said David.

'I'm sorry, David, but if you turn on your TV and see what's happening at the Supacar race, you'll understand,' replied Jake.

'Okay, give me a moment.'

Jake could hear movement down the line.

'Right, what am I supposed to be looking at?'

'The race.'

'There is no race. It's been cancelled,' said David.

'Have they said why yet? Or shown any replays?'

David sat down. 'The commentators are talking about a major tragedy. Ah, I think they're going to replay something.' David was silent for several minutes. Jake could hear David's gasps. 'Oh my god. What happened?'

'That's what we need to find out. The driver of the fireball, Jason Black, died in transit. The other driver, Ulysses David, is listed as stable with severe burns. He rescued the deceased driver from his wrecked car. When I was down at the garage of Balcher Racing- Anhton's brother is Dan Roberts, one of the drivers - I found out that Dan's car had also been tampered with. Anhton convinced me to at least have a cursory look, but soon it was discovered that five other teams have had their cars tampered with. I've managed to take control of the investigation and have closed the racetrack. No one leaves or enters. What I need from you, David, is full mobilisation of every available forensic member and any other defence force personnel required to keep this tight. Ric, Gabby, and Amy are on sight, and I should be speaking with them shortly. I need you to pull some strings for me. The evidence at this site is going to go cold very quickly.'

'What are you suggesting? That the driver was murdered? You do know what you're saying?'

'Yes, I do,' said Jake, with determination.

'Done,' said David. 'I'm so glad you're back, Jake. I'll have every van, kit, body and whatever at the track as soon as I can.'

'Thanks, David, for everything.'

'Is there anything else you need?'

'Yes, I want mobile Lassie,' said Jake. 'You know how well we work together. I also want someone to stay at HQ to assist with Lassie's access. Someone who knows how she works.'

'Done. I'll call you when I know we're leaving. Where is the race today?'

'Phillip Island.'

'Shit! We'll have to fly then,' said David. 'Make sure there's plenty of space to land the craft. In the meantime, maintain the lockdown. I'll have locals arrive to enforce that.'

'We need to get this sorted by sundown today,' said Jake. 'Well, at least have gathered everything we need. We really don't have that much time.'

'I understand how it is, Jake.'

'It'll take as long as it takes.' Jake disconnected, pocketed his phone, and went back inside to the steward's rooms. 'Where's this meeting room? I have to speak to the teams.'

'This way,' said the steward and left the room.

Jake followed him to a large room that was now full and buzzing. As soon as Jake entered, every eye watched him walk to the front of the room.

'Ladies and gentleman, thank you for your attention this afternoon,' began Jake. 'My name is Det.Sgt Jake North and I work for DFIS, the Defence Force Investigative Service. I was not here on the Island for work but for relaxation. For me, it's a matter of being in the right place at the right time. As you are now aware, Jason Black died in transit to hospital after an accident early in the race. My condolences go out to his family and teammates. Whilst an event of this magnitude is always a shock and unexpected, it's something that everyone knows could happen.' People started to speak and murmur and ask questions. 'Please, I will happily address your concerns, but let me finish what I have to say. After the incident, I was in Balcher Racing's garage, as I happen to know Dan Roberts and whilst they were grappling with the loss of their friend, one of the mechanics noticed that Dan's car had been tampered with. Soon I was hearing reports from some of the other garages that their cars had been tampered with. I went to see the chief steward and informed him of what I had been hearing. After a brief discussion, he agreed to lockdown the racetrack. Let me reiterate, no one is to leave the track, and everyone needs to be in contact at any time until you have officially been released.'

The crowded room got even more boisterous.

'Please calm down,' called Jake. A semblance of silence was restored. 'What I'm about to tell you is strictly and absolutely confidential. It might help allay your concerns. With the reports of tampering filtering in and the fact that Jason has died as a result of a horrific accident, I am presuming that everything that has happened has been deliberate. Therefore, we need to gather all the evidence we can as quickly as we can. I have spoken to my commander to mobilise every available resource at our disposal. When they arrive, I will be briefing them on what we have to date. I'm also expecting Def personnel to arrive. They will be appointed guards over each of the garages with strict instructions to let no one enter or leave without permission. When the DFIS personnel arrive, they will be expecting uninhibited access to the garages where cars have been tampered with. I can hear you thinking that if we're only going to investigate the cars that have been accessed, why do the rest of us have to stay? The perpetrator could be one of your own!'

Jake let that hang in the air for a moment. He watched as the team managers and officials looked horrified.

'Please, quiet again. Until we have evidence to prove otherwise, everyone is going to be investigated and interviewed. To make the process move as quickly as possible, I would ask that you encourage everyone on your team to cooperate fully with any defence force personnel that is speaking to them about the events of today. Once this meeting has concluded, I kindly ask that you return to your respective garages and inform your teams of the proceedings. I will be setting this room up as our temporary base of operations. If people want to talk with me, they can come here, and I will speak with them. Alternatively, I'm happy to come to each garage and speak with all the teams in person. Murder is a serious matter; no one is above suspicion. Thank you for your cooperation.'

Jake turned and left the room. Once outside the room, he went directly to race control, knowing that it was a restricted area. Whilst he didn't officially have permission to be there, he was allowed entry. As he stepped inside, his phone rang.

'David, what's the go?'

'You've got detectives and personnel arriving from MetroSouth, MetroEast, and the new DFIS East, as well as some personnel from the naval training base across the bay from you. As for our DFIS crew, we should be there in about an hour or so. Three choppers full of people and resources. Mobile lassie is coming by road and will take longer.'

'Fantastic. I'll get traffic control details for you shortly for the chopper pilots to use when they are approaching,' said Jake. 'Let me know when you arrive so I can show you where to set up. Gabby will have the hardest job, being away from her equipment.'

'She'll survive. She is the best at what she does.'

'We have a disgruntled bunch of teams right now, but they got quieter when I suggested that we were dealing with murder.'

'Hmm. Do you think was wise to suggest that to them?' asked David.

'It served my purpose at the time. We'll see what happens once you arrive.'

10.7

Sunday, May 9, 3:45pm

Jake went back to Balcher Racing's garage. As he walked in, he was swamped with questions from every angle.

He restored some calm and had them gather around.

'I gather by your ocean of questions that your manager has spoken to you,' said Jake. Heads nodded furiously. 'I know its inconvenient, but it has to be done for the time being. As soon as my colleagues arrive, we'll be able to get started on working out what's going on. The more you let us help you, the quicker we can get this done. I especially don't want anyone to move anything in the workshop, or put anything away just yet, etc. We need to investigate each garage as it is. Firstly, I'd like to have a look at Jason's car. Has anyone here had a look yet?' A couple of the guys raised their hands. 'Okay, you'll be with me. I'll need you to answer any questions about construction of the car. What might look out of place for what's happened. Whether it was possible for the car to have exploded on its own or not.' They nodded and began to move to the back of the garage. Jake turned to Anhton. 'Anhton, I want you to start talking to everyone to find out what happened to Dan's car? When it could've happened and where everyone was between the last time anyone was near the car yesterday until the first one arrived this morning.'

'I think I can do that,' said Anhton. 'It'll be harder doing it here for this team, but it's the best place to start.'

'Okay, guys, let's have a look at Jason's car,' said Jake, as he walked towards the two waiting mechanics at the back of the garage.

10.8

Sunday, May 9, 3:55pm

Everyone was silent on the walk to the holding area, but as they got closer, they began to chat, albeit emotionally.

'I want this to be as informal as you are comfortable with. You don't have to call me Det.Sgt, or Det.Sgt North, Jake is fine. You are?' said Jake.

'I'm Jordi Serrano, Jason's head mechanic,' said Jordi.

'I'm Jennie. I've been Jordi's right-hand girl for about five years now,' said Jennie.

'Nice to meet you both,' said Jake.

'Do you really think it's murder?' asked Jordi.

'I hope not, but if I start with that and prove otherwise, that's good,' said Jake. 'Sort of.'

'Why sort of?' asked Jennie.

'Well, from my limited understanding of racing cars, if it's not deliberate sabotage, then it will have been mechanical and that will put the blame squarely on the mechanics looking after Jason's car. That may be harder to prove as they may have been in perfect order but for a chain of unfortunate incidents caused by the accident which amounted to the catastrophic result.'

The mechanics looked at each grimly.

'Alright, here we are,' said Jake.

All three stood outside the roped off area. Beyond the

rope, the burnt and twisted wreckage of Jason's car. Jake used his camera to start taking photographs of the car. They crossed the tape, only to have a race official start yelling at them.

'Hey, you can't go in there,' she called.

Jake waited for her to reach where they stood. He showed her his badge. 'Yes, I can. I have absolute authority until otherwise notified. The only people allowed to cross this line from now are DFIS and defence force personnel and those given interim permission by previously mentioned personnel. If you want more information, talk to the chief race steward. I have his permission.'

The woman backed away and Jake continued to the car. 'Okay, guys, don't touch anything unless I ask you to and please keep your explanations as simple as possible.'

'We'll try,' said Jordi.

'Firstly, as we walk around the car, can you see anything that looks out of place?' said Jake. 'I know the car is a write-off and everything looks out of place, but I guess I'm looking for something more specific.'

'Like what?' asked Jennie.

'Let me ask you this, from what you've seen of the accident, could it have caused the car to explode the way it did?'

'Fireballs can happen when cars are hit hard enough and there's friction,' said Jordi. 'Usually it will start in the engine due to the heat and any leaking fuel, so it's possible. Being so early in the race, Jason's tank would've been almost full too.'

'Okay. From the vision you've seen, did the explosion happen in the engine or somewhere else? Can you tell from looking at the wreckage now where the explosion happened?'

The two mechs looked at the car a little closer. As they did, Jake called Anhton. 'Hey, sweetie, can you have a look at the vision of the crash to see where the explosion took place in Jason's car?'

'I'll have a look at let you know,' said Anhton. 'We may need to commandeer television footage.'

'Do what you have to.'

Jake turned back to the two mechs who were concentrating on a part of the wreckage about the middle of the car. He saw one of them reverse out from underneath.

'See something?' asked Jake.

Jennie, who was under the car, sat up. 'I'm not sure, we need to get the car turned over, or up on a hoist to have a look properly.'

'Do you travel with anything mobile?'

'We do. It'll be in the supply truck. We don't often need a mobile hoist trackside, but we always have one on hand,' said Jordi.

'Can you get it down here and under the car?' asked Jake. 'Any advantage is good. Use whoever you need to get it down here, and some tools, just in case.'

The two mechs dashed off, sensing the urgency of working out what was going on. Once they had left, Jake took more pictures of the car from all sides and varying angles. The mechs returned thirty minutes later with extra bodies and the mobile hoist.

'Here's what I need,' instructed Jake. 'Hoist the car as carefully and slowly as you need to. I want to keep as much of it intact as possible. We need to see the car as it is.'

Everyone nodded and began to get to work.

As they began to hoist, Jake's phone rang. 'David, how far away are you?'

'Oh, I dunno, about ten metres.'

Jake turned around to see David striding across the field with the rest of the DFIS team in tow.

'I send you to all sorts of little cases and they're done within hours. You take a few days off and you get embroiled in grandiose things again. What gives?' asked David, as he shook Jake's hand warmly.

'You tell me,' said Jake. 'Don't know about it being grandiose.'

'So, what's going on here,' said David. 'Where are we at?'

'This is what's left of the deceased driver's car, Jason Black,' said Jake. 'His sister, Jacinta Black, is a driver for one of the other teams. Dan Roberts, Anhton's brother, drives for the same team as Jason. Anhton's interviewing that team and checking on some other details for me. The two mechs who managed to have a quick look at Jason's car when it first arrived here, came back with me for a more detailed look. They wanted to get underneath, so I sent them to bring back their mobile hoist. They're just getting the car up on it now so we can look underneath. If we can leave Amy here, I can show you where we can set up for the day.'

'Amy, take over here from Jake,' said David.

'Yes, sir,' said Amy, kit in hand.

'How many could come down?' asked Jake.

'We have pretty much everyone, including the newbies,' said David. 'Nothing like a baptism of fire.'

'Let me talk to Amy and then I'll show you base camp,' said Jake. He spoke with Amy, introduced her to the two mechs, mentioned what to watch out for and left her to it.

'I've managed to get a hold of the main briefing room,' said Jake, as he led David along the back of pit lane. Ric joined them as they walked along. 'Hi Ric. So, the other teams affected by suspected tampering, along with Balcher Racing, are Saavo Motorsports, APG Racing, Blue Lake Security Racing, Skoel Performance Racing and Broadbench Consolidated Racing. They are the ones we need to check first and find out what's been tampered with on their cars.'

'What do you need me to do, Jake?' asked Ric.

'Ric, can I leave you to organise a team on investigators to check out each of the team's cars?' said Jake.

'What are we looking for?' asked Ric.

'Any signs of tampering, or anything that is out of place. Make use of the engineer's knowledge. Explain succinctly what you need. Only let them touch the cars if asked, otherwise only the investigators. Don't give the newbies a chance to get nervous. This is a single murder on a grand and very visible scale.'

'If I have remaining personnel?' said Ric.

'Hmmm,' thought Jake. 'I've asked Anhton to interview Balcher Racing and try and get a hold of any television footage, Supacar footage, or anything that we can look at of the race. Oh, interview the team members. Use any of the local defs to do that. The quicker we can get through this the quicker we can let people leave and move on.'

'Got it,' said Ric, who turned and headed to where the rest of DFIS was waiting.

'Were other cars involved in the accident?' asked David, when Ric had left.

'A few, but no major damage, most cars seemed to get out of the way when they saw Jason's car go off. The one car that hit him directly, that driver was the one who pulled Jason out. He's in hospital in a stable condition.'

'Very good. You have a handle on things. That's good to see.'

'Ah, we're here,' said Jake. He showed David inside the room.

'This will do nicely,' said David. 'Gabby can set up in here and run things as they come in. We didn't bring mobile Lassie this time. We felt it better to load as much of Gabby's equipment as we could.'

'Who's back at base then?'

'Stevie, I think,' said David.

'That's cool, I've worked with him before.'

'Whilst we didn't bring Lassie down, I do have one of the new mobile link tablets that you can use.'

'I kinda heard about those but haven't got around to working out how to use it,' said Jake.

'Now's as good a time as any.'

'Yes, sir. Let me introduce you to the chief steward.'

Jake led David from the room, and they found the steward in the race control room. Introductions took place and Jake excused himself to get back to work.

10.9

Sunday, May 9, 4:15pm

Jake went from garage to garage to see how the DFIS teams were going. He didn't stay long as he knew he would get involved in trying to instruct them on the way he would've done it. He decided that they needed to work out their own methods. As he walked back towards the briefing room, he met the detectives from MetroSouth and MetroEast. He was reacquainted with Det.Sgt Amita Brookes, from MetroEast and was surprised to see Det.LtCpl Aimee McManus, and Det.Sgt Jared Hood. He greeted them all warmly.

'Thanks for coming to help,' said Jake. 'Good to see you again, Amita.'

'You too, Jake,' said Amita.

'I wasn't expecting to see either of you two,' said Jake.

'We both transferred down to MetroSouth,' said Jared. 'I moved just after Christmas with a promotion and Aimee transferred shortly after, again with a promotion.'

'Congratulations to you both.'

'What have you got for us?' asked Jared.

Jake went over the details of the crash and his initial thoughts and investigations. 'What we need is to interview all thirteen garages and find out what we can. To start with, Saavo Motorsports, APG Racing, Blue Lake Security Racing, Skoel Performance Racing and Broadbench Consolidated Racing need to be interviewed. Anhton is talking with Balcher Racing. His brother Dan drives for that team and the deceased driver, Jason, is from that team. Also check with Ric.'

'A bit close to home,' said Amita, 'but it might also be good for him to spend the time with his brother.'

'We were down here as guests of Dan, so I thought it best to leave him there,' said Jake. 'You might want to check in with David in the control room, which is the main race briefing room on the first level. We want to make sure we get everything we can before everyone starts to get feral. Ah, also, I've placed the racetrack into lockdown. No one is to leave, and no one is to enter. I've spoken with the team managers and explained what I'd like from them. I think we should get cooperation, otherwise they just stay here longer.'

'Totally agree,' said Jared.

'It's good to see you back, Jake,' said Amita.

Jake blushed a little. 'Thanks.'

'Okay, let's get to work,' said Jared. 'If this is murder, then we want to see this resolved.'

Jared, Amita, and Aimee went in search of David. Jake went back to see how things were going with Balcher Racing.

10.10

Sunday, May 9, 4:45pm

Jake walked into the back of Balcher's garage to find everyone sitting quietly peering intently into their personal tablets, or busily writing away on pads. Anhton was in low conversation with his brother to one side. He tapped Anhton on the shoulder.

'Weren't you supposed to come back with an answer to a question?'

Anhton jumped. 'Yes, but I can't work it out. You have a look. It's on a TV in the corner.' Anhton led the way, Dan following.

'Are you okay to watch this again, Dan?' asked Jake.

'It won't be the last time I'll have to view it, but I'd rather not,' replied Dan. 'I want to know what happened as much as you and if I can help in anyway.'

'I appreciate your assistance,' said Jake. 'What's going on with the rest?'

'I hit upon an idea,' said Anhton. 'Rather than try and talk to each one in turn, leaving the others to sit around twiddling thumbs, I sat everyone down and began to speak to them as a group. I asked each one to grab a tablet, or pen and paper or whatever they were most comfortable with and for them to number and answer a series of questions I posed. So we began. The first few were general. Name, age, length of service, qualifications, etc. Then we moved to what they did late yesterday, then this morning, pre-race, during the race, and after the accident happened. The last few questions I wrote up on their whiteboard and left them to it. No one was exempt. Dan had only just finished when you came back.'

'Clever,' said Jake. 'Let's have a look at the footage.'

Anhton pressed play and they watched the cars as they were released from the safety car. They watched it happen in normal time and it looked like it was a simple side on collision with a couple of other cars clipping and crashing as they went past. When Jake slowed it down, he noticed that the fireball seemed to erupt just before Jason's car was hit. Jake slowed the vision even further until it was frame by frame. He moved it along and indeed the explosion happened only moments before the car was hit. Jake checked it against the other angles that Anhton had procured, and it was the same. A small explosion was seen to go off under the car moments before Jason was hit.

'There,' said Jake, pointing at the screen, 'just before car 10 hits him in the side.'

'I think you're right,' said Anhton. 'Now all we need to do is prove what type of an explosion it was.'

'I'll call Amy and get her to look for evidence along those lines,' said Jake.

Jake reached for his phone, but it was already ringing.

'Amy, I was just about to call you,' said Jake. 'What you got?'

'Well, we've been over the car with a fine-toothed comb, almost,' said Amy. 'Short of pulling the engine to pieces we've done as much as we can for now. The guys are saying that to investigate the car in detail, they'd prefer to have it back at their shop and would be happy to have DFIS supervision as they did it. I kinda, sorta agreed, only because they know the cars inside and out.'

'That's no big deal, I'm sure if it comes to that, we can accommodate,' said Jake. 'So, what did you find?'

'Well, the boys are fairly certain that the car had been tampered with.'

'I've just been pouring over the footage of the moment of impact and it's clear that an explosion happened moments before Jason was t-boned by the other car. The impact of the crash only accelerated the fireball. It seemed to come from underneath between the rear door and rear tyre on the driver's side.'

'I'm glad you said that because we did find some anomalous patterns on the right side of the car,' said Amy.

'Have another look knowing that you are looking for a potential trigger point for an explosion.'

'Done. Will call you as soon as I can.'

'Thanks, Amy. Do you have Lassie remote access?'

'Only all year,' said Amy.

'Right, seems I'm the only one who doesn't have it,' said Jake.

'We've been trying all year to get you hooked up, but you kept fobbing us off,' said Amy.

'Sorry about that,' said Jake.

'It's okay, Jake. We understood. I'll get the data loaded as soon as I can.'

'Thanks, Amy.' Jake turned back to Anhton and Dan.

As he did, he saw Anhton grab the right side of his head again. Anhton looked for something to grab on to. Dan caught and helped him sit on the ground.

'What's up? Are you alright, Anhton?' asked Dan.

'It's nothing,' said Anhton.

'Nothing, my arse,' said Jake.

'Talk to me, Jake,' said Dan.

'Quickly, back in March when I got my leg shot up, Anhton was involved in a short scuffle with an offender at a store and hit his head,' said Jake.

'I remember you saying something,' said Dan.

'The hospital kept him in overnight but said that nothing was amiss,' said Jake.

'See, I told you, it's nothing,' said Anhton.

'Promise me you'll get checked again,' said Dan.

'I'll be fine,' said Anhton. 'I'm sure it's only the pressure of today.'

Dan grunted.

'So, what's the go?' asked Anhton.

'The team want to get Jason's car back to the shop so they can strip it and work out what's happened,' said Jake. 'In the meantime, Amy is going to look further and try and pinpoint a trigger point for the explosion.'

'What do we need to do?' asked Dan.

'I need you to get your crew away from the garage. I want them doing something to distract them from what's happened.'

Dan looked at his oddly.

'I want everyone's minds on something else for little while. The only person I want in here is the mech that found the loosened bolts on your car. I'll need him to help me check your car for any other tampering.'

'I understand,' said Dan. 'It'll be a her, Joan, and I'm sure Jonathan will want to stay too.' He moved off to speak to the manager who got everyone's attention and told them what they needed to do.

'You know your job, Anhton,' said Jake.

Anhton smiled, collected the note pads that the crew had been writing on and had those using a tablet send their files to an email address, marked to his attention. Once he had gathered everything, he left the garage. The crew soon left as well, leaving only Jake, Dan, Jonathan, and Joan.

'Let's get to work.' Jake grabbed the kit he'd placed there earlier and began to examine Dan's car with Jonathan and Joan's help. In the beginning, Joan concentrated on the engine bolts. Then she and Jonathan scoured every square millimetre of the engine and found nothing else. Next, they moved to the undercarriage. Jake lay down on one of the sliding boards and rolled underneath with Joan. As the they moved along, Jake suddenly stopped.

'Would anyone have seen anything like this in the pre-race check?' asked Jake, pointing to a small device taped alongside a pipe. 'Also, what's this pipe for?'

'Firstly, that pipe is the fuel line,' said Joan. 'Secondly, things like those would only need to be checked if the car had suffered any undercarriage mishap and as Dan hadn't done that, we probably wouldn't have checked it.'

Jake took photos of the device from as many angles as he could. Close ups, distance, sides. With gloved hands he began to carefully remove the tape holding it in place. As he did, he saw the tiny timing device. Jake gasped. Joan gasped louder.

'How far to the nearest open ground?' asked Jake.

'The infield on the opposite side of the track to where we are now,' replied Joan.

'Right, grab a shovel, go there, making sure you clear a path as I'll need it soon, dig me the deepest hole you can before I arrive and wait. When I give the signal, bury the device, and run.'

'Okay,' said Joan nervously. She slid out from under the car, found a shovel and ran through the front of the garage, across pit lane, across the track and towards the infield on the other side.

'Jonathan, I don't how you do it, but make sure there is a clear path between here at the field I've sent Joan to,' called Jake. 'I'll explain later. Be loud. Be obnoxious. Be whatever you need to be.'

'What's up?' asked Jonathan.

'No time to explain, JUST DO IT!'

Jonathan did as he was told.

With a pair of clippers, Jake neatly cut the device free and carefully rolled out from under the car. Making his way as quickly and gingerly as he could, he followed Joan to the infield. People began to gather around, and Jonathan very quickly got them moved back as far as possible. Jake dropped the device into the hole Joan had made and she began to fill it in with the shovel as Jake did the same with his hands. Jake pulled Joan away and they hid behind one of the barricades alongside the track and waited. A few minutes later, the explosion happened. Dirt flew a few metres into the air and when it had cleared, Jake and Joan stood.

Jake cautiously stepped towards the new crater. As he did, he heard others begin to approach. Jake swung around angrily.

'Are you insane?' he yelled. 'Get back behind the barricades.' He stormed towards the news crew who turned tail and ran. When they were behind the barricade, Jake returned to the hole. He approached just as cautiously as before.

He looked over his shoulder to see that Jonathan and Joan were stopping anyone else from approaching. He could also see David and some of the other DFIS crew running along pit lane. He smiled to himself at the chastisement he was about to receive from David. Jake turned back to the hole and peered in. Only shrapnel remained, but there was still enough for evidence.

Jake looked up from the ground to see a furious and puffing David standing over him.

'Hi, David,' said Jake.

'Don't you "Hi, David," me mister. What in hell's name did you think you were doing?'

'Saving a whole lot of people from being hurt.'

'And you?' asked David.

'I'm fine, as you can tell.'

'We'll talk about this later. Talk to me.'

'Joan and I were underneath Dan's car when I spotted the device,' said Jake. 'I took pictures of it from as many angles as I could, I then removed the tape and took more pics. I had Joan run out to this field and dig me a hole. I then cut the wires of the device and hi-tailed it to the hole. We filled it in and then, boom.'

'Why do you always make it sound so benign.'

'A gift?'

'Keep talking,' said David.

'On the device I saw that it had sixty minutes still to run, but as soon as I snipped the wires, it started to count down much faster. I dropped it in the hole with a few minutes to spare.'

'Anything else?'

'Nope, that's it,' said Jake.

'As I said, we'll talk later.' David leaned in closer. 'Well, done.'

Jake tried not to laugh, got up, dusted himself off and signalled for Joan to come to the hole. 'Keep an eye on this nice little hole. I need to get my kit.' Joan nodded and Jake dashed off to the garage. The news crew tried to catch him, but he brushed past them like they didn't exist. Even on his return journey, he did the same. He also called for some tape and someone to guard the site. The appointed guard arrived moments after Jake had returned.

'Reporting for duty, sir.'

'Yes, thank you. I want you to tape this site off and keep an eye on it until further notice,' said Jake.

'Yes sir.'

Jake got busy bagging and tagging as much of the debris as he could locate. By covering the device with dirt, he was able to contain the debris to a small area. Once he'd finished, he headed back to the garage. The news crew in hot pursuit, only to be snubbed again. With defence force personnel stationed along pit lane, no one could gain access to the garages.

Jake made his way to the DFIS control room and handed over the pile of pieces to Gabby.

'Hey, sweetie, what you got for me?' said Gabby.

'Remains,' said Jake, smirking.

'I heard that someone set off something. Was that you?'

'David wasn't too impressed.'

'I bet he wasn't.' Gabby chuckled. 'What have you got?'

'It was a device I found underneath Dan Roberts' car. When I first saw it, it had at least sixty minutes on it, but as soon as I disconnected it, it started counting down fast. I had only a couple of minutes left by the time we got it to the hole.'

'Hole?'

'Joan, one of the mechanics for Dan's car, helped me by digging a hole,' said Jake. 'I threw the device into the hole, it was covered and then exploded. This is what's left.'

'I could've done more with more, but I'll just have to do great with less.'

'Yes, you will.'

'So the device had a timer?'

'Yes.'

'It was counting down normally before you cut it away?'

'Yes.'

'It started counting down rapidly once it was disconnected?'

'Yes.'

'I see.'

'Yes.'

'Do you know any other words?'

'Yes.'

'Get out.'

Jake raced around, kissed Gabby on the cheek and left the room.

He returned to Balcher Racing's garage to see Joan waiting for him.

'Let's see if there's anything else we can find under there,' said Jake.

'I hope not, that was enough,' said Joan.

'Can I say something?' said Jonathan.

'Sure,' said Jake.

'To me, we were the major target.'

'Without firm evidence, it certainly would seem that way,' said Jake. 'I'll need to see to what degree the other cars have been tampered with.'

'Let's get this sorted. I really want to get home,' said Jonathan.

Jake and Joan got back on the slides and checked everything under the car but found no other evidence of tampering. They continued around the outside of the car once again but found nothing out of the ordinary.

'I think we've done as much as we can for now, particularly for the car,' said Jake. 'Who would be the best person to speak about the rest of the garage?'

'What are you looking for?'

'To know if anything has been touched, put in a different place, tampered with, and so on.'

'By this time, everything would've been touched by a crew member at least once,' said Joan. 'Tools would've been positioned for maximum effect. No matter how it was left last night, it won't be the same now. You can ask the crew if they noticed anything out of place, but Det.Cpl Roberts covered that as well with his questioning earlier.'

'Okay then, but if for some reason, you notice anything, or one of the crew says something, please let us know.'

'Will do.'

'Go and spend time with the crew, we'll let you know when you can leave,' said Jake.

'Thanks, Jake,' said Joan.

Jake watched as Joan walked slowly from the garage. Jake followed soon after, closing the door and marking it as no entry.

Jake stopped Jonathan before he got too far away.

'Will she be okay?' asked Jake.

'Joan?' said Jonathan, watching as she began to climb the stair to the rooms above the garage. 'I think so. Everyone will be shaken and emotional. We are a close family in this team. Everyone knows everyone else. It'll be hard to finish the season, but they will want to do it for Jason, I know that for sure.'

'Let me know if there's anything DFIS can do to help,' said Jake.

'Find out who did this,' said Jonathan.

'I will do my best for you and the team, Jonathan,' said Jake.

'Thank you.' Jake then watched Jonathan climb the stairs.

Jake walked to the DFIS control room to make his notes.

10.11

Sunday, May 9, 5:00pm

As Jake sat working on his notes, David came into the room.

'Hello, bomb-boy,' said David.

'Ha ha. Hello to you too.'

'How's it going?'

'Nothing further on Dan's car, and I haven't heard from Amy about Jason's car yet,' said Jake. 'I'm finishing my notes and uploading them to Lassie remotely. What about you?'

'I've been checking out Saavo Motorsports' garage and nothing as drastic as yours, but as a mechanic was going over the car with me, we did notice that several bolts holding the rear axle assembly had been loosened. Upon checking, it was one of those things that if nothing had happened in the previous day's race, then those bolts wouldn't need to be checked. If left unchecked, they would've eventually worked loose, and the rear axle would release causing all sorts of havoc on the track.'

'We're dealing with someone who has a major grudge against the industry.'

'You think so?' asked David.

'I do, and I think Balcher Racing was definitely the primary target.'

'You're making assumptions awfully early.'

'Perhaps, but it gives us something concrete to work from,' said Jake. 'I had wondered this though, after the target of the jumpsuits last month.'

'Let's wait and see what the other cars and garages produce.'

'Of course. So, who's where?'

'Let me see,' said David. 'Gabby's in here. Amy is working on Jason's car. Dustin is doing APG Racing, and Ric is at Blue Lake Security Racing's garage.'

'Okay, I'll go over to Skoel Performance Racing's garage, and we can send Amy to Broadbench Consolidated Racing when she's done.'

'Where's Amy going?' asked Amy as she walked in.

'How'd you go?' asked Jake.

'You were right, Jake,' said Amy. 'There was an area on the right-hand side that showed that something had happened quite explosively.'

'Well. I found an explosive device underneath Dan's car,' said Jake.

'So that was you blowing things up?'

'Yep.' Jake smirked and David clipped him over the ears. 'Hey.'

Everyone laughed.

'Get your data loaded, Amy, and then head over to Broadbench Consolidated Racing's garage and check their cars,' said David.

'Got it, boss,' said Amy.

'Ulysses David, the guy that pulled Jason from his car, drives for Broadbench Consolidated Racing,' said Jake. 'Have a thorough look at his car. Looking at the footage, his was the car that connected with Jason's.'

'You,' said David, indicating Jake, 'need to get your butt over to Skoel Performance Racing's garage and check their cars.'

Jake rose, grabbed his kit, and walked out the door.

'I'm gonna check in with the detectives to see how they're going,' said David. 'They have thirteen garages to talk to. I may switch over to interviews so we can let these people go.'

'That might be a good idea,' said Amy. 'As soon as I'm done with Broadbench Consolidated Racing's cars, I'll interview them as well. With the size of these crews, that will take a while.'

Jake poked his head back into the room, just as David was leaving. 'Here's a tip; when you're talking to the different crews, ask them to write down all that they know and saw, like a questionnaire. Anhton did it with Balcher Racing and everyone gets interviewed at once.'

'That's pure genius,' said David, and as he left, he grabbed Jake's head and planted a kiss on top.

Jake spluttered, rubbed his head, and left again.

'I've missed that these past months,' said Gabby, once Jake had gone.

'I hear you, Gabby,' said Amy. 'It's good to see him back on his game.'

10.12

Sunday, May 9, 6:00pm

As Jake made his way along the back of pit lane to Skoel Performance Racing's garage, he spotted movement out of the corner of his eye to his right. Ducking between some of the trucks he spied a dark figure.

'Hey, you, stop,' Jake called.

He began to follow the figure. The figure moved faster and refused all contacts from Jake. Jake put his gear up against the rear wall of the garages, drew his weapon and went in pursuit. He began to weave amongst the trucks and for a moment lost sight. He found the figure again when the figure jumped him.

Jake grunted but soon had the upper hand. Jake's gun was knocked from his hand and slid under one of the trucks. The two fought and Jake found it hard fighting someone wearing a full-face helmet. It was constantly used as a weapon against him, but Jake managed to throw the figure against the side of a truck. The figure regained their footing and charged at Jake. He jumped out of the way and tripped the figure as it went past.

The figure lay on the ground, panting and breathing heavily. As Jake approached, it did a sudden round house kick and sent Jake sprawling to the ground. The figure took off and ran through the array of trucks and vehicles. Jake gave chase and soon the trucks hand changed to smaller utes and vans. Keeping track of the figure, he saw it stop at a dark van in the far corner of the parking area and turn and look towards Jake. Jake took off at pace, but the figure had disappeared by the time he arrived at the van. Jake noticed that the only thing beyond the van, and the fence, was a cliff down to the sea.

Jake spotted the hole in the fence, clambered through, and heard a splash below him. Jake carefully crawled on his stomach to the edge, only to see it wasn't as sharp, or as high as he thought. He did see a figure running along the beach, its helmet off. Jake could only catch a glimpse of light brown hair as the figure sped along the beach. Jake climbed down the sloping cliff and jumped the last metre or so to the sand. He looked in the direction that the figure had fled but was gone from sight. Jake turned back and saw the helmet laying partially hidden in some scrub. He picked it up with a handkerchief he had and carefully returned to the top of the cliff. Once there, he went to the van.

Placing the helmet on the ground, he took his phone from his pocket.

'David, I need your help,' said Jake. He quickly relayed what had just happened and David said he'd be there right away.

A few minutes later, he heard David approaching. Jake stood up and retrieved his kit from David's hands.

'They left this behind,' said Jake, holding up the helmet with a now gloved hand. 'I hope Gabby can get something off this.'

'You hope she can,' said David, looking at Jake oddly.

'Okay, I know she will. Happy now.'

'Why this van?'

'The figure seemed to deliberately stop at this van and look back towards me,' said Jake. 'I don't know if it was to see if I was looking, still following or what, but if this was their van, then we should check it out. Also, I lost my gun.'

David shook his head. 'Get it and I'll start here.'

Jake returned several minutes later, gun in hand and opened his kit. David was working in the front section, dusting for prints on the front doors and steering wheel.

'Anything yet?' asked Jake.

'Not yet. See what you can get out of the back.'

'Already on it.'

Jake began to dust for prints, but to no avail. He carefully opened the door to find normal stuff like clothing, a sleeping bag, toiletries, and some magazines. Jake bagged and tagged some samples and put them to one side. Stepping back onto the ground, he noticed that the back of the van was raised. After a brief time, he found the mechanism to release the drawers underneath the platform. This revealed a whole lot more.

'David, have a gander at this,' called Jake.

David came to the back of the van to see a large drawer, supported by legs, waiting to give up its contents.

'If we can't get anything from this, I'll be baffled,' said David. 'Looks like a gold mine to me.'

'Let's hope so,' said Jake.

Once he had finished photographing where everything was in the drawer, he began to bag and tag. There were spare black uniforms, maps of the island, plans of pit lane, lists of whose garage would be where, schematics of the cars that would be targeted, wires, even some more of the devices used on Jason and Dan's cars.

'Gabby will be like a kid in a candy shop once she gets her hands on all this,' said Jake. When he had finished bagging and tagging, he loaded all the pics he had to Lassie by remote. 'Now I want to get back to base to start going through all this.'

'We should call for a pickup of this van too,' said David.

'I've already sent an email requesting an urgent pickup. They should be here in about two hours.'

'What about a guard?'

'He's just about to arrive,' said Jake, indicating the defence private approaching the van. 'The only people to touch this van are DFIS personnel. There is a truck coming in about two hours or so to collect it. When it arrives, I'll bring them down.'

'Yes, sir,' acknowledged the private.

'Let's get this stuff up to Gabby,' said David.

Arms laden, Jake and David carried their bags of evidence to where Gabby had her temporary lab.

Dinner

11.1

Monday, May 10, 3:00am

Jake and Anhton didn't arrive home from Philip Island until midnight. They had left at ten pm when they felt they had enough evidence and information. Even then the Team owners were not happy that they were grounded until further notice.

Jake was restless, even in his own bed. He couldn't sleep. The thoughts of the accident earlier that afternoon, and then the start of the investigation. Everything that had taken place was racing through his mind. At three am, he got up, went to the lounge room, chose his favourite relaxation music, rolled out his yoga mat, placed headphones on his head and sat down.

- *Two cars from the same team tampered with by having an explosive device attached,*

- *One explodes early in race causing death of the driver,*

- *All cars in top ten affected by tampering with potential to cause great damage,*

- *Dark clad figure dares to move through parking lot behind pit lane as investigation happens; possibly feeling desperate at being exposed,*

- *Why would someone want to hurt so many drivers, leading to who would want that,*

- *A massive grudge? A disgruntled ex-employee?*

- *What will the contents of the black van reveal?*

- *Need to find out staffing situations from all teams,*

At four in the morning, Jake packed up his meditation articles and crawled back into bed. Anhton was still sound asleep.

11.2

Monday, May 10, 6:00am

At the delightful time of six am, Jake's alarm began to sound. He hit snooze a few times and then dragged himself out of bed, showered, and fixed some breakfast. As he poured coffee into his mug, Anhton blearily arrived at the kitchen bench. He plopped himself on a stool and grabbed Jake's coffee mug. He took a sip and muttered something about he was now starting to feel human again.

'Would you like a coffee, sweetie?' asked Jake, as he poured another mug.

'No thanks, I have one already.'

'Yeah, mine.'

'What yours is mine and what's mine is mine. Isn't that how it goes?'

'So you would seem to think. Good morning.'

'Yes, what you said.'

Jake picked up his coffee and his breakfast and went and sat at the table.

'Where's my brekkie?'

'No, you can't have mine this time.'

'Don't you love me anymore?' said Anhton, making a comical sad face.

'I'll always love you, baby.'

'I suppose I should put some clothes on.'

'That would be appreciated by all concerned at work. I leave in thirty minutes.'

'How is a girl supposed to make herself look good in thirty minutes.'

'By being the boy that you are.'

'In that case. I'll be back shortly.'

Anhton left the room as Jake laughed and ate his breakfast.

As they got into the car to drive to DFIS HQ, Jake handed Anhton a toasted bacon and egg sandwich. Once they had parked the car, they took the lift to their floor. Jake dropped his satchel on his desk, retrieved his tablet and notes and went to the Glass Room. He pressed his thumb on an almost invisible button in the right corner and waited. When Lassie kicked into life, he removed his thumb.

'Good morning, Jake.'

'Morning, Lassie.'

'How can I help you today?'

'Can you please access all files with the name 'Supacar' in them?'

'One moment.' Lassie began to emit a whistling noise.

'Uhm. Lassie, what are you doing?' asked Jake.

'What you asked me to do.'

'No, I meant with the whistling. You are whistling aren't you?'

'That's what I've been programmed to do when I'm retrieving data,' said lassie.

'How long have you been doing that for?'

'Since December 23 at 10:17 am.'

'Always the precise one,' said Jake. 'How come I haven't heard it before?'

'You have.'

'No I haven't.'

'Yes, you have,' said another voice, entering the Glass Room.

Jake turned to see David standing there.

'Since when?' asked Jake.

'Since December 23 at 10:17am. I heard Lassie tell you the date she was upgraded with that enhancement.'

'I see, yet it is only now that I've heard her do it.'

'I'd say that until recently, there were probably many more things you heard but didn't register hearing,' said David. 'You've been under such a dark cloud for so long we all thought you'd never come back.'

'I came back in March,' said Jake.

'You did, but I don't reckon you had come back fully,' said David.

'Sorry about that,' said Jake.

'That's history now. I was watching you yesterday and I saw the spark that was there the first day you started.'

Jake bowed his head and blushed.

'Ready, Jake,' said Lassie.

Jake looked up to see the various files filling the vertical screen. 'Disseminate and reconstruct as follows. Pictures on the table. Interview notes, collated into the various Teams and listed alphabetically. Evidence notes listed alphabetically. That will do for now, Lassie. Any information that doesn't fall into those categories, create a new file for them.'

'Understood, Jake.' She began to whistle once more.

'Only quieter this time, please, Lassie.'

Lassie lowered the volume and Jake left the Glass Room.

'What's the plan, Jake?' asked David.

'Correlation. I'll try and get the rest of the interview files from the detectives as soon as I can and add them. I also need to scan the paper interviews Anhton gave me from his round of interviews. I'll send emails next to gather what I want. I'll pop down and chat to Gabby and see what she has for me too. Once I know Lassie's finished the current actions, I'll begin to crosslink the data.'

'I can scan the paper and send the emails,' said Anhton.

'There you go, one thing less to do,' said David. 'Make sure you tell Ric what's going on. I'll be out of the office from ten in meetings in town about yesterday. As soon as Ric gets up here, get to work. We have to get this sorted quickly. I was talking to the chief steward last night and he's concerned that the garages won't be able to have their cars ready in time for the next race in four weeks with the embargo you've placed on them.'

'I had to make sure that if we needed access to the cars again, that we'd still be able to see them as they were yesterday,' said Jake.

'The chief steward understands that but is already receiving massive pressure from the team owners,' said David. 'In their game, time is certainly money. Spend a little time in planning who's going to do what and stick to it. Trust in each other.'

Jake nodded and understood the inference. David went back to his office and Jake went into the meeting room they had. He sat at the table and spread his notes. Anhton soon joined him with what he had when Ric crossed the room, Jake got up and called him into the room.

'What's the go?' asked Ric.

'I have Lassie disseminating and re-collating some of the data files we already have,' said Jake. 'I can pause her while we add anything you have. Anhton's going to get the interviews from the various detectives and add those. I'm going down to see Gabby shortly to see how she's going.'

'Good. That gives me time to sort out the rest of the team so that we can have more hands working on this case,' said Ric.

'I can deal with that,' said Jake. 'As soon as we get anything new, we need to add it and have Lassie cross-link it immediately.'

'At least the three of us can work at the same time with Lassie to cross-link,' said Anhton. 'What did you want done there?'

'We need to cross-link the pictures we have with the teams. Perhaps set up a master file for each team, listing all the personnel and any associated picture, interview, comment, etc. Then slowly work through and add the cross-links.'

'That wipes out today, then,' said Anhton.

'Most likely,' said Jake.

'What about potential motives? Suspects?' asked Ric.

'Suspects? I have no idea, other than the dark clad figure I rumbled with yesterday,' said Jake.

'I heard about that,' said Ric. 'Any idea who that was?'

'I'm hoping Gabby can get some DNA off the clothing and equipment for me,' said Jake. 'As to a motive, I have no idea really. When I thought about it at three am this morning, all I could think of was a disgruntled ex-employee, perhaps.'

'Do you know if we asked any of the teams who they've had to let go this year?' asked Ric.

'Or even last year?' added Anhton.

'Worth asking,' said Jake.

'I'll find out,' said Anhton. 'I'll also begin setting up the master files on Lassie.'

'Ten o'clock, coffee and catch up with Lassie?' said Jake.

Ric and Anhton nodded, and the three investigators went their separate ways.

11.3

Monday, May 10, 8:30am

Jake left the meeting room and made his way down two floors to Gabby's lab. As usual, the music was loud and varied as he walked in. As if the lab knew that there was a visitor, the music dimmed.

'Morning, Jake, took you long enough.' Gabby greeted him without even turning around.

Jake smiled and made his way to the bench she was working at.

'What do you mean, "it took me long enough"?' said Jake.

'Firstly, to come down here this morning,' said Gabby. 'Secondly, to snap out of your gloom and get back to work.'

'I have been working.'

'If what you've been doing these past months is work, then I must've been the ruler of a ten thousand strong personal household.'

'I've been back since March,' said Jake.

'Okay, I'll give you that, but it still wasn't truly you.'

'What about that hug, and that damned torch you shine in my face?'

'What torch?' Gabby did her best to look innocent.

Jake shook his head and smiled.

Gabby put her things down, turned and gave him the biggest hug he'd had in an awfully long time, other than Anhton's.

'I knew you'd come back to me one day,' said Gabby.

'Right-o, what have you got for me?'

'So much, yet so little. Where do you want me to begin?'

'What about the bomb fragments?' said Jake. 'Do they match the ones we found in the van?'

'Yes, they do and they're extremely inventive. I haven't had a chance to research anything on those yet, but I'll have something for you by the end of the day.'

'Of course you will. Start with the three robbery sites from the beginning of the year. I reckon you'll find what you need. The van itself? Anything from the minuscule partials? What about the clothing, etc.?'

'See that pile of bags?'

Jake turned to see the evidence bags he and David had collected, sitting neatly in rows inside some tubs, unopened.

'Right. Anything I can do?' asked Jake.

'Yes, leave me alone. I have work to do.'

'Love you too.'

'So you should, young man,' said Gabby.

As Jake left, he met Dustin with a nervous looking intern in tow.

'Morning, Dustin,' said Jake. 'Is that wise?'

'Morning, Jake,' said Dustin. 'Is what wise?'

Jake indicated the intern.

'Indeed it is. I saw how much evidence we had to process, and she can't do it on her own.

'Yes, I can,' called Gabby.

'Not this time, sweetie,' said Dustin. 'Word has it the evidence is required yesterday.'

'Don't I always do that?'

'I have the utmost faith in you, but this time you don't have a choice. Even I'm getting my hands dirtier than normal. Besides. Amy's called in sick.'

'Huh,' said Gabby. 'No time for introductions. Those three tubs of evidence bags are from the black van. They need to be dusted, photographed, analysed, categorised, homogenised and past-your-eyes before lunch.'

Dustin and Jake chuckled, and the intern looked wary.

'You'll get to know her soon enough,' said Dustin. 'She really is a nice person to work with.'

'Damn right I am,' said Gabby.

'Do as your told and you'll survive,' added Jake, leaning into the intern.

'Prove to me that I'm wrong, if you think so, but never just tell me I'm wrong,' said Gabby, smiling.

Jake waved and left the lab. Dustin showed the intern where to get a coat and soon the bags were all over the work bench.

11.4

Monday, May 10, 10:00am

Jake walked back into the Glass Room at ten am, as he had proposed. Anhton was sitting at the table with his tablet resting on top, typing madly. Ric also entered, accessing his tablet.

'What have we got, team' asked Jake.

'The files from the detectives who conducted the interviews should start coming through soon,' said Anhton. 'They'll scan the paper records, add them to a file containing the tablet records and email them across to me.'

'Great, ' said Jake. 'As soon as they come through, load, and cross-link them. The sooner we get the data in, the sooner we can see who was where.'

'I also wondered if there was any video surveillance at the track. I rang the Supacar organisers to discover they did have security. They put me in touch the with company managing the system and they are sending me all security vision they have from midday on Saturday until six pm on Sunday night.'

'That's excellent, Ric,' said Jake. 'When it arrives, get it loaded and we'll have something else to look at.'

They all laughed.

'How's it going with you, Anhton?' asked Jake.

'All the master files have been set up, Lassie's still re-compiling and I've started cross-linking.'

'Very good,' said Jake. 'Once we start getting the data from Gabby, we can start trying to piece together what happened.'

'Looks like we've got the video from the security company,' said Ric, checking his email.

'Get it loaded so we can start watching it.'

'Got it.' Ric tapped madly on his tablet and soon the copy of the data stream from the security company flashed on Lassie's screen.

'Lassie,' said Jake.

'Yes, Jake,' said Lassie.

'Can you please play the data stream from the security company?' asked Jake.

'One moment.' Jake watched the screen and then saw the equivalent of a TV screen open in the bottom right-hand corner. 'Is that large enough, Jake?'

'Bit larger please.'

'How's this?'

'That's fine, Lassie, thank you,' said Jake.

Jake, Anhton and Ric pulled chairs closer to the vertical glass screen where Lassie was playing the data stream.

'Lassie, can you please give us vision controls?' asked Jake.

A series of buttons appeared below the vision and Jake began to move the vision forward until the various garages began to empty out for the night. They concentrated on the vision for Balcher Racing to start with and at about two am, a figure appeared inside the garage.

'This looks good,' said Ric.

'Very,' said Jake, moving closer.

Jake, Anhton and Ric watched as the dark clad figure moved deftly around the garage.

'They've either been in this garage before, or they sure know their way round,' said Jake.

'Agreed,' said Anhton.

They watched as the figure rolled underneath each of the two cars garaged there.

'There's the evidence that explosive devices were placed,' said Jake. 'I wonder if we can get a close up of the face.'

'Or even their height, weight, etc.,' added Ric.

'Something to add to Lassie's list,' said Jake. He paused the vision and noted the time stamp. 'Let's have a look at some more, see if they went anywhere else.' Jake sped up the vision slightly and only stopped it when they spotted the dark figure moving around the other garages.

Jake, Anhton and Ric finished watching the vision and noted all the time stamps they wanted to follow up on.

'Have you had any word yet about the staffing situations over the past 2 years from the teams?' asked Jake.

'They're not so willing to cooperate as I first thought,' said Anhton.

'Keep pushing. If we have to, I'll get David to get what we need.'

'I'll ask again,' said Anhton. 'I can use the "threat" of a court subpoena to get what I want.'

'Be careful.'

'I always am.'

'Let's just see what we can get voluntarily first,' said Jake. 'We do need them sooner rather than later though. Remind the teams that we are dealing with a murder investigation and any hindrance will not be looked upon lightly.'

'That should do it,' said Ric.

'A lot of the files are done, Jake,' said Anhton, looking at the part of the screen not showing the security footage. 'Lassie is still re-compiling, but cross-linking doesn't seem to be hindering her too much.'

'Okay,' said Jake. 'Is there anything else we need to do?'

'I reckon she'll be done after lunch. We can come back and begin to move things around.'

'Lunch it is then.'

* * * * *

When they had come back from eating, Ric sat at one end to the table, Anhton at the other and Jake stood in-between, tablet in hand. Between the three of them, they began to cross-link all the photos they had with the garages they belonged to. Also, the reports they did have, were also cross-linked. Soon there were lines going all over the place. Not to mention the various lists that items were attached to, but all the data accumulated would better help them depending on what type of link they wanted.

'Good, some more reports,' said Ric, answering a sound on his tablet.

11.5

Monday, May 10, 4:30pm

By the end of the day, all the interview reports had been received and about half the teams had sent in their staffing situations for the previous two years. As the data came in, it was added to the massive file of info they had already collected. Then as Gabby's forensics results came through, they were added. Jake was a little disappointed at the results from the black van. Nothing of consequence regarding DNA material, but Gabby was able to pinpoint the origin of the explosive devices. She even provided contact details for the retail outlets they were purchased from.

'Time to go home, kiddies,' said Jake. 'It's been a long day.'

'Yes, it has,' said Anhton. 'And possibly as long a day tomorrow.'

'Depends on what Lassie can find out for me overnight,' said Jake. 'I'm going to program a number of tasks for her to do and we can inspect the results tomorrow.'

Ric left the Glass Room, collected his stuff, and left Jake sitting at Lassie's table. Anhton packed up both their desks whilst it took Jake another thirty minutes to finish typing in the parameters of the searches he wanted Lassie to action. He set her visuals to sleep mode, typed a message for no one else to touch, turn off, interrupt, or otherwise mess up his work overnight.

11.6

Monday, May 10, 5:30pm

As soon as Jake got home he headed for a shower. When he came out, he found Anhton changed and waiting for him.

'You'll need to change; we're going out for dinner tonight.'

'What on earth for?'

'To celebrate,' said Anhton.

'Celebrate what?'

'You getting back to work again.'

'Don't be an ass,' said Jake.

'I'd rather go out with you feeling like you are now than for the previous few months where you've been morose and dark.'

'I have not been morose and dark! I came back in March. Why won't anyone believe that.'

'Yes, you have, sweetie, and we do believe you,' said Anhton affectionately. 'Now, get changed so we can go out.'

Jake smiled, kissed Anhton on the cheek and returned about fifteen minutes later, dressed, and ready to go.

Anhton drove into the city and parked at the casino. They walked through the mezzanine shopping level and walked along the inside alley where a lot of the restaurants were located. Anhton stopped at one, walked in and was greeted by a well-dressed waiter.

'Reservation for two, in the name of Roberts,' said Anhton.

The waiter looked at his sheet, nodded and bid them follow him. Soon the boys were sitting at an outside table. A light breeze wafted along the promenade between the casino and the river. Families, couples, groups of two and three meandered along admiring the sights as they travelled to and from their destinations.

Jake sat back and relaxed, picked up the drink he'd ordered and breathed in deeply.

'Thank you, sweetie, for taking me out tonight,' said Jake. 'It actually feels good to be here.'

'My pleasure,' said Anhton. 'It's been tough, these past few months, but I'd do it all over again to be with you.'

'I'm sorry if I made your life hell.'

'You didn't.'

'Yes, I did.'

Jake turned his head suddenly and looked around the room.

'What's the matter?' asked Anhton.

Jake leant forward and spoke softly. 'Not trying to be rude, but I'm certain I heard someone behind me say, "what's he doing here?". I turned to see who had walked in but saw no one moving. They may have sat down already, so who knows.'

'Funny you should say that,' said Anhton, 'but just as you turned your head, I saw a man's face take on a rather sour expression.'

'Can you describe him to me?'

Anhton casually shifted himself in his chair and Jake shifted sideways. Jake retrieved his smartphone and opened a document.

'Go.'

'Early to mid-thirties. Soft complexion, stubbly goatee. Lightish eyes, refined nose, short brown hair with blonde streaks.'

Anhton shifted in his chair again and mouthed that the man was getting up and moving in their direction. The man passed by the table, making a distinct grunting sound. Jake took note of the clothing and then put away his phone.

Pushing the incident aside, they enjoyed a hearty meal and a sweet banana dessert. They joked about being overstuffed as they made their way back to the car and drove home.

New

12.1

Tuesday, May 11, 8:00am

Jake arrived at work carrying three large coffees and a large box of donuts. Anhton carried both their satchels. People jokingly complained as he went past without offering any to them. Anhton put their satchels at their desks whilst Jake took the coffee and donuts into the Glass Room and waited. When Ric arrived, he was greeted with the smell of the breakfast Jake had brought in.

'What's all this for?' asked Ric.

'To say thanks for yesterday,' said Jake.

'Anything else?' asked Ric.

'No.'

Ric looked at Jake.

'Oh.'

'Here it comes,' said Ric.

'We have a lot to do today,' said Jake. 'Let's have a look at the results of the programs I set for Lassie last night.'

Ric and Anhton took their coffees and grabbed a donut each.

'Good morning, Lassie, what have you got for me?' asked Jake.

'Good morning, Jake,' said Lassie. 'Here are the results of the various programs you wanted me to run.'

Jake looked down his list and selected the one he wanted.

'Open suspect recognition file, please, Lassie,' asked Jake.

'Here you go, Jake,' said Lassie.

The file opened. It showed the image of the black figure in Balcher Racing's garage. At one stage it stood upright and from that, Lassie extrapolated height and approximate weight. As the figure wore gloves, a balaclava and dark glasses, no other features were visible.

'It's a start,' said Ric. 'Why that file first?'

'It may be nothing, and may even missed the intended target,' said Jake, 'but when I was out to dinner last night with Anhton at the casino, not long after we sat down Anhton said that a customer behind me suddenly had a sour expression on their face. Just prior to that, I could have sworn I heard someone, say "What's he doing here?". I looked around but no one else was moving in the restaurant, inside or outside, except the wait staff.'

'It could also have a simple coincidence,' said Amy.

'Perhaps,' said Jake. 'It was very coincidental if that's the case. Anyway, I didn't turn around, but moved my head so that Anhton could look 'past' the table to describe the person. Then they got up, walked past our table, and very audibly grunted. I took note of their clothing and then put away my phone to continue with dinner.'

'What did they look like then?' asked Ric.

'Even though I was sitting down, I'd say that they were about 180cm tall, maybe 90kgs. Anhton had already told me they were in their early to mid-thirties, with a soft complexion, and a stubbly goatee. They also had lightish eyes, refined nose, and short brown hair with blonde streaks.'

'That doesn't mean who you saw last night and who we saw on the tape are the same person,' said Ric.

'I know this. I know this,' said Jake. 'However, would you go so far as to make such faces and deliberate noises when someone sat down near you?'

'Well, no, that would be rude,' said Ric.

'Indeed. So, humour me and let's assume that these two people are the same.'

'Okay, you're the one who's gonna make the ass of himself,' said Ric.

'Granted. If this connection is proven wrong,' said Jake, 'lunch for a week is on me.'

'Deal,' said Ric, shaking Jake's hand.

'I'm in on this as well, thank you very much,' added Anhton, placing his hand on top of Jake's and Ric's.

'Moving on, let's now make a list of suspects,' said Jake. 'Labelling the dark figure as S1, I think we should try and get a copy of any security footage from the restaurant. Perhaps we can get an ID on the person.'

'I'll get onto that, for you,' said Anhton.

12.2

Tuesday, May 11, 12:00pm

After four hours of scanning through comparative list after comparative list, the team finally stopped.

'Nothing. Zilch. Nada. Zip,' said Jake. 'How can we have gathered so much info and come up with nothing?'

Ric and Anhton shrugged their shoulders.

'Let's have some lunch,' said Jake.

They all turned when Ric's tablet buzzed several times in succession. He went back to have a look.

'Good news,' said Ric. 'The rest of the Teams have agreed to our request for staffing over the past two years. We have them all now.'

'Excellent,' said Jake. 'Get them loaded into Lassie and run the cross-link program. Let's see what she has for us after lunch.'

Jake fidgeted all through lunch, and when his phone buzzed with a message from Lassie to say that the recent compile request was complete, he was eager to get back to the office.

He walked straight to the Glass Room.

'Lassie, can you bring the employment file recently loaded showing which team each person belonged to and if they are currently employed by any other team? Please?'

'One moment, Jake.'

Jake tapped his fingers on the tabletop.

'If you're going to be like that, I can easily make you wait,' said Lassie.

'No, no, no. I'm sorry, Lassie,' said Jake. 'I really would like to see the data as quickly as possible. I want to get cracking with this case. Now that I've been rejuvenated, my brain and energies are going into overload.'

'Here you are, Jake.'

The files popped up on screen, with photo's as well.

Jake began to read. 'Let's see who we've got.

• 'Amanda Beston, 34, 180cm. It says that she had been with Broadbench Consolidated Racing for five years and with a now defunct team for five years prior to that. She had previously completed a mechanics apprenticeship prior to joining the defunct team. Was working her way up through the system to be a lead mechanic but was overlooked for a promotion. Was known to be upset when Jason Black moved from Broadbench Consolidated Racing to Balcher Racing at the end of the 2018 season. Reason for departure - was dismissed as had become aggressive, surly, and disruptive.

• 'Christian Boxer, 40, 180cm. Joined his first team at fifteen. That team eventually merged with Skoel Performance Racing. Learnt his trade on the job and became head mechanic at 30. Trained all new crew from then on. Came back to work after his heart attack, but there had been too many changes whilst he was away recuperating and found it difficult to maintain his authority and knowledge base. No one had the time to help him, and he became disgruntled. Reason for departure - health reasons because of the heart attack.

• 'Jack Foreman - 25, 183cm. Joined Saavo Motorsports as a technical assistant working on their computer, electronic and communications systems. Well liked, knowledgeable and efficient. Reason for departure - was discovered trading secrets to Balcher Racing, for whom his girlfriend worked at the time.

'That brings us to;

• 'Leonie Morningside - 24, 176cm. Joined Balcher Racing at 20 and worked with their public relations department. Was also close to all aspects the team. Was active with the promotion of all Team related events and helped organise aspects of the Team's travel itinerary. Reason for departure - was deliberately and knowingly trading Team secrets with her then boyfriend on Saavo Motorsports, Jack Foreman

'Lastly, we have;

• 'Peter Van Gammon, 37, 180cm. Was part of the setup crew for APG Racing, which originally comprised Luke Summerfield and Ulysses David. After the moves, Mark Perrin and Dirk Van Gammon moved to a brand new look APG Racing. Peter was annoyed at having to work with his brother as they didn't really get along, which is why Dirk was always on another team. Management wanted Mark and Dirk and after a few rows with both his brother and management, Peter was let go. The file notes that no other team wanted him, so he drifted away from the sport.

'There we have it, boys. A list of five people who have been dismissed, with one leaving for health reasons over the past two seasons of racing.'

'Makes for some interesting reading then,' said Ric.

'Potential there,' said Anhton. 'Do we interview all of them to see where they were this past weekend?'

'Let's see if we can get current details on them first,' said Jake. 'Lassie, can you please run checks on the five names in this list of former employees and return with their current address and contact details?'

'I can do that, and I will let you all know when I'm done,' said Lassie.

'Thanks.' Jake reached for his phone to see a message that Gabby wanted to see him. 'Can you two keep going with any cross-linking and checking? I'm sure Lassie won't be long with the search of the details. Gabby has something for me to see.'

Anhton and Ric nodded their assent and Jake began to leave the Glass Room. His phone buzzed again.

'I've just been notified that I have an email copy of the autopsy report,' said Jake. 'I'll send it through. Can you also begin to have a look at it?'

'Sure,' said Anhton.

12.3

Tuesday, May 11, 1:00pm

Jake made his way down two levels to Gabby's lab. He walked in to find the intern working on some evidence bags, but Dustin was nowhere to be seen.

'I see you dumped the boss already?' said Jake.

'Too many questions,' said Gabby, 'and the other one is too quiet. I forget he's here, except when he's forgotten how to use one of my toys.'

'What have you got for me, sweetie?' asked Jake.

'Well,' started Gabby, 'those explosive devices are clever little buggers. I was able to trace the retail outlets by the serial numbers. Only four stores across Melbourne have permission to sell these. Whether they were purchased before the new registration laws came in or not, I have no idea.'

'Hmmm,' said Jake. 'Those laws were only ratified in January this year. Does the information you have say when they were purchased?'

'No, you'll have to go to the stores to find that out.'

'That's easy enough to do. Anything else?'

'Yep,' said Gabby, 'the timing devices are even more regulated. There are only two outlets licensed to see those. I'll send the files up to you.'

'You have access to Lassie, don't you?'

'Yeah.'

'Load your files directly to Lassie, using the designation Supacar,' said Jake. 'When I get back upstairs, I'll crosslink the data.'

'You're so smart,' cooed Gabby.

'Stop it, it'll go to my head.'

'In that case, it's too late.'

'Bite me,' said Jake, as he began to leave his phone buzzed. 'Thanks for the information. It's been great.' He looked at the phone. 'Oh my god.'

'What is it?' asked Gabby.

'The autopsy,' said Jake, 'Anhton says it's incredible and that I should hurry back. Bye. Love you.'

12.4

Tuesday, May 11, 1:25pm

Jake left and returned to the Glass Room. As he exited the lift and entered the office area, he bumped into David.

'I was just looking for you,' he said. 'Can I have a word please?'

'I need to view the autopsy report,' said Jake, making to move past David.

'That can wait a few minutes,' said David, indicating his office.

Jake followed David into his office. At first, he didn't recognise the person who was sitting in the chair facing the desk.

'Jake, I'd like you to meet Mr. Tony Cherry, CEO of the Supacar organisation,' said David. 'Mr Cherry, I'd like you to meet one of my best investigators, Det.Sgt Jake North.'

Jake shook Tony Cherry's hand.

'It's a pleasure to meet you, Mr Cherry,' said Jake.

'Tony will be fine.'

Jake nodded.

'Have a seat, Jake.' David sat down behind his desk. 'Tony has come to me today to see what he can do to help get this investigation concluded as quickly as possible. He's getting pressure from the Teams to be able to work on their cars in readiness of the next race.'

'Well, David and Tony,' said Jake, 'the investigation is moving along. We have large amounts of evidence and statements to sift through and we have some leads we need to follow up on.'

'That sounds like something I'd say to my Team managers when I really don't have any information,' said Tony.

Jake smiled. 'I understand, Tony. Would you like to see where we're up to?'

'That won't be necessary,' said Tony. 'If you have no further need of any of the cars by Friday, I want them released form the Island so the Teams can get to work on them.'

'I understand, Tony,' said Jake. 'I will call you myself.'

'That's ok, Jake, let me know and I will call Tony,' said David.

'Is there anything else, David?' asked Jake. 'I'd like to get back to work. My task now is to release the cars by the end of today, if possible.'

Tony looked sharply at Jake.

'I appreciate the urgency of your request and don't wish to hold things up any further than necessary,' said Jake.

Jake stood, shook Tony's hand, and left the office.

12.5

Tuesday, May 11, 1:30

When he got back to the Glass Room, he went immediately to Lassie and accessed the files with the pictures of the six cars that had been tampered with.

'What's the rush?' asked Ric.

'I've just had a brief meeting with David and Mr Tony Cherry, CEO of the Supacar organisation, who wants the cars released by Friday,' said Jake. 'I want to release them by the end of today. The better we stay in his good books, the better chance we have of being able to ask for assistance in the future. I want us to go over all the pictures and make sure that there's nothing else we are likely to need from them. If we do, we need to take pictures of them in their home garages, but if we were as thorough as we usually are, then we probably have enough.'

'So far, the prints lifted all belong to current team members,' said Ric.

'The pictures won't really become required until something concrete is gained from the teams once they have the cars back in their own garages,' added Anhton.

'So you think we can release them now?' asked Jake.

'Don't see why not,' said Ric.

'Perhaps add a proviso that if anything else is discovered, they let us know immediately by providing a full description and detailed pictures of what they find,' said Anhton.

'The main car that we need the most info on, is that of Jason Black's,' said Jake. 'At least their garage is located here in Melbourne. So we're happy to release the cars?'

Ric and Anhton nodded.

'Let's hope that Tony Cherry is still here then,' said Jake. 'Oh, have the autopsy ready for me to view when I get back.'

12.6

Tuesday, May 11, 1:35pm

Jake left the Glass Room and went to David's office. He caught Tony as he was about to depart. He knocked on the window.

'Yes, Jake, what is it?' asked David.

Jake entered. 'I've just been discussing with my colleagues about the cars,' said Jake. 'We've decided that we can release the cars right now, however, we'd like to add the strict proviso that if the teams find anything, anything at all, unusual with their cars, they are to notify us, take appropriate pictures and make detailed notes. For those Teams based in Melbourne, we will travel to their garages and deal with the information. How does that sound, Tony?'

'I'm surprised that you are able to release them so soon, but I'm more than happy to add that proviso,' said Tony.

'Thank you, Tony,' said Jake. 'If you can make sure that all the Teams understand the critical importance of any evidence they may uncover. Anything left out could hinder the investigation. I'm sure they want to see a resolution as much as we do.'

'I totally understand, Jake. I will keep you informed,' said Tony.

Jake nodded and left David's office.

12.7

Tuesday, May 11, 1:40pm

'How did that go?' asked Ric, when Jake returned to the Glass Room.

'Very well indeed,' said Jake. 'We got what we wanted. I doubt we'll have any trouble.'

'Good,' said Ric.

'Where were we?' asked Jake.

'The autopsy,' said Anhton. 'You won't believe what they found.'

'Let me guess,' said Jake. 'The ME found a quantity of an unknown substance that he eventually discovered was a synthetically boosted serum for mental acuity?'

'No,' said Anhton.

'Oh,' said Jake, puzzled. 'So what did he have to say?'

'That he found a large quantity of an unknown substance that he eventually discovered was a synthetically boosted serum for mental acuity.' Anhton smiled.

Jake looked Anhton with a small amount of disdain. 'Do we have the ME's number?'

'It's at the top of the report,' said Ric.

Jake scrolled the report until he got to the phone number. He grabbed his phone and dialled.

'Good afternoon, this is Det.Sgt Jake North, DFIS. I'd like to speak with Mr. Charles Tanaka, please.'

'This is Charlie Tanaka. How can I help you Det.Sgt?'

'Jake will be fine. I've just learnt that you discovered a quantity of an unknown substance. What made you think to look at the mental acuity angle?' asked Jake. 'I'm putting you on speaker, so my colleagues, Det.Cpl Anhton Roberts and Det.LtCmdr Ric Harding can also hear. They are assisting with the investigation.'

Greetings were dealt with quickly.

'Please go ahead, Charlie,' said Jake.

'When I saw the formula, something triggered in my mind,' said Charlie. 'I had a vague recollection of knowing what some of the components of the substance were. It took me some time, but I eventually found the chemical formulas for the natural herbal remedies for mental acuity. When I compared them, I could see that someone has been experimenting with enhancing and synthesising those formulas. In effect they have boosted their capabilities.'

'Were you able to determine if there might be any side effects?'

'Not really, but the brain is a funny organism. Every person's chemical makeup is different to another's. No two people are the same. Therefore, any synthetic substance, or any natural substance for that matter, will have different reactions to the chemical makeup of the individual.'

'I think I know what you're saying,' said Jake.

'What are you trying to work out, Jake?'

'I'm trying to find out if the serum that Jason Black took had any effect on his ability to drive. Whether his concentration and focus were over-affected as result.'

'If you like, I can have a look at some brain tissue samples? I still have the body. I haven't released it to the family yet,' said Charlie.

'I'd appreciate that, Charlie. Email me the results as soon as you can.'

'Done. Is there anything else I can help you with?'

'You've done more than enough. Thank you,' said Jake, and he disconnected the call.

'That makes for an interesting turn of events,' said Ric.

'It also makes for a more interesting conversation we need to have with Dan,' said Jake. 'How are you feeling Anhton?'

'I'm shocked and surprised at Dan,' he said. 'I never thought he'd resort to supplements. It's like cheating. If they had of stuck with the herbal remedies, then I wouldn't have a problem. Now that's it's synthetically enhanced, I'm not so sure.'

'Ric and I can handle the interview, if you like?' said Jake.

'No, I need to be there,' said Anhton.

'Very well,' said Jake. 'Oh, has Gabby sent anything through yet, Lassie?'

'Nothing received from Gabby just yet, Jake,' said Lassie, 'but I do have some information on those in the suspect file.'

'Let's have a look, Lassie,' said Jake.

The screen began to populate with each of the files. Listed below the picture were all the details they had.

Addresses, driver's licences, health records, anything that Lassie had access to.

'Jake?' asked Anhton. 'Have a look at this one.'

'Whose?'

'Amanda Beston's file. It seems that after June 2019, she ceased to exist yet there is no death certificate.'

'We'll focus on that one for a while, as that's strange,' said Jake. 'So we have an address?'

'The last known address is shown,' said Anhton.

'Right, let's go, Anhton,' said Jake. 'We're gonna take a little drive this arvo. Ric, Gabby's file should be here soon. Cross-link and cross reference anything you can. She was saying that she had addresses of the four outlets that were licensed to sell the explosives and the only two outlets licensed to sell the timers. I'll bet anything that the first three retails outlets investigated this year are on those lists.'

'Seems odd that four can sell the explosive but only two can sell the timer,' asked Ric.

'True. See what you can make of it,' said Jake. 'Go visiting if you have to.'

'Done,' said Ric.

12.8

Tuesday, May 11, 2:15pm

Jake and Anhton headed for the basement garage, signed out a DFIS Forden AV and mapped out where the address was.

'Should take us about an hour to get there,' said Anhton.

'When we get there, I'd like you to be as an impartial observer as possible,' said Jake, as he steered the Forden onto the road.

'Why so?'

'I want you to take note of words, expressions, tonality, intonation, perhaps hidden meaning, between the lines stuff.'

'So you want the less conspicuous stuff, or the stuff you might miss because you're engaging with the person we're talking to?' said Anhton.

'That's it. Then when we get back in the car, we can compare notes. Perhaps even try and record the conversation.'

'That's a bit sneaky.'

'I know we can't use it as evidence, but it can help us recall when comparing notes,' said Jake. 'It might even jog our memories to things we forgot.'

Anhton began to search around in his backpack. 'Yep, I think I can do that. I can use the headphones from my phone to make it look like we're waiting for a phone call or something, but in fact when I hit record, the mic will pick up what's said.'

'Hmmm.'

'Uh oh, I know that sound.'

Jake smiled. 'There's an electronics store close to our destination. I want to stop there and see what sort of ultra-discrete cameras they have. Like in a pair of glasses, for example.'

'You really do like to push the limits.'

'Sometimes you have to.'

'Let's hope it works,' said Anhton.

'To check, we're going to the address of Amanda Beston, correct?'

'Yes, that's right. What, do you think someone else is going to be there?'

'I don't know yet, but I have this odd gut feeling,' said Jake.

12.9

Tuesday, May 11, 3:45pm

After getting kitted out at the electronics store in Ashwood, they checked their final directions and drove the last few kilometres to their destination. With weapons ready but hidden, they checked that everything was working and recording as required. They walked up the footpath and then the steps to the front door of a modest inner-eastern suburban home. A neat front garden greeted visitors. Plants along the porch made the front look fresh and welcoming. Jake knocked on the door.

'One moment,' came the voice from inside.

Seconds later, the door was open by a man with brown hair and blond streaks. Jake was momentarily surprised.

'What do you want,' said the gruff voice.

'Have we met before?' asked Jake.

'I don't think so. Who are you?'

'Det.Sgt Jake North, and Det.Cpl Anhton Roberts, DFIS.'

'Like I said, what do you want,' repeated the occupant of the report.

'We're looking for a Ms Amanda Beston. Does she live here.'

The occupant was taken aback for a moment. Anhton caught movement off to his left and when he casually looked in that direction, a curtain was hurriedly closed.

'She doesn't live here anymore,' said the occupant.

'I see. I gather that you bought the house when it was for sale?'

'Something like that,' said the occupant, wiping his brow.

'Thank you for your time, Mr...?' asked Jake.

The occupant grunted and closed the door. Jake and Anhton walked back to the car and as Jake climbed in, he looked up at the house to see a curtain close hurriedly. He started the AV and drove around the corner. Once they had stopped, they turned off their equipment. He then drove to some shops nearby where they found a quiet corner of cafe. They unpacked their small equipment on the table and waited for the drinks to arrive.

'That was interesting,' said Jake. 'What did you make of it all?'

'By the tone of the opening comment, they definitely knew who we were.'

'He was the person from the restaurant on Monday night.'

'He was very defensive throughout the brief chat,' said Anhton. 'His eyes were concentrating on you the whole time, and I thought they looked a little angry, perhaps resentful at something.'

'I did my best to stay cool though.'

'You did that well.'

Jake nodded. They stopped talking when their coffees were placed on the table.

'Then when you asked about Amanda, I thought he was going to jump out of his skin,' said Anhton.

'Yeah, I kinda got that impression. Then when I suggested he must've bought the house, he neither confirmed nor denied it. To me that says it was never for sale.'

'This could be true. I'll see what I can dig up on records of ownership and the like from local council.'

'Now we have to work out who the other person in the house is,' said Jake.

'You noticed that as well?'

'I felt you move behind me at one stage but wasn't sure why until I was getting into the car. Just before the curtains closed, I distinctly saw two faces, but I couldn't make out the sex of the second. One I knew would've been the man who answered the door.'

'The second is definitely female,' said Anhton. 'I'll bring up the vision of my camera to see if we can get a description.'

'Use Lassie and Gabby if you have to.'

'I intend to. Do you think that was Amanda?'

'No I don't,' said Jake.

'Why so sure?'

'It's that gut feeling I said I had before we left.'

'Can I ask what your gut feeling is?' asked Anhton, taking a sip of his drink.

'Sex-change.'

Anhton almost spat his coffee across the table. Jake chuckled.

'Sorry about that,' said Jake. 'Didn't mean for you to do that.'

'A sex-change? Where on earth did that come from?'

'Apart from left field?'

'Yes, apart from left field,' said Anhton.

'The very close similarities between the builds of Amanda and our occupant of the house. Both are about the same age and height. Although Amanda was much slimmer, and our man in the house is larger, I daresay that could be simply for the fact that he may have tried to bulk up as a man, or has put on weight with little activity after an op.'

'I thought sex-change operations took years to be completed. You know, lots of counselling and preparation.'

'We don't know that the sort of prep you're talking about hadn't already taken place,' said Jake. 'I think we need to go and have a chat with the management of Broadbench Consolidated Racing about what Amanda was like leading up to her dismissal. The report says that she became aggressive, surly, and disruptive.'

'That would make sense if she was on any hormone treatment to assist with the sex-change operation. Hormones can play havoc with emotions.'

'We also need to find out if Amanda has travelled overseas in the last two years.'

'Let me email Ric now and he can get started,' said Anhton. He began tapping away on his tablet. 'Done.'

'Let's have a look at the vision we collected.'

Jake pulled out his tablet, hooked up his phone remotely and downloaded the vision. As he did that, Anhton did the same. Both tablets dinged about the same time to say that their downloads were complete. Jake turned his tablet sideways and hit play. They watched the face of the man in the house and Jake paused it at a point near the end.

'See here, he's sweating now,' said Jake. 'That's when I asked about the sale of the house. This almost makes me feel sure that the house never sold and that it merely underwent a change of ownership. As the man was reluctant to give us his name, we'll just have to find other ways.'

'You mean like taking a photograph of his mail?' Anhton pulled his smartphone out and accessed his photos. He slid it across to Jake.

'You sly bastard,' said Jake. 'When did you take that?'

'As we left. I spotted several letters sticking out of the letterbox. I pretended to stumble and crash into it. Thankfully, they fell out, so as I was picking them up again, I snapped a photo.'

'I wondered why you were on the ground near the front gate. I thought you were tying your shoe or something.'

'I was,' said Anhton, with a wink. Jake smiled and nodded.

'Our mystery man now has a name?'

'He sure does,' said Anhton. 'Mr. Reuben Villaman.'

'We need to get this name into Lassie for a check,' said Jake. 'I'll send that in now with the command to run a check on him, listing all available information ... and ... done.'

'Let's have a look at my vision,' said Anhton. He got his tablet ready and hit play.

They watched as he captured most of the interaction

between Jake and Reuben, but it also captured the time he turned to see the face in the window.

'Yay, we at least got half a picture, and it is female. Mid-late twenties, reddish-blond hair, pulled back from her face. Pretty, with not a lot of make-up. If what you're saying is true, I wonder if she knows about Reuben's past?'

'Let's make sure of our facts first,' said Jake. 'We need to get this back to HQ and get it loaded.'

'Or load it from here so it's ready for us by the time we get back.'

'Or we can do that too.'

Anhton smiled as they finished their coffees, sent their files to Lassie, packed their things, and headed back to DFIS.

12.10

Tuesday, May 11, 4:45pm

Jake and Anhton parked the AV and checked it in. They collected their gear, including their new surveillance toys, and headed for the Glass Room. When they arrived, they saw a message flashing on the screen.

'Access message please, Lassie,' asked Jake.

'One moment,' replied Lassie. 'Here it is;

Hi Guys,

Have gone to talk to some of the stores selling the explosives and timers. I'm going to take pictures of both Amanda and the guy from the restaurant - the vision came through - to see if the retail staff can identify either of them as having purchased the items. David is preparing warrants in case we need them to obtain the records, but I think I'll be able to get to see the details without the warrants. If I don't make it back by knock off, I'll see you tomorrow.

Ric.

End Message.'

'Thank you, Lassie,' said Jake. 'Let's see what mister Ric can dig up for us this arvo. In the meantime, let's check on what we have and get it cross-linked.'

'All the files we sent have been received,' said Anhton. 'I think we may even have an answer back about Reuben already.'

'That was quick.'

'Well, if he's technically only existed since the year before last, then there won't be that much on him.'

'Agreed. Let's hope we get what we want from the search on Amanda,' said Jake.

'Reuben is listed as the owner of the house at the address we visited. Title was changed over in September last year. Guess who's listed as the previous owner?'

'Ooh, I don't know. Maybe Amanda Beston.'

'You only have ten questions left to win the two million dollars,' said Anhton.

Jake laughed. 'What else is in Reuben's file?'

'A new passport was registered in his name in the August.'

'Documents?'

'Listed but not shown,' said Anhton. 'Let's see, a bank statement, utility bill and a change of name form.'

'Well, well, well.' Anhton opened his mouth. 'Don't say it,' added Jake quickly. 'I want to see that change of name form because I know exactly what I'll find there.'

'Are you so sure about that?'

'Pretty much. Lunch for you for a second week if I'm not and vice-versa if I am,' said Jake, holding out his hand.

'Deal,' said Anhton, taking the wager.

'Lassie, can you please access Office of Records please? Authority; D-F-I-S-J-N-5-7-2.'

'Accessing now,' said Lassie. After a few minutes, Lassie responded. 'Access granted. Which department?'

'Change of name.'

'Access granted. Original name?'

'Beston, Amanda.'

'Accessing.' Jake watched as Lassie provided a sliding green line on the screen for him to watch. When it reached the end, he was still startled by her voice. 'Record appearing now.'

'Can you also take a copy of this record for our files please?'

'Done.'

The record flashed onto the screen.

'Yes. I'll have soup on Monday, a steak sandwich on Tuesday, ...'

'Okay, okay, you win,' said Anhton. 'Amanda Beston became Reuben Villaman. Do we still need to confirm Amanda's travel plans and dates then?'

'It would be good, just to make sure.'

'The next question is though, is Reuben the man we're looking for regarding the suspected murder of Jason Black?'

'We won't know that part until we see Ric and the results of his chats this afternoon,' said Jake. 'Lassie, please merge Amanda and Reuben's files and add a speculative note to the new file; Paperwork from Office of Records confirms that Amanda Beston, female, changed her name to that of Reuben Villaman, male. The descriptions we currently hold for both Amanda and Reuben are very close, except for weight.

Hair colour can be easily changed, but in this case doesn't seem to have been done to any great detail. Still waiting results of information search for Amanda. Also waiting on investigations from Det.LtCmdr Ric Harding to see if either Amanda or Reuben, but most likely Reuben, have purchased certain explosive devices and timers from licensed outlets in Melbourne. Close note.'

'So merged and noted, Jake,' said Lassie.

'Have we had any information, or even run the license plates from the van yet?' asked Anhton.

'That's a very good question,' said Jake. 'Lassie, has Gabby run the license plates from the data retrieved from the black van yet?'

'Checking now.' Lassie's green line reappeared. 'Here are the results.'

The files popped up on the screen.

'It's a rental,' said Jake.

'In the name of a Donna O'Neill,' said Anhton. 'I wonder if that's the girl we saw at Reuben's house?'

'Let's see if what her driver's licence has to show.' Jake clicked on the licence number attached to the rental form to have the details flash on the screen.

'This is getting better,' said Jake. 'That picture pretty much matches the half pic you saw in the window, but let's make sure.'

'Let me get the vision up.' Anhton tapped away at the glass tabletop and soon he had frozen the vision he'd captured of the half face in the window. 'Looks like a match to me. I'll just add the notes to the file.'

'What about we run the image of Donna against the faces of the women caught on film at the three stores?' said Jake. 'I'm confident it's the same person. Lassie, can you run a picture analysis of the images taken from the three store robberies and do facial recognition against the image on the driver's licence of Donna O'Neill please?'

'One moment please, Jake.'

'I think we still need to visit Broadbench Consolidated Racing's garage and have a chat to them about Amanda,' said Jake. 'I'll do that first thing in the morning. If you can see what Ric has and get the data up to date, hopefully I can add some more light to the situation when I get into work.'

'Sounds good to me,' said Anhton.

'Your information is ready, Jake,' said Lassie.

'Ah, thanks, Lassie. Let's see what you found.'

Jake and Anhton looked at the four pictures and then watched as Lassie ran them on top of one another. Allowing for minor distortions in the vision, the four pictures matched perfectly.

'Now we have our accomplice,' said Jake.

'We sure do,' said Anhton.

'Lassie, can you send Donna's picture to Ric? Add a note to ask him to show it as he visits the stores?' said Jake.

'Will do, Jake,' said Lassie.

'On that note, I'm calling it for the day,' said Jake.

Jake and Anhton packed their satchels and left DFIS HQ.

Revelations

13.1

Wednesday, May 12, 2:30am

Jake was enjoying a warm and comfortable sleep when both he and Anhton were awoken by Anhton's phone going crazy for the third time. Anhton reached over and answered it.

'Hello,' he said groggily. 'Dan, what's the matter. Slow down.'

Jake was wide awake by now and trying to find out what was wrong with Dan.

'Okay. Dan, we'll be there as soon as possible.'

'What's the matter, sweetie?' asked Jake.

'Dan's panicking,' said Anhton. 'He was staying at the garage as Jason's car had come back and someone broke in and tried to destroy the car again. Dan's managed to corner them, but he doesn't know for how much longer.'

'Why are we still here then,' said Jake.

They threw on some clothes. They each grabbed their guns and raced to the car. Jake drove while Anhton fed the address into the navigator. Soon they were on their way to Balcher Racing's garage in the north of the city. As it was almost three am, there wasn't a lot of traffic and as Jake's car isn't fitted with lights or sirens, he couldn't use those. A couple of regular defence cars began to follow him.

When they pulled up, they began to race to the side entrance Dan had told Anhton to go to, however the pursuing defence officers tried to stop them, Jake got out his credentials, as did Anhton, and the officers relented. Jake also barked orders for reinforcements from the closest station.

Anhton opened the side door and could hear the commotion happening on the far side of the complex. They moved in closer and soon found Dan, breathing heavily and extremely nervous.

'Where's the person?' asked Jake.

'Over there,' said Dan, pointing to a storeroom.

As Jake moved closer, he could see an array of items strewn around the doorway.

'Whoever you are,' Jake called, 'it's time to come out with your hands behind your head. DFIS and defence officers are all around the building.

The commotion went quiet, and they relaxed slightly. Suddenly there was a manic cry and the person inside the storeroom charged out. Seeing Jake, his gun raised, the person turned suddenly to their right and barrelled into Anhton. Anhton was knocked over and Jake gave chase. The figure ran around the inside of the building, throwing things down as they went. Jake deftly dodged each attempt and was soon chasing the figure outside.

This caught the officers outside off guard and although they fired, they missed each time.

'Follow as best as you can,' ordered Jake. 'I need something from my car.'

Jake rummaged around in the rear of his AV and was soon back in pursuit, night vision goggles on his face.

He stopped at the edge of dark forest track. 'Which way?' Jake asked. The officer pointed down the track. 'Bugger.'

Jake headed down the track carefully, gun at the ready and looking from side to side. He decided to move fast along the track and as he turned a corner, he spotted his target up ahead. He fired one shot, saw the figure duck, and then disappear to the left. Jake pursued and when he got to the point of the turn, he couldn't see anyone or anything moving.

Turning suddenly at a sound on the right, the figure jumped out in front of him, waving a branch above his head. Jake ducked out of the way and the branch hit the ground. Jake swung his legs around and brought the figure to the ground. With the figure winded, Jake was able to jump on top and started to pin them down. The figure fought back, and Jake realised it was the same man he'd fought with at Phillip Island.

Sensing a lapse, the figure kicked hard and managed to dislodge Jake. They began to wrestle, and the figure started punching. Jake fended them off and with the energy he had, lunged one last time, bought the figure crashing down with a loud grunt and a crack.

The figure began crying out in pain and began to writhe around on the ground. Jake stood up and saw that the figure's right leg was bent at a very wrong angle. Jake winced. Jake saw lights approaching and so he removed his night goggles. Anhton arrived, followed by several officers.

'We might want to call for an ambulance,' said Jake. 'Our friend here on the ground has a broken leg.'

'Did you have to be so hard on them, Jake?' asked Anhton.

'It was either him or me.'

'You bastard. I'll sue you for this,' cried the man on the ground.

'I don't think so, Mr. Villaman,' said Jake, shining a torch on his face.

The gasp was so audible, it caused everyone to go quiet.

'Cuff him,' said Jake.

One of the officers complied and two of them stood guard.

13.2

Wednesday, May 12, 4:00am

Once the ambulance had arrived, Villaman was brought back to the parking lot and officially arrested. The two officers who had stood guard over him followed the ambulance to the hospital and stayed by his side as often as they could.

Anhton pulled Jake aside after the ambulance had left. 'How did you know who it was?' he asked.

'I had a hunch,' said Jake. 'Are you alright? Did you hit your head again?'

'Yes, I was only partially winded,' said Anhton. 'My head is fine.'

'How's Dan?'

'Very shaken.'

'Is he up to talking?' asked Jake.

'I think so.'

Anhton led Jake to where Dan was sitting on a couch in the office area inside the complex.

'We got him, Dan,' said Jake, placing a hand on his shoulder.

'Is he the one who killed Jason?' asked Dan.

'That's what I'm going to find out,' said Jake. 'I'll go into the hospital and have a chat to him later this morning. Now, can you tell me what happened here tonight?'

'Sure, I'll do my best,' said Dan.

'That's all I ask,' said Jake. 'I'm going to place my phone down and record what we say. I can transcribe it later and you can re-read it and verify the statement. Is that okay?'

'Yeah, it's cool,' said Dan.

Jake activated the record function and set it down on the table between them. 'Record of interview with Dan Roberts at Balcher Racing's racing complex at 4:17 am, Wednesday May 12. Dan, in your own words can you please tell me what happened here tonight, from the time you first came to the complex.'

'Okay,' said Dan. He sat and thought for a moment. 'It started about six pm last night. We finally got word that the cars were being released and that mine and Jason's would be coming back to the garage. I arrived about an hour before the cars did. I helped get mine in bay 2, where it lives. Then we dealt with Jason's. We've only been in this complex a few years and we deliberately left a couple of large open spaces at the back, so we parked Jason's car in one of those so we could work on it from this morning. We were also aware of what we had to do if we found anything unusual, as per the directive from DFIS. Every member of the team was present when we placed Jason's car out the back. We are a big family, even if some of us are new, so it was sad for all of us. We ceremonially placed Jason's helmet on top of the car and left quietly. His funeral is listed for Friday this week, provided the hospital releases the body. Once we had finished with our private ceremony for Jason, my mechanics and I came back to my car and began to go over it with a fine-toothed comb. We decided to strip it completely and make sure nothing else had been tampered with. By midnight, we had everything off or out, except the engine. Most of the guys left after that, but I asked if I could stay the night. The manager said it was okay. We left the security cameras operating, but the back to base alarm wasn't turned on and the security company was duly notified.

I ordered a pizza about one am and waited for them out the front. I left the side door open so I could get back in. I obviously didn't see anyone get in as they must've come up by the parkland, which is more to the back than the front of the complex. Anyway, I went into the office, ate my pizza and I must've dozed off. I woke suddenly when I heard noises. They were faint, having to come through so many walls, so I investigated. When I stepped onto the landing, I could hear it clearly. I raced to where I heard it and saw someone moving around in the shadows. I called out but they didn't stop, so I went down to confront them. By now, I was feeling heated, not to mention emotional.

'As I approached the figure, they started throwing things at me, so I returned, trying not to throw anything valuable. I seemed to have them cornered when they tried to go into a room. I knew I had them as it was a storeroom with only the way out was the way they went in. That's when I called you, I mean DFIS. While I waited, I was able to keep them in the room. That's' when you, DFIS, arrived and took over. I think the rest you know.'

'You didn't get to see who it was at any stage?' asked Jake.

'No, it was dark and even though I turned the lights on low, I still didn't get to see their face. Do you know who it is?'

'We'll inform you at the proper time, Dan,' said Jake. 'Is there anything else you'd like to tell us about tonight?'

Dan thought for a moment. 'No, I'm sure that covers it.'

'Thank you, Dan. If there's anything you happen to remember, please make sure you let us now,' said Jake. 'I'll conclude this interview now. Time is 4:27am, Wednesday May 12.'

Jake turned off the phone and put it in his pocket.

'Thanks for that, Dan,' said Jake. 'I'll get Anhton to take you home. You need a good night's sleep.'

'Is your car out front, Dan?' asked Anhton.

'Yes, it is, but I want to stay here,' insisted Dan.

'I'm taking you home, you will have a hot shower and you will go to bed,' said Anhton. 'Do you want me to call mum to come over?'

Dan turned sharply. 'Kick a guy when he's down.'

'You may be younger, but this time I'm definitely saying what you have to do,' said Anhton, standing up to his brother.

Dan hung his head.

'Let's go,' said Anhton.

Jake gave Anhton a hug. 'I'll give you a call later, make sure he's ok.'

'I will,' said Anhton. 'Love you, sweetie.'

'Love you too.'

Anhton escorted Dan from the building with Jake following. Flashes of light started going off in all directions. Anhton forced their way through the media throng now gathering and hustled Dan into the car. As Jake watched Anhton and Dan leave, he retrieved his forensics kit and began to get some evidence. He had the defence officers close the gates to keep everyone well back. He dusted the side door, the door of the storeroom and several items inside the storeroom. He retrieved several fingerprints and photographed several items. After he'd finished, he waited until someone else from Balcher has arrived. Once they had arrived to secure the promises, Jake left and went directly to DFIS HQ.

As he got close to HQ, after being forced to ditch trailing media, it was just after seven am, so he detoured and got some breakfast. Sitting at his desk, he began to doze off. He jumped when he felt a tap on his shoulder. Realising he'd fallen asleep, he wiped his chin and sat up.

'Did you sleep here last night or something?' asked Ric, trying not to laugh.

'So not funny,' said Jake, tidying himself. 'I had a call out this morning from Dan Roberts, reporting a break in at Balcher Racing's garage. As it turned out the perpetrator was none other than Mr Rueben Villaman.'

'Villaman, what on earth was he doing there?'

'As soon as we can get to the hospital, I intend to ask him.'

'What have you done to him?' asked Ric.

'I did what I had to do.'

'You sure did. What happened?'

Jake recounted the events from the time they arrived at the complex to answer Dan's call, right up to when Jake tackled Villaman to the ground, inadvertently breaking his leg in the process.

'You will probably get into trouble for this,' said Ric.

'More than likely, but that bridge will be crossed when it happens. In the meantime, I have evidence to get down to Gabby.'

'Where is it now?'

'Just here. Why?' asked Jake.

'North! My office. Now!' bellowed David.

'That's why,' said Ric. 'I'll drop the stuff down to Gabby for you.'

Jake stood, tidied himself, out of uniform as he was, and walked over to David's office. The ringing of the slammed door still in his ears. He knocked once and entered.

As Ric walked past, he could only hear David's angry voice dressing down Jake. When he returned several minutes later, it was a much quieter scene inside the office with Jake now sitting and David looking a lot calmer. Ric waited by his desk for the longest time and Jake eventually exited David's office and crossed the floor.

'Do you still have a job?' asked Ric.

'Of course I do,' said Jake.

'What happened in there? When I took your evidence down to Gabby, David was tearing shreds off you. Then when I came back it seemed as if nothing had happened.'

'He didn't quite tear shreds off me. He was pissed off though. Moreso that I didn't send him, or you for that fact, a message about Dan's sudden call and Anhton's and my eventful morning. He heard it over the radio. I didn't think. It was a sudden and urgent decision. Dan reached out for help from his brother, and we attended. When David had cooled a bit, he gave me the chance to explain and so I did. I even played him the recording of interview with Dan, which I also need to load to Lassie.'

'At least you still have your job,' said Ric. 'Gabby says hello, and she'll have your evidence scanned, tested and sorted when she can.'

'Thanks. Guess we'd better get to work. I'm sure we'll have reason to visit the hospital later this morning to interview a certain man.'

'Will David let you do that interview?'

'Yeah, he's cool with it,' said Jake. 'You know the best bit, even though it was dark, and I really couldn't see Villaman's face, I called him by name as he lay on the ground. The gasp was so audible I knew I had him. That's when I shone the torch on his face. It was indeed Mr. Reuben Villaman. I'd like to hear what he has to say about this incident.'

'Please take me when you interview him. I want to see him squirm.'

Jake laughed. 'Of course I'll take you.'

'What about me?' asked Amy, as she came into the office. 'I know, I should be downstairs with Gabby working all the evidence, but I had to see you first.'

'Morning, Amy,' said Jake. 'Wait until you hear about what sort of night I had.'

'I already have,' said Amy. 'Some nosey parker neighbour near the complex had the news crews there. I saw the early morning news; they were all over the street.'

'Where were these neighbours?' asked Jake.

'They say they were working late in a factory nearby,' said Amy. 'They heard the Def cars arrive and so began to keep an eye out. They must've called the news agencies. You still don't look any better now than you did on TV this morning.'

'Gee thanks,' said Jake. 'I suppose I should go home, shower and put my uniform on. Especially if I have to go interview a suspect today.'

'Yeah, you do,' said Ric.

'I'll leave you to hold the fort for an hour or so,' said Jake. 'Ric, I've loaded the record of interview to Lassie, can you crosslink it please?'

Jake left and when he got home, he called to make sure Dan was ok. Anhton assured him Dan was asleep at that he'd stay there for the rest of the day with Dan. Jake said he'd bring over some of Anhton's stuff when he came over for dinner that night. Jake relaxed in the shower and after he'd dressed, he sat down at the kitchen table, opened his tablet, and played that day's Super Quizzler puzzle. He returned to the office just on lunchtime.

13.3

Wednesday, May 12, 5:00am

Anhton pulled into Dan's driveway and helped him inside.

'Go and have a shower. I'll put the kettle on,' said Anhton.

Dan trudged his way to his bedroom and was soon returning having showered and changed.

'Sit, drink and eat,' said Anhton placing a cup of tea and some toast in front of Dan. 'While you're sitting there, you can think about how you're going to explain to me why you started taking this serum?'

Dan shot Anhton a look of anger, tinged with sadness and regret.

'I know I should have Jake here, but I want to hear this brother to brother, not def officer to witness. No badge, no titles, no airs, or graces. We're brothers who need to talk.'

Dan dropped his shoulders, sipped the tea, and sighed.

'We were first approached back in February, before the first race, by Balcher,' said Dan. 'Johan, Jason, Jonathan, and Jordi were also at the meeting with Balcher. They've helped us in the past, but this is the first time they've asked or offered to help with our driving performance.'

Dan paused. Anhton sat and listened.

'Jason was all for it. We always knew he was competitive with his sister and now that she's becoming a successful driver, I think he'd become a little jealous. He denied this of course, but I could see it. We talked with Balcher and initially declined. In the minivan back to base, we discussed it, again Jason was all for the idea. It was then suggested we try using the natural herbal remedies to see if they worked. They seemed to, as we began to always finish in the top ten. I even had a win, but then I had a bad weekend and finished way down the list.

'Just before the super race weekend in March, we agreed to let Balcher administer the serum, called Menac, which is short for mental acuity. At Phillip Island, Jason and I had taken the shot for the Saturday races, and I knew there was more than enough for the following day. We even had extra in case the engineers monitoring our stats wanted to use it. They always refused and so we always returned any unused serum to Balcher.'

'Did you ever think it wasn't working or was bad for you?' asked Anhton.

'I must admit that I never really felt anything,' sad Dan. 'Yeah, I was able to focus a little more clearly and managed to concentrate for much longer than the length of the race, but I never felt unwell or never noticed any side-effects.'

'What about Jason?'

'He was always tetchy, but with the stress of driving and competing, he seemed slightly more on edge.'

'Why were you so edgy last Sunday when we saw you in the garage after the accident then?'

'I dunno. Maybe because the serum was kicking in finally and we'd normally be in the heat of the race where its effects are better felt. I was ready to go but stopped suddenly.'

'Did you notice anything out of the ordinary with Jason that day? Did he seem to be acting unnaturally?'

'I don't know about unnaturally. He did seem a little more reclusive as he prepared. His eyes were darting all over the place, he was speaking to himself more than normal.'

'Did you speak to him about it?'

'Not really, I was getting ready for my own race.'

Dan paused and looked deeply thoughtful.

'Have you remembered something?' asked Anhton.

'There was one funny thing. We always kept the serum for each weekend locked in a fridge at the back of the garage. Johan, Jonathan, and Jordi were the only people who had access to it. They were the ones tasked with administering the serum to us before the race. I did notice that soon after we arrived on Sunday morning, that Jason was remonstrating with Jordi about something. Eventually Jordi relented and they headed in the direction of the fridge. I had Jonathan take me there soon after for my shot. There was only one left when there should've been at least half a dozen.'

'Are you saying that Jordi let Jason have more than he was supposed to?'

'I guess so.'

'That can't be good.'

'Can I go to bed now?'

'Sure. I'll crash on the couch,' said Anhton.

Dan trudged off to his room and closed the door.

Anhton lay down on the couch and it took him a while to fall sleep. His mind was racing with so many questions.

13.4

Wednesday, May 12, 11:45am

Jake wandered into the office like he was on holiday.

'What happened to an hour or so, mister?' asked Ric.

'I took my time,' said Jake. 'I needed to relax.'

'Ah, you dozed off again.'

'I did not.'

Ric looked at him.

'I did not!'

Ric looked at him again.

'There goes your free lunch,' said Jake. 'Grab your stuff and let's go. Did you get to hear the interview from this morning?'

'Listened to, transcribed and cross-referenced,' said Ric.

'Let's get going,' said Jake, and he and Ric headed downstairs to get a DFIS vehicle.

13.5

Wednesday, May 12, 1:00pm

They drove to the Northern Memorial Hospital, and once they'd found out what room Reuben was in, they proceeded to speak with him. As they turned the corner, they saw two defence officers standing outside a room.

'What do you think, Ric?' said Jake. 'Perhaps he's in that room?'

Jake went to the nurse's station. They identified themselves and had the room confirmed. They showed their IDs again to the two officers and Jake and Ric entered the room.

'You,' spat Reuben. 'You'll be hearing from my lawyers soon.'

'Bring it,' said Jake. 'Now, we have a few questions we'd like you to answer.'

Reuben clamped his mouth shut and turned away.

'I see we're going to play this game. Okay, here are the rules. I will ask a series of questions. If you answer them with silence, a refusal, a shake of the head, a grunt, we will take that as a yes.'

'You can't do that.'

'You wanted to play the game; I gave you the rules.' Jake retrieved his phone from his pocket. 'Record of initial interview with Mr Reuben Villaman in the presence of Det. LtCmdr Ric Harding and Det.Sgt Jake North, conducted at the bedside in Mr Villaman's hospital room at the Northern Memorial Hospital, at 1312 hours on Wednesday May 12. Are we speaking with Mr Reuben Villaman?'

'Pigs.'

'The interviewee has answered with a refusal and so by the rules of the game that he has decided to play, that is a yes. Next, were you in the vicinity of Balcher Racing's headquarters this previous evening.'

Reuben spat on the ground.

'Another refusal, answer - yes. Right, we're doing well here today. Next, did you illegally enter the aforementioned premises?'

Reuben gritted his teeth and closed his mouth.

'Again, Mr Villaman has refused to answer, so yes is the answer.'

The more this went on, the more Reuben's face reddened.

'Okay. What was the purpose of your illegal entry into the premises of Balcher Racing?'

No answer.

'Once again we are met with silence, so we will presume that the intentions were sinister.'

'How dare you presume?' spat Reuben.

'Then tell us why you were illegally inside the premises?'

Silence.

'Very well. Just before I conclude this interview, I will say it on record that whilst you are resting in the hospital, your room will remain guarded and no one, other than medical staff or Def personnel will be allowed to enter the room. Interview ceased at 1325 hours.' Jake switched off his phone.

'You cannot deny me visitors.'

'Yes, we can, and we will,' said Jake. 'Then, Mr Villaman, once you are released, the defence officers outside your room will have strict instructions to escort you directly to DFIS HQ for further questioning. Good day.'

Jake nodded at Ric, and they turned and left the room to a hail of protests from Reuben.

When they closed the door behind them, he spoke with the defence guards. 'Under no circumstances is anyone to enter or leave this room except for medical staff or Def personnel. Check ID tags if you must. I will leave the same instructions with the hospital as well. If anyone has issue, refer them to DFIS. Understood?'

'Yes, Det.Sgt,' said the two officers in unison.

Jake and Ric left the hospital after speaking with the nurse's station attending to Reuben and with Reception. Jake left his details if anyone had any queries regarding the instructions.

13.6

Wednesday, May 12, 1:45pm

Jake and Ric climbed into their car and began the drive back to DFIS HQ.

'Interesting game,' said Ric, once they were on the road.

'No messing about sometimes,' said Jake. 'I reckon we should get the lady who was with him that day in for a little chat.'

'Should the local station handle this one?'

'Probably. I'll have to see who it is.'

'Oh, and you're supposed to have a chat to Broadbench Consolidated Racing about Amanda/Reuben,' said Ric.

'Yes, I do,' Jake glanced at the time on the vehicle. 'We can do that now.' Jake's phone rang through the vehicle's Bluetooth connection. 'Hello, this is Det.Sgt Jake North.'

'Hello,' said the female voice. 'I'm Sr Janet Deacon, head of nursing on E-Ward. You came in to visit one of our patients just a short while ago?'

'That's correct, a Mr Reuben Villaman,' said Jake. 'Is there a problem? Do we need to return the hospital?'

'Yes, Mr Villaman. No there's not a problem as such. I thought I should inform you of some results of tests that we conducted.'

'Isn't that a breach of privacy?'

'Technically, it is, however, it is my discretion to make such a decision and since you are defence, I felt it the right thing to do,' said the nursing director.

'What information do you have?'

'Basically that when we did a check of Mr Villaman, we discovered that he was once a female,' said Sr Janet.

'I thought he only had a broken leg?' asked Jake.

'Yes, he did, but he was complaining of other aches and pains and so we gave him a sedative,' said Sr Janet. 'We advised him that we would do some checking to make sure there were no other injuries. He reluctantly agreed. We took some blood for testing and the results showed elevated levels of artificial testosterone. Also, when we conducted further tests, we discovered that Mr Villaman has undergone extensive reconstructive surgery of the reproductive organs. Namely the removal of a womb and vaginal passage and the addition of a penis.'

'Interesting. Thank you for the information,' said Jake. 'Does Mr Villaman know that we know?'

'We have informed him that there were no other major injuries and that he might have some bruising as a result of the fall that broke his leg,' said Sr Janet. 'We have not told him of our finding as his choices are his own.'

'Thank you, Sister,' said Jake.

'You're welcome, Det.Sgt North. I just thought you needed to know.'

'We'll make the necessary notes in our file and will keep the information confidential.'

'Thank you.'

Jake turned to Ric once the call had disconnected.

'We already knew that, didn't we?' said Ric.

'It's always nice to receive independent confirmation,' said Jake. 'Now, do you have the address of Broadbench Consolidated Racing?'

Ric punched an address into the navcom. Jake had a quick look at the directions but allowed the voice to instruct him on where to turn.

Jake called ahead to make sure that someone would be available for them to speak with, and they were assured that the team manager would be waiting.

13.7

Wednesday, May 12, 2:15pm

Jake pulled into one of the parking spaces out the front of Broadbench Consolidated Racing's offices. They walked inside, introduced themselves to the receptionist and were shown into the board room.

Jake and Ric both turned when they heard the door open, and a mid-thirties athletically built man walked in.

'Hi, I'm Vern Jacobson, team manager for Broadbench Consolidated Racing.'

Jake and Ric shook his outstretched hand. 'I'm Det. Sgt Jake North and this is my colleague, Det.LtCmdr Ric Harding.'

Vern indicated they take a seat each.

'How can I help you today?' said Vern.

'As you know, we're following up on the tragedy that occurred this past Sunday,' said Jake.

'Such a loss to racing. He'll be sadly missed.'

'Yes, he will,' said Jake. 'As part of our investigation, we've come across a name and we're hoping you might be able to assist.'

'Oh, who's that?'

'Amanda Beston.'

'Hmm. Yes, an interesting and troubled woman,' said Vern.

'How so?'

'I joined the team at the beginning of the year. Even
then I knew I'd have trouble with her. Mind you, she knew
her way around the garage, the cars, and the toolboxes, but
whilst she never talked about her personal life, there was
something happening away from the team.'

'There certainly was,' said Jake.

Vern raised an eyebrow.

'I'd like to hear what you thought of her and the events
that led up to her dismissal before I taint your thinking.'

Vern nodded. 'As the year went on, she became more
troubled. Of course this started to affect her work. Thankfully,
nothing serious, but a lot of trivial things. She started to drop
a lot of things, as if she had become clumsy. Those who were
above her tried to talk to her, but she became stand-offish.
As the pressures of that race year progressed, it increased
her tensions.'

'How do you mean?'

'She became more disruptive, less disciplined, she back
chatted more, and was more aggressive,' said Vern. 'As soon
as the year was over, we let her go. Thankfully, we could do
it as part of our annual review, but hers was the easiest to
decide and the hardest to deliver.'

'Did she get even more aggressive?'

'Verbally mostly. She accused us of being male
chauvinists and that we didn't want women in the industry.
This is farthest from the truth. She wasn't the first woman
to work in the team and she won't be the last, but she was
certainly the most disruptive. We had no choice but to let her
go. She was so angry, that as she left, she caused thousands
of dollars of damage to the cars and other equipment.

Management made the decision not to pursue her for it but to repair the damage and wipe the slate clean.'

'How was morale in the team?' asked Jake.

'It was amazing after she left. Even though she had caused so much damage, everybody chipped in their time, and we've never looked back.'

'Have you hired any woman engineers since?' asked Ric.

'Absolutely we have. We have three particularly good women on the team now. In fact, I need to make sure I do my job well as one of them could easily run the team.'

They laughed.

'So, what do you have to tell me about Amanda?' asked Vern.

'We have reason believe that Amanda was going through mental and physical preparation to become a man,' said Jake.

Vern looked shocked. 'Are you serious?'

'We are now,' said Ric. 'Certain news came to us today that confirmed it, even though we'd seen other evidence to back that up.'

'I can't believe it. I guess I can understand everything now. If she had of talked to us, I'm sure we could've helped.'

'We'll never know,' said Jake.

'Who did she become?' asked Vern.

'As that's a matter of an ongoing investigation, we'd rather not say right now.'

'I understand.'

'Thank you for your time, Vern,' said Jake, getting up from his chair, Ric following.

'I hope I was able to help,' said Vern, rising as well.

They shook hands.

'We need to get back to base,' said Jake. 'This information has been helpful, thank you again.'

13.8

Wednesday, May 12, 3:15pm

Jake and Ric made their way back to DFIS HQ in Newport.

'She was one angry lady back then,' said Ric.

'She sounded like it and it seems to have spilled over to Reuben as well,' said Jake.

Jake's phone rang.

'This is becoming a habit suddenly,' said Jake. 'Det.Sgt Jake North.'

'Jake, Vern here from Broadbench Consolidated Racing.'

'Yes, Vern.'

'I just thought of something else that happened that year,' said Vern.

'Yes?'

'Jason Black moved from us to Balcher Racing and I have this vague recollection that some of the guys would also tease Amanda as she had a crush on Jason, but as he was married, he treated her like one of the boys.'

'Very interesting, thanks for that, Vern.'

The call disconnected.

'Unrequited love?' said Jake.

'Probably not, but definitely so strong a crush that she was probably going mad and the fact that she was also going through the whole sex-change process, she was obviously battling with sexuality too,' said Ric.

'Man, that must've been sending her round the twist,' said Jake.

'Perhaps we could lay those cards on the table when we talk to Reuben next?'

'Thems powerful cards, miss Ric.'

'Where did that come from?' said Ric.

'Uhm too much TV?'

'Ya think?'

They laughed.

'Seriously, I think we can use that,' said Ric.

'We'll have to be careful using such information in that manner, it could push Reuben right over the edge.'

'Since when have you become so caring?'

'It'll have to be a last resort if he won't talk and we need to be ready for whatever shit flies out of that mouth when it happens,' said Jake.

'True.'

'For now, we need to get someone to bring the lovely Donna O'Neill in for a chat.'

They drove back to DFIS HQ, dropped off the vehicle, loaded what they had collected into Lassie and went their separate ways.

Meditation

14

14.1

Thursday, May 13, 7:00am

Jake rose early, moved quietly about the house, gathered his yoga mat, phone and earphones and stepped onto the back deck. He set himself up, started off with some warm-up exercises, then proceeded with his yoga routine. When he had finished that, he sat comfortably on the mat, chose an appropriate music track, and begin to meditate.

What do I know so far;

• Three stores robbed of explosives,

• Explosives and timers were stolen,

• Death of the sales assistant at the third store, first count of murder,

• Theft of blank security passes from Broadbench Consolidated Racing,

• Fuel lines on the two Agile Motorsports Supacars delicately cut using explosive devices stolen earlier,

- *Uniforms stolen from Balcher Racing's offices,*

- *Use of explosive devices at Phillip Island Supacar race, resulting in death of one driver and serious injury to another,*

- *Subsequent investigations prove sabotage - second murder count, first grievous bodily harm, first count of attempted murder,*

- *Altercation with a dark clad figure during afternoon investigation at Phillip Island,*

- *Impounding of suspect van, subsequently little clues,*

- *Van was rented by a Donna O'Neill, no apparent links to any of the teams,*

- *In course of investigation, discovery that Amanda Beston used to work for Broadbench Consolidated Racing,*

- *Images captured at first three robberies show a woman distracting the sales assistants each time to allow a second person to steal the goods required,*

- *Analysis shows that woman at all three stores is the same woman,*

- *Suspect in Reuben Villaman, who used to be Amanda Beston, former crew member at Broadbench Consolidated Racing,*

- *Need to find evidence specifically placing Reuben at the store robberies, the robberies at Broadbench Consolidated Racing and Balcher Racing and at the racetrack on both days,*

- *Need to get any security vision of spectator areas at both races,*

- *Need to work over the black van from Phillip Island,*

- *Donna confirmed as being present at the home of Reuben Villaman, which also happened to be the home of Amanda Beston,*

- *Need to see ownership papers for house,*

- *Need to wait for results of interview with Donna O'Neill,*

- *This should be a simple case to solve but for lack of incriminating evidence.*

Jake sat for some more time in silence. That's where Anhton found him. Facing the east, the warmth of the sun soaking into his skin. Anhton coughed politely.

Jake smiled and slowly stretched out, allowing his legs to resume blood flow. He slowly stood and greeted his partner.

'Welcome home sweetie. How's Dan?' said Jake.

'Better today. He dropped me off and has gone back to work,' said Anhton. 'What earth-shattering decisions did we come to this morning?'

'This should be an easy solve, but it's not.'

'Talk to me.'

Anhton sat on one of the lounges on the back deck. Jake spilled his thoughts on the case to date.

'By the way, you get to interview the delightful Ms O'Neill,' said Jake. 'She's in MetroEast's jurisdiction.'

'I see. When does this interview have to take place?'

'As soon as possible.'

'Before we do, I need to confess and share,' said Anhton.

'What have you done?'

'Well, when I got Dan home, I told him to shower. As he did, I made him some tea and toast. He drank and we talked, brother to brother. I told him there were no titles, no defence force badges, etc.'

'You know I wanted to talk to Dan.'

'Yes, I know, sweetie, but I wanted to hear it from him as his brother. Well, he spilled alright.'

'Did you record it?' asked Jake.

'No. I wanted to, but I had basically said that it was off the record.'

'What did he say?'

Anhton retold the information Dan imparted to Jake.

'We need to speak to him officially and as soon as possible,' said Jake.

'Yes, we do,' said Anhton.

Interview  15

15.1

Friday, May 14, 8:00am

Jake and Anhton pulled into the car park underneath DFIS HQ. As Jake got out of the car his phone rang.

'Det.Sgt Jake North.'

'Det.Sgt North, we need you at the hospital immediately,' said the officer at the other end. 'A woman is insisting on seeing Mr Villaman.'

'Don't let her in,' said Jake. 'I'll be right there.'

'What's up?' asked Anhton.

'We need to get to the Northern Memorial. I think Ms O'Neill has made a fatal move. She's trying to get in to see Villaman.'

They pulled out of the car park and made haste for the hospital. Soon they were parking at the Northern Memorial and heading directly to the ward where Reuben Villaman was being kept. As they exited the lift, they could hear the commotion. As they turned the corner, they could see the two officers barring the door and a woman wailing on them with her fists. Another fifteen minutes or so and she would've prevailed.

As Jake and Anhton arrived, backup defence officers from MetroCentral arrived. They deftly moved in front of the current guards who then stepped aside, much relieved. With the fact that there were new guards blocking the door, the woman crumpled to the floor. Jake and Anhton helped her to her feet and guided her to a lounge area the nurses indicated.

'Is there anything we can help you with, ma'am?' asked Jake.

'They won't let me in to see my boyfriend,' said the woman.

'Who's your boyfriend?' asked Jake.

'Reuben Villaman. I've only just found out he's in here and I want to see him.' She started to wail on Jake this time.

Jake held her hands until she stopped.

'I'm sorry ma'am, but you can't see him just yet,' said Jake.

'Why,' she screamed. 'Why not,' she said little quieter.

'What's your name, please? Mine's Jake.'

'Donna, Donna O'Neill. Please tell me what's going on?'

'Why don't you come with us, and we can talk about it in a better location,' said Jake.

'Where are you taking me?' asked Donna.

'To DFIS HQ. I'm Det.Sgt Jake North and this is Det.

Cpl Anhton Roberts.'

There was a slight gasp when she heard the names. Jake stood and helped Donna to her feet.

'Am I in trouble?' asked Donna.

'No, but we'd like to speak with you all the same,' said Jake.

'When can I see Reuben?' asked Donna.

'We'll let you know when you can talk to him again. This way.'

Jake led Donna down to the car and sat in the back with her as Anhton drove them back to DFIS HQ in Newport.

15.2

Friday, May 14, 10:00am

When they arrived, Donna was shown to an interview room, given some tissues and a coffee and informed that someone would be with her shortly. Jake showed Anhton the room next door. As they entered, they watched as Donna stood in front of the mirrored window facing her and fixed her hair and makeup.

'Stay here and see how things go until I return,' said Jake.

'I can do that. Do you want me to help interview her with you?'

'I may go in there alone, or I may even see if Amy can do it. I haven't decided yet. With either of us, her feminine charms won't work. Amy might try and side with a fellow female and Ric, well, he's all testosterone sometimes.'

Anhton laughed. Ric and David walked into the viewing room.

'What have we here, Jake?' asked David.

'Ms Donna O'Neill. I got a call from the Northern Memorial saying she was insisting on seeing Villaman, claiming she's his girlfriend. Anhton and I went there immediately and brought her back here. There were plans to bring her in for questioning anyway today.'

'Who's going into talk to her?' said david.

'Let me, please,' said Ric.

'No!' said David. 'What about Amy?'

'She was one of the possibilities,' said Jake.

'Get her in here and we'll see what she says,' said David.

Jake made the call and soon Amy came into the viewing room. She was briefed on the situation.

'Do you think you can do this, Amy?' asked David.

'I reckon I can deal with this,' said Amy. 'I've been keeping up with the case since day one and as we now have a face to match a number of pictures, I can put that in front of her and get her to talk.'

'Take it easy though,' said David. 'Record it all. You may want to take someone else in. Someone she might try and schmooze up to.'

'We can't send a rookie in there, David,' said Jake. 'She'll eat them alive.'

'Don't be so sure about that,' said David. 'We've got to blood the newbies at some stage.'

'Who did you have in mind?'

'Det.LtCpl Samuel Munro.'

'Oh, that's cruel, David,' said Amy. 'She'll be all over him like a rash.'

'Then you can just scrape her off him,' said David.

'Let's see what happens,' said Jake.

'I'll get him,' said Ric, who left the viewing room.

'Ok, Amy, let's get you up-to-date and armed with the questions I need answers for,' said Jake. 'I particularly want to know where she was on Wednesday night this week. Also back on Tuesday March 30 with the burning car.'

'Got it,' said Amy.

Jake and Amy left the viewing room and returned about twenty minutes later.

Just before they came back, Ric delivered Samuel to the viewing room. Samuel was 190cm tall, short black hair, tanned skin, goatee, effervescent pale blue eyes, broad smile, the hint of a larger tattoo just above the neckline of his uniform and a couple of rings in one ear. He's also very fit and can be seen in the DFIS gym either before or after his shift every other day. He's made many a woman swoon as he's moved around the office, not to mention a few of the men, although they've mostly been jealous.

Jake smiled and shook his head.

'Is something the matter, Jake?' asked Samuel.

'Hey, Sam, nothing's wrong. Has Ric mentioned why you're here?'

'Not really. All he said was that I was needed to help with an interview.'

'That part's correct,' said Jake. 'Have you been in an interview like this yet?'

'No, and I've not really spoken to people on the road either. I've only collected evidence for the others or taken photos.'

'That's fine. This is what I would like you to do. Det. Cpl Amy Hilton will be conducting the interview. Apart from listening and learning, I really want you to sit there and be as charming as you can. If you look through the window, you'll see who we're interviewing today.'

Samuel bent slightly and looked at the woman sitting at the table, wringing her hands.

'Amy will do most of the talking, but we have a suspicion that with you sitting beside her, the woman may try and deflect and use you to dodge the answers. If you are asked a question, defer to Amy, especially if it relates to the case, unless it's something you know for absolute certainty.'

'I understand,' said Samuel.

'You ready Amy?' said Jake.

'We'll soon find out,' said Amy.

'Samuel?'

'I think so.'

'Amy, one more thing, did you see the update we had from the Northern Memorial the other day?' asked Jake.

'Just now,' said Amy.

'I don't think Ms O'Neill has any clue of Villaman's past. If she becomes stubborn and refuses to answer, find out how much she knows about Villaman and how long they've been together, etc.'

Amy nodded, touched Samuel's arm and in they went.

Jake breathed and watched. Anhton, David and Ric turned to see what was going to happen.

15.3

Friday, May 14, 10:30am

Amy opened the door and walked in, followed by Sam. She indicated where to sit and they sat across the table from Donna. Donna in turn looked at Amy and then at Sam and began to smile.

'Yes, this might just work,' said Jake.

'Now, Ms O'Neill, Donna O'Neill, isn't it?' said Amy.

'That's right. Why am I here? Why can't I see my boyfriend in hospital?'

'You can see him as soon as we can arrange it for you, but I need you to answer a few questions for me.'

'What's it regarding?'

'I'll start from the beginning.' Amy slid the images captured at the three explosives stores, along with her driver's licence and the half image caught at the house. 'Let's start with these; different contact lenses, different makeup, different hair, same facial structure. Look familiar?'

Donna was hesitant. 'No, not really.'

'Okay then, how about this?' Amy slipped a copy of the composite image across the table. Different contact lenses, different makeup, different hair, same facial structure.'

'Th-th-they're not me,' said Donna.

'Now I want to add an identikit image made from descriptions taken from witnesses at an event back on Tuesday March 30 of a woman supposedly injured when her car conveniently exploded near a particular building. Another car happened to screech around a corner, stop beside the damaged car, this woman then got up and hurriedly ran to the second car on the signal of three horn blasts.' Amy slid the image across the table. 'Different coloured lens, different makeup, different hair, and the same facial structure. Now, either there are, let's see, five of you running around, or we have a problem. So are you part of quintuplets?'

'That's absurd,' said Donna.

'Fair enough, then how did your image appear on three security cameras at three stores that happened to have been robbed whilst you were there? How do those same three images seem match the image drawn from eyewitness accounts at a supposed crash scene, which is now obviously a fake scene? Those same four mages just all happen to have the same facial structure as the picture on your driver's licence?'

Donna was silent. She looked at Sam and batted her eyelids. He smiled politely and in his smooth, deep voice, asked the lady to politely answer the questions.

'They're not me!'

'Okay, we'll move along then,' said Amy. 'Now for the next thing we need to try and workout. A black van was hired out in your name using your driver's licence and parked just outside the fence of the Phillip Island Raceway. Did you go camping there this past weekend?'

'I don't go camping. Someone must've stolen my identity.'

'I see. So, someone just happened to steal your driver's licence, which you obviously haven't missed and therefore have been driving around technically unlicensed, and you haven't reported any such theft?'

'I guess so.' Donna started wringing her hands again and when she realised, she moved them to her lap.

'Another question. Where were you on Wednesday evening, May 12?'

'I was at home watching TV.'

'You say you're Mr Reuben Villaman's girlfriend?' said Amy.

'That's correct.'

'Do you live with him?'

'We're planning to very soon,' said Donna.

'That would explain your presence at his house the other day?'

'I wasn't there. I haven't been there for a while.'

'So this isn't you then?' Amy indicated the half picture, which Donna made no comment on earlier.

'It's very fuzzy,' Donna said.

'Not so fuzzy that we couldn't find a match to your driver's licence though. We know you were there.'

'It's not me! I wasn't there.' Donna's voice cracked.

'It'll be disappointing to see that pretty face get marked,' said Sam.

'Why should it get marked?'

'The women like pretty faces,' added Amy.

'What women ...' Donna's face went white. 'You don't mean pris...?'

'I can't promise anything, of course.'

Donna looked from Amy to Sam several times. Panic beginning to set in her eyes.

'I think I'm going to be sick,' said Donna. Without warning, Donna leant over the side of her chair and vomited on the floor.

'Blech,' said Jake, as he turned away from the viewing window.

Amy and Sam helped Donna to her feet and led her to the nearest bathroom. Amy went inside with her, whilst Sam stuck his foot out to hold open the door. Jake had already called for the cleaners to come in and mop the place out. Amy and Sam brought Donna to a small waiting room where they let her lay down on the lounges. Amy sent Sam to get some cool towels. When he returned, Donna was sitting up, although she still looked pale. Amy wet Donna's forehead and gave her water to sip.

Jake, Anhton and Ric were back at Jake's desk when David came over to see how things were going.

'Amy was starting to get through, and then she threw a magnificent curve ball,' said Jake.

'What did Amy say?' asked David.

'Something about having a pretty face the women would like,' said Jake.

'I didn't think she knew that line,' said David. 'She surprises me all the time.'

Jake nodded.

'Did the woman spill?' said David.

'Literally,' said Ric.

David looked at Ric.

'She threw up, David,' said Ric. 'All over the interview room floor.'

'Well, that's a first.'

'Hopefully a last too,' said Jake.

'Where are they now?' asked David.

'In the waiting room,' said Jake. 'I'll head back down there soon and see how it's going.'

'No need to,' said Sam, his voice echoing across the office. 'Once she'd calmed down and some colour had returned to her face, she admitted everything. The pictures were of her in all three stores, and at the house this week. She wasn't with Villaman on Wednesday night but did become worried when he didn't come home. She only found out this morning that he was in hospital. It was on the news Thursday night and as they didn't say where he was taken, she'd been ringing all the hospitals until someone told her. The rest you now.'

'Thanks, Sam,' said Jake. 'I hope it wasn't too traumatic for you?'

'That's nothing. I've been on the frontline, remember.'

Jake nodded. Sam went to his desk and Jake went downstairs. He spotted Amy coming out of the waiting room.

'Nice move, wrong reaction, good result,' said Jake.

'It worked, didn't it?'

'Yes, but I didn't need to see it.'

'Diddums,' said Amy.

'Let's get the data loaded into Lassie so we can get to work on Villaman. Have you got the official statement out of her yet?'

'That's next,' said Amy. 'I've left her in the lounge with an officer while we get the statement ready.'

'Sounds good,' said Jake. 'We need to go back and have a chat to Villaman again. No doubt he would have heard the commotion at the hospital and with no one telling him anything, he'll be in a state.'

'I can guarantee that. I'll send you the statement as soon as she's signed it.'

'Good idea. He can have a read of it, and we'll take it from there.'

Jake went back to his desk as Amy went back to Donna.

Anhton walked up to Jake as he approached his desk. 'Dan's just called to remind us that Jason's funeral is at one this afternoon.'

Jake looked at his watch. 'We'd better get going then. I'll have a chat to David.'

Jake knocked on David's door. 'Enter.' Jake walked in. 'Ah, Jake, what's up?'

'I've just been reminded that Jason Black's funeral is at one this afternoon. I'm going with Anhton, unless you have a very real objection.'

'It's fine with me. You've done well this week. It's great to have you back.'

Jake blushed slightly. 'I'll be going now. I want to go home and get ready, then we have to travel across to Sandown where the funeral is.'

'See you Monday.'

Jake left David's office and soon he and Anhton were heading home.

Breach

16

16.1

Saturday, May 15, 8:00am

Jake went for a jog soon after Anhton had left for work. After that, he reviewed all the information he had on the case, including going over Donna's statement. He ate some lunch then went to work in the back yard. After a while, he began to hear noises coming from the front of the house. He walked through, cleaning himself up on the way and opened the front door.

Immediately he was assaulted with camera flashes and a barrage of questions from the media crews that had gathered. Jake slammed the door shut, locked it, and went and closed all the curtains both downstairs and upstairs. He raced through and locked the back of the house. As he did, he heard a chopper fly overhead.

'Great. This is all I need today, and it's my day off.' He went into the office near the front of the house. 'Let's see what's going on out there.' He manoeuvred the camera to see who was out the front. He spotted all the major news networks and some of the cable ones as well. He recognised

some of his neighbours. *They're probably out for a sticky.*
He panned the camera around a bit further and was struck
by the small group at the left-hand fence line. It seemed he
had aroused the attentions of the transgender community in
Melbourne. They had signs saying who they were and some
rushed signs denouncing Jake's actions. *That's a bit unfair.*
They haven't even come to speak to me about it.

Jake picked up his phone, scrambled it and dialled a
number.

'What's up, Jake?' said Anhton. 'Why the scramble?'

'I'll be brief. Don't come home for a while, or at least
until I tell you. News crews everywhere. Nosey neighbours.
Transgender community protesting as well. Will call local
defence station. Love you.

'Hey, wait up. Don't you want me beside you?

'Of course I do, but I also don't want you to get mixed
up in this,' said Jake.

'Grrr. We're in everything together, remember?'

'I know, sweetie.'

'Settled. I'll be home as soon as I can,' said Anhton.

'Okay. Thank you. Come in by the back lane. It should
be free enough.'

'Deal.'

Jake then rang the local defence station, and they
dispatched a couple of cars. Once they had cleared the scene,
they spoke briefly to Jake and then left. The only people left
were the transgender protestors. Jake went and relaxed
and as soon as Anhton came home, had something to drink.
Anhton noted that the transgender protestors were still out

the front.

Jake stepped outside and they became vocal. He managed to gain clam and invited the small group inside. They refused but eventually agreed and sent two people in to talk with Jake. He offered them seats in the lounge.

'How can I help you?' said Jake.

'Why are you mistreating Reuben Villaman?' said the first woman.

'I'm not mistreating him.'

'You're holding him in hospital against his will and without any visitation rights,' said the second woman.

'This is where I get serious,' said Jake, sternly. 'Firstly, why did you not simply call DFIS and ask to meet with us, rather than make these false assumptions. Secondly, Mr Villaman is person of interest in an ongoing DFIS investigation. The details of which I am not at liberty to divulge, but suffice to say that if proven, the fact that he is transgender will not matter.'

The two women were affronted at Jake's sternness.

'Keeping him in hospital without visitation rights is inhumane,' said the first woman.

'He is in hospital because he has a broken leg. He has no visitation rights because of the investigation. As soon as he is discharged from hospital, he will be taken to DFIS HQ for further questioning.'

'Even in jail, he would be allowed visitors,' said the second woman.

'The point is moot,' said Jake. 'The decision is final. If you like, I'm happy to invite you to our HQ in Newport and to meet with my superior, Cmdr David Castle.'

'Yes, we will take you up on that,' said the first woman. 'This needs to be resolved.'

'Come to the office at ten a.m. on Monday and you will be able to speak with him.'

'We'll be there,' said the second woman. The women rose and Jake escorted them to the door. They left without even a polite farewell.

'What fresh hell is this?' said Jake, collapsing onto the couch.

'Political points gathering,' said Anhton.

'How in hell did they even get my address? It's restricted.'

'We'll find out. Ask them directly on Monday?'

'I may just do that,' said Jake. 'Then there's the information they had that Villaman's in hospital. How did they know that? Does Donna know about his past? Did the nurses blab? I need to find out.'

'Let's get some dinner and chill out.'

16.2

Sunday, May 16

Jake and Anhton stepped from the lift on their level and into a quiet office. Only a handful of officers were rostered on, and they were keeping to themselves and their tasks.

'Tell me again why we're going in to work on a Sunday?' said Anhton.

'Amy's already rostered to work and Ric was happy to come in and help out,' said Jake. 'He knows we need to get this sorted as quickly as we can and with what happened yesterday, it's even more important. If information is leaking, we need to get this resolved so it can be closed.'

Jake and Anhton dropped their satchels at their respective desks and took their tablets to the Glass Room.

'Thanks, Ric, for coming in on your day off,' said Jake.

'It's cool man,' said Ric. 'We need to get this sorted. So, what happened yesterday?'

Jake explained from the time he opened the front door until the women left his house.

'Do you know how they knew?' asked Ric.

'That's what I want to find out,' said Jake. 'I'll ask them directly tomorrow and hopefully they'll comply. Otherwise, we have a problem.'

'A very serious one,' said Ric. 'Where do you want us to begin?'

'I was hoping that you and Amy could go over to the

Northern Memorial and have a chat to our friend?' said Jake. 'Provided Amy hasn't got anything that needs to be tested, tagged, printed or whatever in the lab.'

'We can do that,' said Ric.

'Take Donna's statement and let him read it and make sure he understands it,' said Jake.

'We will,' said Ric, as he left the office.

Jake continued to work with Lassie to make sure he had everything covered.

A couple of hours after they left, Amy and Ric returned.

'How'd it go?' asked Jake.

'As we supposed,' said Amy.

'Not without my lawyer, was all he said repeatedly,' said Ric.

'Even after reading Donna's statement?' said Jake.

'Even more so after that,' said Amy.

'We'll just have to wait until he's discharged and have a chat to him down here,' said Jake.

'We have more though,' said Ric.

Jake raised an eyebrow.

'As we were leaving, we happened to overhear some nurses chatting,' said Ric. 'One was saying how she thought the restriction of visitors to Villaman was almost criminal.'

'She even mentioned DFIS by name,' said Amy. 'Anyway, we interrupted and pulled the one nurse aside and spoke to her.'

'She confessed that she was a friend of the trans community and that she told them about the treatment of Villaman, of course they were refused entry to visit him when they arrived,' said Ric.

'We then gave the nurse a caution that any more talk like she had done would lead to an obstruction of justice charge,' said Amy. 'That seemed to shut her up immediately as she'd started to reiterate his alleged mistreatment by us.'

'That still doesn't tell me how they got my address, let alone the news crews,' said Jake.

'I wouldn't be surprised if they tipped off the news, but chose to arrive late,' said Ric.

'They did manage to get a small spot on the news that night,' said Amy, 'but as they couldn't speak to you, they of course speculated no end. David may need to release a press statement about the investigation. Thankfully, they have no idea we're holding Villaman over last Sunday's murder. Wouldn't that put fuel in their engines?'

They all laughed and updated Lassie with all the info they had.

Meetings

17.1

Monday, May 17

Jake and Anhton arrived at the office early. Jake was busily working when he looked up to see that David had already arrived. He went across the office and knocked on the door.

'What is it, North?' said David.

'A quick word, if I can?'

'Sure.'

Jake explained the events of the previous Saturday and said that he'd invited the transgender people to meet with David.

'Some notice on Saturday night would've been better than a couple of hours, but I can manage that,' said David. 'The last thing I want is for us to have our name tarnished by misinformation.'

'We almost need another department to look after that,' said Jake.

'We do, public relations, but this isn't as bad as there is no link with the murder investigation from last Sunday,' said David. 'Is there anything else I need to know before they arrive?'

'Not really. I'll meet them and then bring them up.'

David nodded and Jake left the office.

17.2

Monday, May 17, 10:00am

At ten o'clock, Jake received a call from reception to say that the women had arrived.

He went downstairs to greet them and took them to a waiting room lounge first.

'Before I take you up, I have a question I need the answer to,' asked Jake.

'How can we help?' said the first woman, officiously.

'How did you come by my address?'

The women looked at each other.

'I don't believe we need to divulge that,' said the first woman.

'Actually, you do,' said Jake. 'My address, as a DFIS officer, is restricted. It's not even allowed to be listed in phone directories, so unless you have the appropriate government clearance, you have obtained my address illegally.' Jake sat back to let that sink in.

'How dare you accuse us of anything illegal,' said the second woman.

'Then how did you get my address,' said Jake. 'This can be done the right way or the hard way.'

'Excuse me?' asked the first woman.

'You can cooperate and give me the information now or I can get a court subpoena to interview each one of you and your staff under oath.'

The women were once again affronted by Jake's questions.

'Can we speak with your supervisor now?' said the first woman.

Jake rose. 'This way.' He escorted them up to David's office.

After introductions, they women sat down, and Jake went to leave.

'I'd like you to stay, Det.Sgt,' said David.

'Yes, sir,' said Jake. He stood to one side.

'How can I help you, ladies?' asked David.

'To begin with, we'd like you to dismiss this arrogant young man,' said the first woman. 'He's done nothing but accuse and harass.'

'Indeed,' said David, looking at Jake. 'Please explain.'

The women recounted the brief conversation when they first arrived and how Jake had virtually threatened them with court orders to divulge their sources.

'Unfortunately, ladies, the Det.Sgt is correct,' said David. 'Our private information is restricted and should not be available to anyone in the public arena unless expressly given out by the defence officer themselves. So, we really do need to know how you came by this information.'

The women looked at each other.

'We are not trying to harass you, we are here to help and the fact that the private residence of a defence force member was exposed to the media and had been revealed is of great concern. All I want to do is be here to help. I'm more than happy to address your concerns over Mr Villaman, but first we need to be on mutual terms.'

'Fair enough,' said the first woman. 'My apologies, Det.Sgt North. We only ever seem to be on the wrong end of justice and our defences kick in automatically.'

'I understand and my apologies if I came over too strong,' said Jake. 'All I want to know is how you came by my address?'

'We have a number of supporters who often come in and do volunteer work for us,' said the first woman. 'Last Friday, one such supporter was helping us with some office work. During the afternoon, we received a call from a nurse at the Northern Memorial hospital informing us of her belief that a Mr Reuben Villaman was being mistreated by DFIS by not allowing him any visitation rights. When we pushed for information about who authorised such a restriction, the Det.Sgt's name was mentioned. This supporter recognised the name. When we asked how, they said that they lived in the neighbourhood of the Det.Sgt and knew where he lived. They provided us with the address and the rest you know.'

'Thank you, ladies,' said David. 'As Det.Sgt North has already mentioned, defence force personnel's private details are restricted. Whilst no action will be taken this time, please be aware that if you come by such information in the future, please contact the appropriate defence station before acting on the information. It may very well be something we can assist with. We don't need the wrong people getting hold of this sort of information.'

'Are you saying we're the wrong people?' said the second woman.

'No, not at all,' said David. 'It was a general comment

339

aimed at people who may have a grudge against the defence force, or even the government. In your case, it was innocent, and the person thought they were helping you out. I understand that.'

'Thank you,' said the first woman.

'As to Mr Villaman,' said David, 'he has restricted visitation rights because he is a suspect in a murder case. I know that Det.Sgt North did not go that far when he told you on Saturday about the continuing investigation, but it is my decision to bring you into the strictest of confidence. Also, until we know for sure what's happening, we need to make sure that anyone else involved with Mr Villaman doesn't speak with him so that any information we gather is not tainted or coached. Do you understand?'

'Most certainly,' said the first woman. 'We know Mr Villaman and find it hard to believe that he would do that to someone else.'

'Everyone is so different,' said David. 'We have come across that many times during our investigations. Is there anything else I can help you with?'

'No, we're happy with the information we have,' said the first woman.

'Please, let us know if there is anything we can help you with,' said David.

'We will,' said the first woman.

'Det.Sgt if you would be so kind as to show these ladies back downstairs.'

'Yes, sir,' said Jake.

Jake escorted them back to reception to sign out and bid them a good day.

17.3

Monday, May 17, 10:45am

Jake had only just got back to his desk when he was buzzed by reception. He returned to reception to see a man waiting by the desk. He introduced himself as Reuben Villaman's lawyer and Jake took him directly to David's office.

It lasted only a few minutes, but David called Jake in once the lawyer had left.

'We need to deal with Villaman as soon as possible,' said David. 'It seems Donna O'Neill contacted the lawyer on Villaman's behalf, and the lawyer has demanded we allow visitation rights. I want to know when he's coming out of hospital and I want him brought directly here and interviewed, preferably without the lawyer.'

'I'll do that now, David.'

Jake went to his desk, called the hospital, and found out he was due to be discharged that afternoon. Jake advised that DFIS would be collecting him and that he was not to be released to anyone else. Jake informed David and the vehicle was duly dispatched.

Villaman refused to enter the building upon his arrival at DFIS HQ but was wheeled in all the same and placed in an interview room. Jake was notified.

He walked into the Glass Room where Ric and Anhton were working. 'We have Villaman downstairs in an interview room. Are we up to date with our information? Anhton, you'll be with me when we speak with Villaman. We'll need to be on our best game. He's a hard nut, but I reckon we can do it.'

'I'm ready,' said Anhton.

'Ric, I'd like you in the room next door as well. Watch for any signs of a crack in the armour.'

'Will do, Jake,' said Ric.

'Let's print out anything we need to show Villaman, then we can see how the stew is,' said Jake.

When Jake had finished sending his requests to the printer, he left the Glass Room and walked towards the printer room. As he did, he saw Det.Sgt Brad Mallinson of MetroWest walked into David's office.

Jake gathered the printouts, put them in a folder and called for Anhton.

'Let's do this,' said Jake.

They took the lift down to level one where the interview rooms were.

They strode into the interview room to a hail of protests from Villaman. Jake dropped the large file onto the table. Villaman stopped momentarily.

Jake retrieved his tablet, laid it on the table, accessed a program and tapped a red button. 'Interview commencing at 1430 hours, on Monday May 17. Det.Sgt Jake North and Det. Cpl Anhton Roberts in attendance. Interviewing Mr Reuben Villaman.'

Villaman then resumed his tirade of abuse. Jake and Anhton sat down and said nothing. They let Villaman rant for a few more minutes until he stopped.

'Aren't you going say anything?' said Villaman.

'We were waiting for you to run out of steam,' said Jake, coolly. 'We can sit here as long as we need to.'

'Bastards, all of you. I have the right to my lawyer being present.'

'You see, that's the problem. We've been having some trouble contacting him, so we're going to start,' said Jake.

'Bullshit,' said Villaman.

'Be that as it may, I'm gonna start with Donna O'Neill.'

'Don't know her.'

'Indeed. Try this. It might jog your memory.' Jake slid across the table, the picture showing half of Donna's face in the window.

'That could be anyone's picture.'

Jake slid the various pictures of Donna captured from the three stores, then her licence and then the composite picture of all of them and how it matches the half-picture they have.

'Different coloured eyes, different makeup, different hair, and the same facial structure,' said Anhton.

'You made that up,' said Villaman.

'Then read this for me?' said Jake.

'I've already seen that. It's a pack of lies. Probably garnered under duress too.'

'I see it's game time again,' said Jake.

Jake took a deep breath. He opened the file, spread the various pictures and documents he had and slid them across to Villaman. As Villaman leafed through them, Jake noticed a distinct change in his face.

'Yes, we know who you are. Who you had a crush on.

Where you used to work.'

'I don't know what you're going on about. These are all lies and rubbish.'

'Is this a lie as well?' Jake slid across a copy of the results from the hospital confirming that he used to be a woman. 'DNA is undeniable, Villaman, or should I call you Amanda.'

'That person no longer exists,' spat Villaman. He crossed his arms, closed his mouth, and turned his wheelchair to one side slightly.

'We also have the problem of the break-in at Balcher Racing's premises on Wednesday night last week,' said Jake.

Silence.

'I see how it is.'

Jake rose when there was a repeated knocking on the interview room door. He opened it to see an extremely excited Gabby.

'Det.Cpl, can you please come with me?' Jake stepped back to the desk. 'Interview paused at 1450 hours.'

Jake had a guard step inside with Villaman. David, Ric, and Brad stepped into the hallway from the viewing room.

'Where's Gabby?' asked Jake.

'I dunno,' said David.

'Did you see where she went, Ric?'

'Probably back to her lab,' said Ric.

Jake and Anhton headed to the lab in the far corner of level one and walked in.

Gabby rushed to Jake and hugged him tightly when he arrived.

'I did it, Jake,' said Gabby. 'I found some evidence.'

'How? Where? What? Whose is it?' asked Jake in quick succession.

'I was getting frustrated that I couldn't find anything,' said Gabby, 'so I went over the clothing again from the van. This time I found a hair, with live DNA, trapped underneath the collar. I ran it through the systems, and it came back with a match to an Amanda Beston - DNA doesn't lie. Anyway, I went through the file on Lassie to discover that Amanda Beston had now become Reuben Villaman, therefore we have DNA on Villaman for you. I kept on going through the van and its contents and found some more DNA. It matched the first sample, so I knew then that we had what we needed. I also found O'Neill's DNA in the cabin of the van. I reckon she only drove the van down and Villaman made some other arrangements of getting down there or was simply tucked away in the back. Either way, he was in the van.'

'You're a gem, Gabby,' said Jake, kissing her on the cheek. 'Do you have a printout?'

'Right here, Jakey.' Gabby handed him a sheet of paper from her desk.

'I'll come back later with some champagne for you.'

17.4

Monday, May 17, 3:05pm

Jake and Anhton left the lab and returned to the interview room.

'Interview re-commenced at 1505 hours,' said Jake, accessing his tablet.

'I see you have more lies,' said Villaman.

'Not this time, Villaman,' said Jake. 'We have DNA evidence from the jumpsuit you left behind in the van after we wrestled last Sunday week. DNA doesn't lie, Amanda.'

'I told you that person doesn't exist.'

'Maybe on paper, but DNA will always come up as female, Villaman. We also found other DNA evidence in the van.'

'I demand you contact my lawyer,' said Villaman.

'I'll make sure I tell him which cell you're in,' said Jake.

The door opened and Brad walked in.

'Det.Sgt Brad Mallinson now entering the interview room. As I have been listening to the interview, I'm convinced we have evidence enough for a conviction. Mr Reuben Villaman you are under arrest for ...'

Jake took his cue. 'Under arrest for the murder of Jason Black; the attempted murder of Dan Roberts; the attempted murder of Ulysses David; the three store robberies; the murder of Jospeh Strassman; the robbery at the offices of Broadbench Consolidated Racing; the illegal entry at, and the theft of uniforms from Damacles Textiles; the assault on Joe, one of Damacles Textiles' staff members; and the illegal entry at Balcher Racing.'

Two officers were brought into the room.

'Cuff him to his wheelchair and take him to the holding cells,' said Brad.

The two officers nodded and wheeled Villaman from the room.

'Interview concluded at 1525 hours,' said Jake.

Jake and Anhton collected the material they had and returned to the Glass Room. They began to update the file with the information they had and to record the arrest of Villaman. As they worked on that, David and Brad walked in.

'Congratulations, Jake,' said Brad.

'Thanks to Jake and the team though,' said David.

'Thank you, Brad.' Jake blushed a bit.

'I was glad to hear that you were working on the case,' said Brad. 'I can only imagine what you've been going through these past months. I for one am happy you're back.'

Jake shook Brad's hand.

'I need to head back to my office. I hope to see the files this afternoon, Jake?'

'Absolutely, Brad. We need to make sure we have everything up to date and they'll be sent across tonight.'

David showed Brad to the lift and then returned.

17.5

Monday, May 17, 4:30pm

Once Jake had finished updating the file with Ric's and Anhton's help, he sent a copy to Brad, closed Lassie for the day and walked to his desk.

'Jake, I want you to know that I am grateful for your work on this case,' said David. 'It's been a tough time for you.'

'Thankfully, I'll be fine now,' said Jake. 'I needed a push to get going and this did it. When it sort of became personal, I had no choice.'

'I have one more job for you.'

'What's that, David?'

'I need you to arrest Donna O'Neill.'

'In what respect?' asked Jake.

'I thought you would've known that already,' said David. 'As Villaman's accomplice. You said yourself that the woman at each store robbery was the same woman and that woman matched the half face of Donna O'Neill you captured at Villaman's address.'

'Do we have a warrant?' asked Anhton.

David handed over a piece of paper.

'That was quick,' said Anhton.

'We already wanted to bring her in, so we had this prepared in a case we needed it with Villaman.'

'I guess we had better go and pay her a visit. We'll head down there tomorrow.'

Jake grabbed his satchel off his desk and he and Anhton left the office.

Balcher

18.1

Tuesday, May 18, 8:30am

Just after eight-thirty am, Jake and Anhton parked in front of the Balcher Research Building on the Mornington Peninsula.

It was nothing spectacular. An old building. Five storeys high, with a simple entrance. Plenty of trees surrounded the property.

'You'd think they wanted to be hidden with all these trees about,' said Jake.

'This was supposedly an old military research facility that was bought by the Balcher group,' said Anhton.

'Perhaps we need to watch for booby traps then,' added Jake laughing.

'It was decommissioned long before Balcher got it. It should be clean.'

'How do you know this much already?'

'I read it online last night,' said Anhton.

'Ah.'

They walked up the few steps to the door and walked in.

As they approached the desk, Jake noticed that the receptionist kept darting her eyes everywhere and was upset. She jumped slightly when they stood at her desk.

'Is everything okay, miss?' asked Jake.

'S-s-s-ure,' she replied.

'We're here to see a Miss Donna O'Neill.'

'She should be back shortly, if you want to wait?'

'Thank you, we will.'

As Jake and Anhton walked towards a couch near the reception desk, they, along with the receptionist, looked suddenly towards the staircase and up to the next level.

'What's going on?' asked Jake.

'I'm really not sure,' said the receptionist. 'Soon after Donna asked me to watch the desk, the noises began somewhere near the rear of the building.'

Gunshots were clearly heard coming from the level above them. They stopped as quickly as they started. The receptionist screamed and ran through a door and disappeared.

Jake and Anhton drew their weapons and approached the staircase.

18.2

Tuesday, May 18

Jake stopped at the bottom of the stairs and looked upwards. They both quickly crouched and aimed their weapons upwards when they heard more noises of a fight in progress.

'They seemed to have moved away from the stairwell, but I'm not sure where to,' said Jake.

'Maybe they went up?'

'No, I think we would've seen them.'

Without hesitation, they both spun around and aimed their weapons at the now opening lift.

A face appeared, Jake was a little surprised that there was a distinct lack of fear or dread on the face. The person indicated for them enter the lift.

Jake and Anhton cautiously circled around until they were directly facing the lift. The only person they could see was the man who had shown his face long enough to indicate for them to travel with him.

They entered the lift and watched as the man furiously pressed the button for the third floor.

'What's going on?' asked Jake. 'Who are you?'

'I'm Lance Reeve, senior research assistant and member of Westbrook,' said Lance.

'Hi,' said Jake quickly. 'I'm ...'

'... we know who you are,' interrupted Lance.

Jake was taken aback.

'You still haven't answered my question?' said Jake.

'We've been broken into and attacked by a group known as Calderwood. They want what we have and that's not going to happen while I'm alive. It's now your job to do that.'

'I don't think so,' said Jake. Jake aimed his weapon directly at Lance. 'Who are you and who do you work for?'

'We don't have time for that, we're here.'

The lift doors opened and in contrast to what they'd heard earlier, it was quiet.

'Watch him, Anhton,' said Jake.

Anhton took over the guarding of Lance whilst Jake cautiously peered out of the lift.

'Looks like it's clear,' said Jake.

Lance raced past him, turned to the right and ran into a laboratory. Jake and Anhton followed closely, watching for any signs of those who had attacked the building.

18.3

Tuesday, May 18

Jake and Anhton watched as Lance checked two vials of liquid that sat on a rack on the bench. Lance was visibly relieved.

'What are they?' asked Jake.

'They are the future, Jake North,' replied Lance.

Jake was not expecting to hear Lance use his full name.

'This is getting very creepy,' said Jake. 'I demand to know what's going on here. How do you know my name? Anhton's as well? Do you know his last name?'

'Of course I do,' said Lance, as if everyone knew his name. 'Think for a moment. Doesn't the name Balcher ring any bells anywhere other than here?'

Jake was too focused to think of such things.

'Of course he'd know our names, dummy,' said Anhton. 'Balcher sponsor Dan's racing team. I'm Dan's brother. We've been guests of Dan at some of the races already this year. For us to have the passes we did, they would've had to do background checks on us.'

Jake grunted.

Just then noises were heard coming from the floor below. They all ducked to hide behind a work counter. Without thinking, Lance grabbed a small container form a cupboard nearby, placed the vials inside and deftly pushed them down his pants.

Jake and Anhton looked at him strangely.

'They'll most likely be safer there than if they were simply in a pocket,' said Lance. He rearranged himself so that the bulge looked almost natural. 'There. Anyone would be happy to see me like this at a bar.'

Anhton smiled, but Jake was unimpressed.

Suddenly the noises they had heard spilled from the stairwell and filled their floor. Jake indicated for Lance to take cover.

Jake crawled along the floor and peered out of the door. Immediately he was shot at, and he ducked inside safely. Anhton was by his side, and they quickly found a place where they could return fire.

Jake took aim and one of the assailants was struck and crumpled to the floor. Another assailant went to his aide and was quickly shot by Anhton.

Using only sign language, Anhton indicated he would creep through the lab and see if he could get behind those who were on the attack. Jake nodded and watched as Anhton left his side. Jake watched him until he could see him no longer.

Jake was perplexed by a strange feeling that things would not be the same by the end of the day.

Jake looked out of the door once more and was disturbed to see Jeremy Pyke crouching by the top of the stairs. As Jake spotted Jeremy, Jeremy spotted Jake. They both fired at each other, missed, and ducked for cover.

Jake took several deep breaths, gritted his teeth, stood, and stepped into the hall, gun at the ready in front of him. 'Jeremy Pyke, you have some nerve showing your face back in Basslea.'

Jake watched as Jeremy stepped from his hiding place, gun before him, aimed at Jake.

'I still see your assisting doomed enterprises,' said Jeremy.

Jake refused to respond.

'Jeremy Pyke, you are under arrest for the murder of President-elect Danika Wordsworth last November 18.'

'How do you propose to enforce that?'

'I'm not known for missing my targets,' said Jake.

'I see.'

Jake lowered his weapon and fired. Jeremy didn't move but noticed that the bullet had landed perfectly on the floor between his feet.

'Impressive. I have more people coming. You'll never get out of here alive. Face it, North, you failed again.'

Jake, with his gun aimed directly at Jeremy once more, move it slightly to the left and fired. This time bullet whizzed past Jeremy's right ear.

'I see how it's going to be. Only one of us is coming out of this alive today,' said Jeremy.

'If that's how it is, then so be it.'

'If I remember correctly, you know how to fight hand-to-hand?'

Jake was silent.

'We had a tussle the night I reduced the senate by a couple of members.'

Jake remained silent.

'I propose we finish this without the use of our guns. What say you?'

Jake remained focused on Jeremy's face, his gun in front of him.

Jeremy flipped his gun on his finger and slowly bent down to place it on the ground.

'Fire if you have to. It'll show on record that I was unarmed. I know you have someone coming up behind me. In a court of law, they will have to tell the truth.'

Jake blinked and then placed his gun on the ground.

Jake and Jeremy stood about twenty metres apart. Jeremy began to move. Then Jake did. Soon they were racing towards each other. Before Jake knew it, Jeremy had removed a hidden knife and was preparing to use it on Jake. Jake had enough time to move sideways, deflect the blow and knock the knife from Jeremy's hand.

It made a loud noise and it skittered across the tiled floor.

The punches began to fly. As many as Jake was able to land on Jeremy's body, Jeremy landed some on Jake. Jeremy, however, seemed to land his on more vital parts than Jake was doing. Learning quickly, Jake began to apply punches to those same areas on Jeremy.

With an almighty push, Jeremy forced Jake to retreat. Jeremy also took a moment to take a few steps back.

With eyes focused, Jake began to approach Jeremy once again. This time they applied their martial arts abilities on each other. High kicks to the chest and back. Low kicks to the legs disguised to unbalance the opponent. Punches and jabs that connected were equally deflected. Jake could feel the bruising beginning to take effect on his body.

Through gritted teeth, he prepared for another assault. As he watched Jeremy carefully, he deliberately ignored the momentary appearance of a face at the top of the stairs.

Jake took a step forward to attack.

'Shoot him, you bastard,' cried Jeremy.

A shot rang out and Jake clutched at his left leg and crashed to the ground.

Just as quickly, Jake head two more shots ring out. He was able to see the person at the top of the stairs collapse as a bullet pierced the brain. Jake looked up and through his pain, watched as Jeremy turned and was shot in the shoulder. He collapsed to the ground as Anhton raced past him and gathered Jake in his arms.

As Anhton dragged Jake into the lab, Jake saw Donna appear from the lift and drag Jeremy inside.

18.4

Tuesday, May 18

With Anhton holding Jake in his arms and Jake holding the wound on his leg, Lance appeared with a first aid kit.

'I don't think that will be enough,' said Anhton angrily.

'It'll be fine,' said Lance calmly. He quickly wrapped a bandage tightly around Jake's leg. 'This will hold things in place until people can assess the leg properly.'

The pain in Jake's leg and the application of the dressing caused him to pass out.

As Anhton sat and watched Lance work, he suddenly grabbed the right side of his head.

'Are you okay?' asked Lance.

'I'm fine,' said Anhton. 'I had a fall at an investigation a few months ago and hit my head. I was cleared at the time, but every now and then, when I get stressed, it comes back.'

Lance looked from Jake to Anhton. He then reached inside his pants, retrieved the small container, and removed the vials.

'Here, take this,' said Lance. 'It'll help.'

'What is it and how do you know?' asked Anhton.

'It's the latest serum we've been working on. It helps with healing, and quickly. I'll give the other one to Jake.'

'I don't think so.'

Anhton grabbed his head in pain once more.

'Just take it.'

Lance opened the vial and handed it to Anhton. Lance encouraged him to drink it. As Anhton held the vial, Lance opened the second one and administered it to Jake. Anhton reluctantly drank the vial of liquid as another headache hit him.

'Help me get Jake to the lift,' said Lance.

'We can't go out there,' said Anhton.

'No, not those ones,' said Lance. 'The one now opening in the corner of the room.'

Anhton looked to his left and saw the wall sliding open.

18.5

Tuesday, May 18

Carrying Jake between them, Anhton and Lance walked slowly to the waiting lift. Reaching over, Lance swiped his card and entered the level he wanted to go to.

'How many basement levels are there?' asked Anhton, as the lift moved quickly down.

'I've found four, but there could be more,' said Lance. 'It'd take a dedicated team of people to fully search the building. I only found the one we're going to by accident one day and have kept it my secret.'

'For times like these?'

'For times like these.'

The lift stopped and Lance took a quick glance outside. 'All clear.'

As Anhton stepped from the lift, he faltered slightly.

'Hang on, Anhton, we're almost at the car.'

Lance opened the door of the large car remotely. Anhton was surprised to see two stretchers in the back, as if waiting for this very moment.

As Anhton and Lance placed Jake on one of the stretchers, Anhton collapsed onto the other, unconscious.

Lance quickly checked Anhton's vital signs, administered a sedative to both men, and was satisfied that all was well. He strapped both men securely and safely to the stretchers. He closed the rear door and climbed into the driver's seat.

Driving slowly across the car park, he activated a button on a small unit sitting on the centre console of the car. The far wall began to slide open revealing a tunnel that was now beginning to light up. Lance drove carefully through the opening and pressed the button once more to close the wall.

Travelling along at a safe speed, Lance didn't need to check his rear-view mirror as he knew no one would be following. To make sure, he pressed another button on the console. This time he did look in the rear-view mirror to see a small explosion and a cloud of dust head in his direction. He did this twice more before driving up a ramp and into a large farm shed.

Closing the tunnel behind him, he activated the main door of the shed and drove out onto a little used track.

18.6

Tuesday, May 18

Lance followed the track until he got to a farm gate. Stopping momentarily to send off a message, he casually drove through the gate, turned onto the road, and drove away from the farm.

Heading north, he travelled until he came to the highway he needed. At this point he turned eastwards and travelled for about three hours before turning north again and heading into the mountains in the middle of Gippsland.

After stopping for groceries at a small town, he drove on until he came to a white fence, indicating a driveway. Lance turned and passed through the gate and threaded his way along the winding driveway until he pulled up in front of a large farmhouse.

As he stepped from the car, he looked up to see a helicopter approach. Unconcerned, Lance opened the front door of the house, took the groceries in, and returned to greet the single occupant of the helicopter.

With their help, they stretchered Jake and Anhton inside. Anhton was placed into a room on his own.

Jake was taken to another room where Lance went to work immediately on Jake's wound. Once the surgery was finished, Jake was settled onto another, more comfortable bed.

Lance then spent time hooking up monitors to track the vital signs of the two patients in his care. Satisfied that all was well and that the two men were sleeping soundly, Lance went and ate a meal with his visitor.

18.7

Wednesday, May 19

Before breakfast Lance took blood samples from Jake and Anhton and took them to the small lab at the rear of the house. He placed them in the lab's fridge and went in search of something to eat in the kitchen.

As he was cleaning up, he heard noises coming from one end of the house. He went to investigate and as he grew closer, he knew that one of the patients was awake.

He entered the room and saw Anhton forcibly removing the cables and looking for his clothes.

'Where am I? What have you done to me? Where are my clothes? Did you do tests on me without my knowledge?' Anhton was angry and distressed.

'How's your head today?' asked Lance calmly.

'It's fine,' snapped Anhton. Walking around the room naked, he opened a closet and found his clothes. He dressed quickly and walked towards Lance. 'Now, how do I get out of here.'

'You can't leave just yet.'

'You have no right to hold me here.' Anhton stepped right up to Lance and stared at him.

'Is everything okay, Lance,' called a voice from the far end of the hall.

'It's all good. One of our guests has woken and wants to leave,' said Lance, stepping away from Anhton.

Anhton looked around Lance to see who else was there. 'Hey you, can you get me out of here?'

'Why would you want to leave? Where would you go? Do you know where you are?' replied the voice.

'I know you can't hold me against my will, so I have the right to leave,' said Anhton.

'Technically correct.'

'Why don't you settle back down on the bed, and I'll bring you some food?' said Lance.

Anhton became aggressive and lunged at Lance forcing him to the ground. Anhton grabbed Lance around the throat. 'Do you have a car?' Lance barely nodded. 'Where are the keys?' Lance pointed back down the hall. 'Fat lot of good that is. TELL ME!' Lance grabbed Anhton's forearm to remove it from his throat. Anhton relaxed. Lance took a few sharp breaths.

'The keys are on the stand, by the front door.'

Anhton threw Lance onto the floor roughly and stormed off down the hall. As he approached the main hall, he saw a figure appear opposite.

'Let him go, Joel,' rasped Lance.

Anhton began to throw things off the top of the hall table and then from the drawer until he found the keys. He ran through the front door, climbed into the car, and screeched down the driveway and away from the farm.

18.8

Thursday, May 20

Lance was working in the small lab when someone knocked on his door. He turned to find the other resident standing there. 'Yes, Joel?'

'Our other guest is awake.'

Lance looked over at a monitor to see that Jake was indeed moving in his bed. 'I'll go and check to see that he's okay.'

'Let's hope he's a little more amenable than Anhton,' said Joel.

'I don't think we have to worry about Jake,' said Lance.

Lance left the lab and made his way to Jake's room.

'Good afternoon, Jake, how do you feel?' said Lance.

'I'm not sure,' said Jake. 'Very tired.'

'You have been asleep for over forty-eight hours now. What do you remember?'

'I remember going to Balcher Research with Anhton. Anhton, where is he? How is he?'

'We'll come to that shortly. I need to know how you are first?'

Jake went to get up when he realised he had nothing on. 'Where are my clothes?'

'In the closet. I've even mended your pants where you got shot,' said Lance.

Jake suddenly realised that he had been shot and pulled back the sheets to inspect his leg.

'What the ...! What's going on? I should have a wound the size of Australia on my leg but all I see is a red mark and almost no scar. How long did you say I'd been out for?

'Over forty-eight hours. When you arrived here at the farmhouse, I operated on your leg to remove the bullet. The rest was the serum. I told you it could heal.'

'No you didn't, did you?'

Lance thought for a moment. 'Sorry, I told Anhton about its healing properties.'

'So, if I'm healed, then I should be able to stand and walk normally,' said Jake.

Lance nodded and stepped up to remove the cables that were attached to the monitors.

Taking the sheet and wrapping it around himself, he stood. Taking a few steps he discovered that there was no pain and that in fact he felt very well indeed. He walked over to the closet and removed his clothes. He indicated he wanted to get dressed and Lance left the room.

Once he was dressed, he opened the door. Lance turned and indicated that Jake should follow him. Leading him to the kitchen, he prepared him a meal. It was several minutes before Jake recognised that there was someone else in the room, leaning up against a wall partially hidden by the door. He was startled but settled.

'Who are you?' asked Jake. 'Again, where is Anhton?'

'When you've finished eating, I will tell you what you need to know and show you what happened to Anhton.'

'Is he okay,' said Jake, concerned.

'You can decide that. Follow me.'

Jake finished his meal and followed the stranger along a hall to a lounge.

'Have a seat,' indicated the stranger. 'My name is Joel Westbrook and I own this house.'

'Westbrook. I've heard that name mentioned recently,' said Jake.

'Quite possibly. Lance said he mentioned it the other day amid the chaos at Balcher. Anyway, I own and operate a group simply known as Westbrook. Outwardly, we have many legitimate faces. Privately, I run an organisation of operatives that, whilst not above the law nor a law unto themselves, exists to make sure that things are kept safe and out of the wrong hands.'

'Who decides what the wrong hands are? To me it sounds like that you are a law unto yourselves, deciding what is right and what is wrong.'

'It's never that black and white, unfortunately. Mostly we are trying to keep things out of the hands of Calderwood, who seem dedicated to undermining everything. They will tell you the same thing about me; that they exist to keep things from getting into the wrong hands. What they won't tell you is that as long as those things get into their hands, they will stop them from getting into anyone else's.'

'I'm still confused. How does this relate to Anhton?'

'Before I get to him, let me tell you about the serum.'

'What serum?'

'The one that Lance administered to you and that

Anhton took before you came here. Perhaps I should let Lance explain the serum. He did help create it.' Joel stood and walked to the door. 'Lance, can you come in here please?'

A few minutes later, Lance walked into the room.

For the next hour, Lance explained the development of the serum, which also included the development of Menac, which Jake remembered from the investigations over the recent death of Jason Black. Jake tried to protest but was quietened quickly.

When Lance had finished, all three sat in silence for a few moments.

'Thank you, Lance,' said Joel. 'Also, we're calling the serum *Raptorlin.*'

Lance rose and left.

'So, I have this serum, Raptorlin, inside of me and as a result, my wound has healed in less than forty-eight hours instead of several weeks?'

'So far you get it.'

'Anhton also has the serum inside of him?'

'Yes.'

'So, what happened?' asked Jake calmly.

Joel picked up a tablet from the table beside him, accessed a file and handed it to Jake. 'Press play when you're ready.'

Jake did and watched the video of how aggressive Anhton was towards Lance. Tears welled up in his eyes and he let them flow freely down his cheeks, even after the video had stopped. Joel took the tablet from Jake's hands.

'I have to find him and tell him it's going to be okay,' said Jake.

'Yes, you do, but I would like you to consider an offer first?'

'What's that?'

'Come and work for me,' said Joel.

'Why would I do that?' said Jake defensively. 'I have a good job with the Basslea Defence Force working for their investigative service.'

'I know you do, but you can do both. You work for them and if I need you, you work for me. You'll get paid for it too.'

'I need to find Anhton first before I decide anything,' said Jake.

'I understand.'

Jake sat upright in his chair. 'What happened to Jeremy Pyke?'

'We don't know.'

'The last I saw he was being dragged into the lift by someone Anhton and I had gone to Balcher to arrest.'

'Who was that?' asked Joel.

'Donna O'Neill. She was to be arrested as the accomplice of Reuben Villaman, the man we charged with a number of things, but no less than the murder of Balcher Racing driver, Jason Black.'

'I see.'

'What does that mean?' said Jake.

'It means that Donna O'Neill is a known operative of Calderwood, and I daresay, so is Jeremy Pyke. More than likely they are long gone, or if not, in deep hiding.'

'Is there any way I can get back to the city this afternoon?'

'Follow me,' said Joel.

They rose and Jake followed Joel out through the front door and across the driveway. Jake saw the helicopter sitting in the paddock opposite the house, as the sun began its final descent over the hills round the house.

'Is that yours?' asked Jake.

'Yes, it is, and I can take you back to the city. Tomorrow when it's daylight again. If you'll at least let me know that you'll consider my offer.'

'A conditional offer of a trip home.'

Joel smiled and shrugged his shoulders. 'Is there truly ever a free ride?'

www.ingramcontent.com/pod-product-compliance
Lightning Source LLC
Chambersburg PA
CBHW070203120726
47909CB00001B/228